Guideposts
Best Loved
Stories

A Treasury of
Guidance and Hope

Introduction by
Fulton Oursler, Jr.

Volume One

BROADMAN
& HOLMAN
PUBLISHERS

Nashville, Tennessee

19.99

Gift

Aug. 1999

Contents

Chapter Four: Faith for the Family

Chapter Five: Help on the Job

Chapter Six: Pass It On

Chapter Seven: Don't Ever Give Up

Chapter Eight: Glimpses of His Presence

Introduction

When I came to *Guideposts* almost five years ago, my secretary was also newly hired. One day, after she had become familiar with the magazine, she came into my office with a question. "Are these stories real?" she asked. I assured her they were. At first she seemed unsure of my reply or at least troubled. Then she said, "aren't you afraid you'll run out of them?"

I had to laugh. Almost 50 years earlier, our publisher, Ruth Stafford Peale and her husband, co-founder of the magazine, Norman Vincent Peale, had told a friend that they had asked themselves the same question. That friend was my mother, *Guideposts'* first executive editor, Grace Perkins Oursler.

Today the question might seem to be even more burning, because we have not only *Guideposts*, but a slew of publications in our stewardship — *Plus, Positive Living, Angels on Earth* and *Guideposts for Kids* — packed with life-changing stories. Occasionally, I confess, I have been tempted to wonder what would happen if the stories stopped arriving.

For thirty years I worked at the *Reader's Digest* where I could call upon scores of professional writers. When I arrived at *Guideposts* I was concerned that it would be difficult to find the unprofessional but irreplaceable authors we seek: plain, unpretentious people who have had extraordinary adventures in faith.

I shouldn't have worried. For over the last few years I've witnessed a sort of miracle of editorial regeneration. It happens in issue after issue because when one person tells his story, others find their hearts opened and they write to us and their stories inspire others.

Let me tell you about a letter that just crossed my desk from Laura Taylor, a reader in Elkridge, Maryland. Laura writes:

My husband, Dean, is a cement truckdriver. Dependency on the weather to perform his job often results in financially trying winter seasons. After one particularly trying day, I lay in bed and asked God to give me a sign if he really existed. The next day I went to work and found a Guideposts *magazine in my "In" box.*

I realized it had come from my friend Becky. She had given me magazines from time to time, but never Guideposts. *I have to admit when I discovered that* Guideposts *was a "religious" magazine, I was rather insulted. I had nearly abandoned my faith after several traumatic events when I was young, including the death of my father when I was ten. Now I was receiving this magazine. Then I remembered that I had asked God for a sign. Was this it? I took the magazine to lunch with me and read while I ate.*

The more I read, the more I realized that Guideposts *is a magazine about ordinary people, like Dean and me, whose lives have improved from inviting God into their hearts. I went back to work with a new outlook and my faith has grown with each new issue. You have truly changed my life. Dean and I have even experienced what we consider our own personal miracles...*

I can't think of a better argument for what we do. Our stories come from our readers, and in this volume we've collected your recent favorites from all our magazines. You'll meet people who discover, as one writer puts it, "The Puzzling Power of Forgiveness." You'll experience the excitement of those who uncover the mystery of faith anew, like John Wren-Lewis meeting the angel of death in "The Dazzling Darkness." You'll see how some people put their faith to work both at home and in challenging work situations. And you'll be inspired by those who meet God in the most desperate of circumstances, such as Shony Alex Braun who plays "The Magic Violin" in a German prison camp.

Will we ever run out of stories? No, not as long as people continue to search for God, struggle to grow in their faith, see the surprises of grace and glimpse the mysteries of the beyond. And it will be our pleasure to present in these pages, year after year, the ones that readers like you have loved best.

— Fulton Oursler, Jr.

Guideposts
Best Loved
Stories

Chapter One

When Loving Is Hard

Dear Lord and Father of mankind, Forgive our foolish ways;
Reclothe us in our rightful mind; In purer lives Thy service find,
In deeper reverence, praise.

– John Greenleaf Whittier
(1807-1892)

Bubba

by Bert Clompus, Douglassville, Pennsylvania

I was about five when I first realized that Bubba—Yiddish for "grandmother"—was not on good terms with Mom. Whenever Dad drove us to Harrisburg, Pa., to visit his mother, it was always the same story. If Bubba spoke to Mom at all, her words were clipped and cold. Then on one visit Mom and Bubba were washing the dinner dishes when a teacup slipped out of Mom's hands and shattered on the floor. A look of disdain clouded Bubba's broad face. "Mollie," she grumbled, "you never were good enough for my son!"

I was shocked. How could Bubba talk like that? My eyes welled with tears as I watched Mom bite her lip and look to Dad. He was red-faced and wordless; but my grandfather's eyes blazed at Bubba. "You apologize to Mollie!" Grandfather demanded. Bubba, a large woman who dwarfed my short and wiry grandfather, merely folded her arms and pursed her lips stubbornly.

Our visit ended abruptly, but not before my grandfather steered me down the steps of the small apartment to his grocery store below. He slid open the door at the back of the candy case. "Here, Bert, take one," he said, as if the sweetness could purge the bitter aftertaste of Bubba's outburst. I shook my head, then relented, selecting a cherry sour ball.

I was still rolling it around in my mouth and resisting the urge to bite into it as we drove home. Mom must have been doing the same thing with Bubba's words, rolling them around in her mind and fighting the urge to complain to Dad. About the time I finally crunched the sour ball, Mom blurted out, "Ike, why didn't you say something?"

Dad didn't answer. He only gripped the steering wheel a little tighter and drove a little faster. At last Mom cried out, "So is that what you think too? I'm not good enough?"

I was nearly thrown off the backseat as Dad slammed on the brake pedal and swerved to a stop on the shoulder of the road. "How can you say that, Mollie?" he gasped, grabbing her hand.

"I know I had only a third-grade education when I came to this country," Mom sobbed. "I know I had to sew in a sweatshop to help support my family. I know you are your mother's favorite son. But does that make me not good enough, Ike?"

My father's face, usually so stern, softened. "Are you through?" he asked quietly. Mom nodded, rummaging in her pocketbook for a tissue. Their eyes finally met and Dad kissed his fingertips and touched them softly to Mom's lips. I knew things were all right again. But I also knew how Dad felt, torn between the two women he loved most in the world, not wanting to hurt either one.

The next time we went to Harrisburg, Mom insisted on waiting in the car while we visited with Bubba.

"I'm staying with Mom," I declared loyally.

"Go with your father, Bert," Mom ordered.

"All right," I said, giving in, "but I'm not speaking to Bubba."

Bubba pretended to be disappointed that Mom wasn't with us. When she smiled and spread her huge arms wide for me, my resolve evaporated. I melted, all the while feeling like a traitor. But what five-year-old can resist a grandmother's hug? When Dad and my grandfather went downstairs to the store, I mustered my courage and asked Bubba why she didn't love Mom. She refused to answer.

"But you love me, don't you?" I persisted.

Bubba pulled me onto her lap. "Sure I do!" she said fiercely.

"Well, if you love me, why can't you be nice to Mom?"

Bubba shrugged. "It's different," she said, "and you're too young to understand." Just then Dad came upstairs and said it was time to leave.

Not long after, Bubba took ill with a severe case of the flu. Stubborn as always, she refused to go to the hospital or stay with any of her children nearby. My grandfather had his hands full working 12-hour days tending the store, so my dad offered to bring Bubba to recuperate with us, in the home of her favorite son. To my surprise, Mom agreed. My stomach knotted at the prospect of the two of them under one roof.

The next day Dad followed Bubba into the house, carrying a battered brown valise and a large paper bag. He put the bag on the kitchen table. "What's this?" Mom asked.

"I brought my own food," said Bubba, punctuating her statement with a series of hacking coughs.

Mom emptied the bag of its contents: a large jar of pickles, another of sauerkraut, and six cans of store-bought chicken soup. "This isn't food for a sick person," Mom said, glancing dismissively at Bubba. The tension between them made my knees weak. *Lord*, I prayed desperately, *please let them get along just this once. Please.*

5

"I'll get Bubba settled in the guest room," Dad interjected quickly, taking my grandmother by the arm.

"She's not eating *this* food, Ike!" Mom called after them.

"I will too!" Bubba coughed.

"I don't want her dying in my house!"

"I wouldn't dream of it, Mollie!"

"Both of you—that's enough!" Dad shouted, pulling Bubba up the stairs. When he returned he took Mom aside. "You've got to try to show my mother respect while she's in this house," he whispered hoarsely. Then he stomped off to work.

Red-faced and silent, muttering a prayer, Mom swept aside Bubba's groceries and went to work herself—chopping and slicing, preparing a big pot of her homemade chicken soup. While the glorious concoction bubbled and simmered on the stove, Mom baked a fresh loaf of challah—the sweet braided bread she usually made for the Sabbath. When it was all done she fixed a tray with her best china and carried it up to Bubba. There was something almost defiant about her as she climbed the stairs.

I tiptoed behind and watched Mom silently hand Bubba the tray. There was a long nerve-racking pause before Bubba croaked, "For me?" Mom didn't answer. Instead she briskly smoothed the covers on Bubba's bed and left.

Downstairs I asked Mom why she had gone to such trouble for Bubba. "I thought challah and soup was just for Fridays? I mean, Bubba isn't even nice to you."

"That doesn't matter, Bert," she said. "She's still your father's mother and she's still my guest. That's how we'll treat her; apparently that's what God wants."

Later I went up to get Bubba's dishes. "Isn't Mom's chicken soup the best?" I asked her.

Bubba hemmed and hawed and shifted in bed. "It's not half bad," she finally admitted, as if the words were torture to get out.

"Mom," I said, handing her the tray downstairs, "Bubba said your chicken soup is the best."

"She did?" Mom said, failing to mask her surprise. This was high praise coming from Bubba, and I thought Mom straightened a little bit with pride.

Every day, from then on, Mom made Bubba soup and fresh challah, and served it on her best dishes. It was good medicine, and not just for Bubba's flu. Each time Mom took Bubba her tray, they lingered together a little longer. One afternoon, while I listened outside the door, I heard Bubba say, "Mollie, I have six daughters and not one of them makes chicken soup to match yours."

"Oh, go on, Bubba," said Mom modestly. "Can I get you some more?" I peeked into the room just in time to see Bubba raise herself from bed and give Mom a good long hug. I knew how that felt.

Mom was blushing when she came out and scooted me away. But later she took me by the shoulders and said, "Bert, if I grumble about the girl you marry, just tell her to keep trying to love me anyway. God will do the rest."

I think Bubba stayed on a few days extra just because she was having a good time. Seeing his wife and mother get along at last lifted a huge burden from my father. And I was glad God had heard my prayer and helped bring Mom and Bubba together. If we treat one another with respect and love, even if it's difficult, he'll look after the rest. That's what the two women I loved most in the world taught me when I was five years old.

"Someone Hates Us!"

by Julie Michael-Weisser, Lincoln, Nebraska

We received the first call right after we moved into our new home. It was a Sunday morning in June 1991, and we were sipping coffee in our eat-in kitchen, half-uncrated boxes littering the floor. The phone rang and my husband, Michael, picked it up. Almost immediately I could tell something was wrong.

Michael slammed down the receiver. Anger squeezed his voice. "That guy just said, 'You will be sorry you ever moved into 5810 Randolph Street, Jew boy.'"

Just then our 16-year-old son, David, walked into the kitchen. "Why would anyone do something like that?" he asked, his face paling. He had picked up the phone in his bedroom downstairs and had heard the man's words too.

Someone hates us, I thought. We had come to Lincoln two and a half years earlier so that Michael could become the cantor of B'Nai Jeshurun, one of two synagogues in town; most of the people we had met had been warm and welcoming.

It must be some crackpot, I told myself, and tried to put the incident out of my mind.

Two days later, coming home from my job in a doctor's office, I retrieved our mail and found a thick brown manila envelope addressed in block letters to "RABBI MICHAEL WEISSER."

Calling to Michael, I tore open the package. Rubber bands held together a thick stack of brochures. On top was a card that read: "The KKK is Watching You, Scum." One bilious tract denied the "Holohoax," another called Jews "the Great Masters of the Lie." There were caricatures of Jews with huge hooked noses and black people with gorilla heads. "Your time is up," threatened one note, incriminating us as "those responsible for the suffering of our white race."

I felt invaded, repulsed, sickened. The police came to investigate and one

8

officer explained, "We suspect the person who sent this package is the local head of the KKK." Now I was frightened: There was a real person behind the ugliness.

His name was Larry Trapp, a Grand Dragon of the Ku Klux Klan. He was severely diabetic, legless and going blind. He was also considered extremely dangerous. Holed up in a dingy apartment, he kept an arsenal of loaded guns and Nazi paraphernalia. Both the FBI and the Lincoln Police Department had him under surveillance.

Among those he had already harassed, I learned, was his next-door neighbor, a 35-year-old journalist, William Rush. Unable to walk or talk because of cerebral palsy, Rush depended on his computerized voice synthesizer. When Trapp heard Rush playing a tape of Martin Luther King's "I Have a Dream" speech through the thin apartment wall, he went into a rage. Using his CB radio, he broadcast scurrilous comments that were picked up by Rush's voice synthesizer. He continued the verbal assault night and day.

Trapp made a name for himself in the community by sponsoring a white supremacist video series, "Race and Reason," on the local public access station. Publicly he claimed he wasn't against blacks or Jews, he just wanted to preserve the white race. But privately he had mailed hate-filled messages to a prominent black woman in town. Recently, Vietnamese immigrants had moved to Lincoln, and he launched another sordid campaign against them.

We did not discover all of this right away. But it was clear we were being threatened. Following the police's advice, we installed dead bolts on our doors and began to lock our car. I carefully checked the mailbox before reaching in. We started being extra cautious with our three children, making sure we were aware of their every movement. But how can you steel yourself against such hatred?

What makes him do this? Why is he so bitter and angry? Michael had seen Trapp once—at a meeting of a town group called the Coalition Against Racism and Prejudice. Wearing a baseball cap with a KKK logo, he spoke out against the coalition. Trapp was so intense, so powerful, so focused that Michael said, "At first I didn't even notice that he was in a wheelchair."

What's wrong with the man? I thought. He had once been a patient of the doctors I worked for, so I knew where he lived. One day on my way home, I found myself making a detour to drive by his apartment at 817 C street. Gazing at the plain brown one-story building, I wondered how he had become so evil.

At home I turned to Proverbs, my favorite book in the Bible, and came across the passage: "A worthless person, a wicked man, goes about with crooked speech . . . continually sowing discord; therefore calamity will come upon him suddenly; in a moment he will be broken beyond healing" (6:12-15, *Revised Standard Version*). I saw Larry Trapp's apartment in my mind's eye and I asked myself, *when will he be broken?*

Michael was also becoming obsessed. Not one to sit on his anger, he told me he was going to call Trapp. After dialing Trapp's number, Michael listened to an 11-minute message, "Vigilante Voices of Nebraska," a recorded tirade of hate. Michael called again and again, to keep the recording playing so no one else could hear it. He kept it up for a week—until a friend told us that tying up someone's telephone line is illegal.

The next time Michael dialed Trapp, he left his own message: "You better think about all this hatred you're spreading, because one day you're going to have to answer to God."

After that, whenever he thought about it, Michael called Larry and left a message. Once he said, "Why do you hate me? You don't even know me, so how can you hate me?" Another time, after seeing Larry interviewed on television, standing in front of the Nazi flag, Michael said, "Larry, with your disabilities, the Nazis would have made you the first to go."

Michael continued his calls for months. One night in early September when we were eating pizza in our kitchen I had an inspiration: "If Larry ever answers the phone, tell him you want to do something nice for him."

Several weeks later, right after one of Michael's brief messages, Trapp picked up the phone and accused my husband of harassment.

"I don't want to harass you," Michael said. "I was thinking you might need a hand with something. Can I take you to the grocery store?"

There was silence at the other end. Then Larry's voice changed slightly. "I've got that taken care of, but thanks for asking . . . "

Maybe Larry was softening. Maybe all the messages were having an effect. I realized they were having an effect on us. We had started out contacting him in hurt and anger, but we were coming to care. *In a moment he will be broken beyond healing*, Proverbs had promised. I didn't want him to be broken irreparably. I wanted him to heal.

In mid-November the local newspaper carried a story that gave us hope: Larry was taking "Race and Reason" off the air. "I'm not backing out of the Klan or the white movement," he was quoted as saying, "but I think we should work for equal rights for all."

"He's waffling," Michael said.

Michael called up Trapp. "Larry," he said, "if you want to talk about this change of heart, I'd love to help you."

"I'm not having a change of heart," Larry insisted. But there was something different about his voice.

At the time, he was facing a judge's sentencing for harassing Bill Rush. On his way into court on November 15 Trapp was surrounded by TV reporters. "I don't talk to Jews!" he shouted to the cameras, rolling past in his wheelchair. He was fined five hundred dollars and given a two-day jail sentence, pending an appeal.

He left furious, but that night when Michael called again, Larry was apologetic.

"Do you still want to rethink things?" Michael asked.

"Yes, but I'm going to do it myself," he replied.

That same evening at synagogue, after naming several ill members and friends, Michael suddenly turned to the congregation, "Pray tonight for someone who is sick from the illness of bigotry and hatred. Please pray that he can be healed." *Please pray for Larry.*

The next night the three kids went out. Michael and I were trying to decide on a movie to see, when the phone rang and a man asked for "the rabbi." It was Larry Trapp.

What I could hear of the conversation left me stunned. This was a greater change than I could have prayed for. He would allow us to visit him. "He wants to get out of it," Michael said.

We got into our station wagon and drove downtown. I knew the block and the apartment building only too well. We knocked at his door. It opened slowly. There was Larry sitting in his wheelchair, a huge Nazi flag hung behind him, his piercing blue eyes looking up at us. "Hi, there," we said, awkwardly. Then Michael extended his hand.

At the touch of Michael's hand Larry burst into tears. We knelt down and hugged him, all three of us crying, as Larry repeated over and over again, "I'm so sorry. I'm sorry for all the things I've done . . . "

He had us take away his KKK and Nazi paraphernalia. Over the next months he apologized to the people he had harmed with his words and anger. On Martin Luther King Day he even joined us at the synagogue for an interracial service.

Larry became part of our family. With Michael's help and instruction he studied Judaism. As his health deteriorated, he moved in with us, where we could help care for him. The doctors didn't give him many months to live, so I took time off from my job to be with him. I came to know about the horrors of his childhood and forgave him. More important, he forgave himself. One day when he was still mobile he disappeared on a mysterious mission and returned with a bouquet of a dozen yellow roses and a note that read: "To the most beautiful woman, who helped me in my transformation from a dragon to a butterfly."

The morning he died Michael sat at his bedside holding his hand. I miss him. But the lesson of his life remains: God-inspired love will always defeat fear and hatred. Always.

My Irascible Aunt Alice

by James F. Marsh, Little Rock, Arkansas

"I 'm going down to visit Aunt Alice," I said, staring out the apartment windows to the courtyard five floors below. I was up from Atlanta visiting my parents in Port Chester, N.Y., and I always tried to call on family members when there, but I could guess what my mother was going to say about this errand.

"Why do you want to go see her? You know how Alice is."

I knew only too well. If everyone in our family got good marks in arguing, Aunt Alice was the valedictorian. Naturally abrasive, easily roused, chronically critical, she was a tangled ball of emotions, impossible to love. But she was Dad's sister, and she lived only three floors downstairs from my parents' place. I figured I could make a quick visit and escape before my patience had been too sorely tried.

"I'm going down," I repeated.

In the elevator I girded myself for the questions that would come. Everything I did seemed to meet Alice's disapproval: my move away from home, my work with prisoners, my faith. I stood staring at the door to apartment 204. I sighed deeply and leaned on the doorbell, saying a prayer for strength.

Her squeaky, arthritic footsteps seemed slower this year. Then they were drowned out by her call: "I'm coming! Hold your horses." She cracked the door wide enough to show her derisive scowl.

"Oh, it's you," she said, through pursed lips. "C'mon in." Only four feet eleven inches tall, she could knock you out with one of her caustic comments.

Pointing me to a seat at her cluttered dining table, she immediately served up a complaint: "Why doesn't your father ever visit me?"

"Alice, why don't you ride the elevator up three floors and ask him yourself?" I said, snapping at the bait.

"Well, he never asks me to come. And why doesn't your brother Bill ever write or call? And what about your sister?"

12

I could feel myself becoming heated. "Look," I complained, "I live in Atlanta. I don't know what goes on here in Port Chester. Why are you so cranky?"

Trying to tune her out, I glanced around the apartment. It hadn't changed much. The sink was cluttered with plastic foam meal trays and unwashed cups. The living room couch displayed handmade afghans, guarded by stuffed dolls. In one corner stood a mahogany bookshelf holding a hundred miniature china dogs.

I thought back to when I was a seven-year-old boy, fascinated by the dogs. One day when I thought she wasn't looking, I picked up a tiny black terrier. Suddenly I heard her scream, "Put that down!" Startled, I dropped the pooch. She swooped down and inspected all the canines. "Don't you ever touch those again," she cried. "They're mine!" Even now I squirmed at the memory.

"Let's have some Irish soda bread and tea," Alice announced. This was another ritual. She brought out some stale bread and weak tea. Then she watched carefully to see how much butter and jam I used. When we finished, she made her usual request, "How about a game of Scrabble?"

Staring at me from the table was the *New York Times Magazine* crossword puzzle, completely finished, a rite she repeated every Sunday. I wiped jam from my lips and she took out the Scrabble board.

I spelled *cat, dog* and *boat*, and she laid out *xylophone, zephyr* and *parquet*. Each time she put down a good word, she'd rub it in with a nasal snicker, adding points to the already lopsided scoring column, her gnarled fingers wrapped around the pencil.

Throughout the torturous match there were more barbs: "The priest hardly ever comes, and when he does, he rushes out." "Your mother hardly ever comes." "My sister Agnes never visits."

"Look, Aunt Alice," I blurted out, "I don't know about our relatives. They don't come to see me either. But you don't see me whining about it, do you?" My blood was boiling. "What is your problem?"

With that Aunt Alice turned her guns on me. "So when are you going to get married? Is there a woman in the picture?" My hands were shaking by now. Alice sat quietly for a moment, then looked right at me, saying, "And stop sending me those Bible references to look up. I don't like having to look things up in the Bible."

That did it. "Alice, I have to go. Good-bye."

I hurried out to the elevator, wishing her the worst. I couldn't love her. I couldn't even like her. She made me feel as trapped as the prisoners I ministered to.

Back in Atlanta I put her out of my mind. Three weeks later I was attending a training conference for work. "Is there anything hindering your relationship with God?" the speaker said. "Is there any person who makes you feel angry? Ask for God's forgiveness. Give up your resentment."

I closed my eyes. There in my mind I could see Aunt Alice, but oddly enough, she seemed to be holding a fishing rod, reeling the line in. Then I understood. I always went for the bait, lured by her accusations and complaints. She had her hook in me.

"Lord," I prayed, "forgive me. I've been trapped in my anger. Let me just accept Alice as she is, feisty and opinionated. Forgive me for my impatience. Let me see her as a person."

Six months later I went back to Port Chester. Standing in front of apartment 204, I felt a curious eagerness to see my aunt again.

"Oh, it's you," she said. "Come on in. Your father hasn't been down in months. Why?"

"I don't know, Alice. But it's good to see you." I kissed her forehead and looked into her lonely blue eyes.

"Well, what about Bill? He never comes. And Roberta might as well be a total stranger. Not even a call."

"I don't know," I said, noticing her eyes searching mine for an emotional response.

"I haven't heard from Patricia in years."

"I haven't either."

"Uncle Tommy comes but doesn't stay long."

"I'm sorry."

The next five minutes were almost fun, like playing tennis but not having to win. "Aunt Alice," I interrupted, "let's have some Irish soda bread and tea. I'll fix it if you'll set up the Scrabble board."

She smiled and cleared the table.

During the game I said, "Alice, tell me about the time when you were a telephone operator." For the next hour she chattered about her life at the phone company. While talking she didn't make one complaint. Then she described the sudden death of her husband and her own fears. "When Ed died I had nobody. No children. I didn't know where to turn." Her eyes lowered.

"It was hard when my father died too," she continued. "I was just a teenager and I had four sisters and a brother to look after. My mother had to take in boarders to make ends meet." Staring at her fingers, she related how arthritis had plagued her over the years. Day after day she'd make herself get up and go.

Suddenly before me I could see a valiant person with remarkable coping skills. No wonder she was so bossy. She was a survivor.

As I left I gave Alice a big hug. Over her shoulder I noticed the china dogs and chuckled to myself. "I love you, Aunt Alice," I said and kissed her cheek. She kissed me back and said, "I love you too."

A maturing process happened that day. I learned how to look beyond a lonely woman's verbal combat to discover the person God knew—a strong and giving person, a soul needing love and affirmation, my aunt Alice. And to think, I could have missed knowing her.

The Girl Nobody Wanted

by Stephanie Fast, Aloha, Oregon

After the end of the Korean War I was conceived by the union of a Korean woman with an American soldier, probably in the city of Pusan. As a child of mixed blood, I was considered a nonperson. I was abandoned at about the age of four and began living on the streets. Many orphaned children of mixed blood were killed; others were picked off the streets and sent to America by adoption agencies. I wasn't.

I learned to snatch morsels from food stalls, to be at butcher shops when they threw out the bones, and to roast grasshoppers on rice straw. At night I'd roll myself into a straw mat and sleep under a bridge. I never dreamed of acceptance from adults; I was a half-breed—a dirty *toogee*—an ugly reminder of an ugly war. Even other street children taunted me. They'd send me to steal food, reasoning that as a nonperson I wouldn't feel the pain of a beating if I got caught.

Once I was tied to a waterwheel and nearly drowned. Another time I was thrown down an abandoned well. I screamed for help until I had no more voice, then watched as the patch of light at the top turned to darkness. I found a stone sticking out of the wall and sat there, cold and numb. I wondered how long it would be before I was dead. Then I heard the voice of an old woman: "Little girl, are you down there?"

After she hauled me out with the well's bucket, she hurried me to a barn and covered me with straw. Kind as she was, she didn't want to be seen helping a *toogee*, for fear of what her neighbors would do to her. That's why she had waited till dark to help me. "You sleep now, little girl, but before daylight, run to the mountains. If they find you here tomorrow, they'll kill you."

At dawn I fled to a mountain cave and hid. That night, huddled alone, I peered out at the stars. *Why am I so bad,* I wondered, *that people want to kill me? Why can't I be like other children, who have a mommy and daddy?*

15

I began going from village to village, thinking, *Maybe my mom lives in one of them and will recognize me.*

One day I went to the train station and stood on the platform, waiting until a train pulled in. People began spewing out of the cars, and forgetting all caution, I scurried among them, craning my neck and peering into the women's eyes so the one who was my mother could recognize me.

Any moment now, my mind raced, *a woman's face will light up and she'll say, "My little girl! At last I have found you!"*

But no one stopped. Time after time women brushed me out of their paths. Instead of lighting up, their eyes narrowed. I knew what they were thinking. *Toogee.* The platform emptied. Just a few American soldiers stood about. *Maybe one of them is my daddy.* I went to them. But none of the soldiers even saw the American in me. To them I was just like all the other little beggars who filled the streets of Pusan. One of them gave me a chocolate bar that I wolfed down.

I was about seven when a cholera epidemic swept Korea. One day I fainted in the street. When I woke up I was on a mat in a bright room filled with children. A Swedish nurse had brought me to the World Vision orphanage in Taejon. I recovered and was soon strong enough to wash diapers and help feed and care for the babies.

One day the nurse told me that an American couple was coming to adopt a baby boy. I took extra care with my boys to make them look appealing. We were out in a courtyard when they arrived—huge people with pale faces like moons. The man came over, picked up one of my boys and lovingly stroked the baby's face. Then I watched in disbelief as tears welled out of the man's eyes.

I inched closer to get a better look at this strange man. He placed the baby gently back in his basket, turned to me and then began to caress my face. My heart thumped wildly; his touch felt so good. But I had never, ever been touched except to be beaten or kicked. Child of the streets, I slapped his hand away, spit at him and ran.

The next day this man and his wife returned. They talked to the nurse and pointed at me. Even though I was nearly nine, I weighed only 30 pounds. I had worms, my body was covered with scars, my hair crawled with lice. I had a lazy eye that flopped around in its socket. But David and Judy Merwin chose me.

When I entered their house, I thought I'd come to a palace. I was overwhelmed by their kindness and love. Patiently, painstakingly, they taught me English and helped me with my lessons at the American school. After a while they took me back to America, provided the best home life, the best education; they gave me their all. I was living in a fairyland, and yet I was not a part of it. Deep down I still felt like a *toogee.*

I learned early that Americans like it when you smile, so I did a lot of smiling.

As a young teen in Rockport, Ind., I made many friends. Everyone loved the pleasant Korean girl who sang in the choir, taught Sunday school and got academic awards. I smiled to please everyone because I never wanted to go back to street life again. But deep down the gnawing fear always lurked: *If they only knew who I really am they would hate me.*

My mother and father were disappointed when I insisted on bleaching my hair and buying deep-blue contact lenses so I could look more American. My orange hair looked strange and I lived in a dark-blue world, but I thought it was an improvement.

I put up a pretty good front in public, but at home I became withdrawn and irritable. I had temper tantrums, and I spent a lot of time in my room, brooding under the covers. I hated it, but the toogee began to take over my life. When Mom questioned me, I clammed up. Mom and Dad should never, never find out about my life as a street kid. I was convinced that if they did they'd shun me.

One night after Mom confronted me about my sullenness, I ran to my room, so upset that I didn't dare speak to her for fear I'd lash out and ruin everything. I looked in the mirror behind the closed door of my bedroom. "You haven't changed anything," I hissed at myself. "You're still nothing but a dirty *toogee*, a piece of trash."

I ran to my bed and buried myself under the covers fully clothed. *Now you've done it,* I thought, cringing. *Mom and Dad are probably wishing they'd taken that little boy . . .*

My bedroom door opened, and my father called softly, "Stephanie."

I pulled the covers away from my face and looked at him. His face was grave. *Oh, no. He's going to tell me they want me to leave . . .*

He sat in a chair by my bed and reached for my hand. "Your mother and I want you to know that we love you very much, but you seem to have a hard time accepting that love. The time has come for us to release you to God. You know the Bible; I don't have to tell you that God loves you . . . "

He fell silent, his jaw working as he groped for words. Finally he said, "Think of Jesus, Stephanie. He has walked in your shoes. He knows exactly how you feel. He's the only one who can help you." My father hugged me and left the room.

For a long time I lay there, turning over in my mind what Dad had said about Jesus. He was born in hard circumstances, straw was his blanket as it had been mine, and he had to flee because, like me, some people wanted to kill him.

For the first time in years I felt a strange sensation on my cheeks. Tears. Deep inside me something hard and cold had broken—something that had been standing between me and the love of my dear family and God.

I wept for Jesus, who understood about love but had to die for us anyway. I wept for the girl who finally had been loved, but still had chosen to listen to the

17

voices that taunted her. And I wept in relief: Jesus knew all about me and still loved me.

A sprout of self-worth started growing in me that afternoon. As my anger melted away, so did my sullenness and outbursts. I let my hair grow back naturally and threw away the blue contact lenses. And then one day I looked in the mirror, regarded the face smiling at me and said, "God thinks you're beautiful, Stephanie, and so do I."

"Will You Forgive Me?"

by Victoria Baker, Huntington, West Virginia

I was nervous the day we drove from my home to the Work Release Center in Charleston, W.Va. "It's not too late to change your mind," my husband, Don, said. He hadn't wanted us to come, didn't believe I should meet the man whose image had haunted me for a dozen years. He had tried to dissuade me from the moment I mentioned the visit, but I was resolute. If I was going to live, truly live, I had to see James Whitsett again face-to-face.

Twelve years earlier, on a wintry evening in 1982, I was parking my car near Don's apartment on Huntington's South Side. Back then Don was my fiancé and he had invited me over for dinner. I closed the car door and took a few steps. Abruptly someone grabbed me, pinned my hands behind my back and threw me to the icy pavement. I looked up and saw a pair of wild, drug-crazed eyes.

The man yanked my hair and punched my face. I tried to scream, but he clamped his hand on my bloody mouth, silencing me. Angry, frightened, I bit his hand and he howled in pain.

"Give me your purse," he snarled. I flung it at him, scared for my life. He stuffed it inside his jacket and ran, leaving me bruised and bleeding on the deserted street. I dragged myself to Don's apartment, finding some solace in the knowledge that I could identify the man who had assaulted me.

By the time I married six months later, the bruises and wounds had healed, and James Whitsett, my attacker, had been given a life sentence. But even with him behind bars, I was haunted by fears. I still trembled at the mention of his name. Once at the supermarket I thought I saw him and abandoned my half-filled cart in the middle of an aisle, hurrying out of the store in a panic. Another time I had stopped my car at a crosswalk when a man who looked like him walked by. I felt a surge of anger and for a split second considered gunning the engine and hitting the innocent stranger.

I lived in terror for myself and, after Don and I had children, for our family.

I locked all car doors, and even double-bolted the front door in our safe neighborhood. Four years after the attack, I was still fighting James Whitsett. Other, graver fears intruded in my life, but they could not erase that one primal fear or relieve me of the image of those drug-crazed eyes. Nothing terrified me more, not even learning in 1986 that I had cancer. The tumor was successfully removed, but the cancer came back. I had more operations and radiation therapy, but the malignancy returned, ever threatening. By 1993, it had spread to my lungs and I was told I had less than a fifty-percent chance of living more than five years.

Around the same time I received word that James Whitsett was up for parole. I told Don, "Do everything you can to make sure he stays in prison." In April I went to Ohio State University Medical Center in Columbus for intensive radiation therapy, requiring a three-day stay in an isolated, cell-like room. While there, I lay on my bed, saying prayers for my health.

I saw the radiation as light, spreading through my body. "By his stripes we are healed," I repeated, and I imagined every part of my body touched by the healing blood of Jesus. But I never offered any prayers for the anger and fear that were also riddling my body; I held onto my hatred for the man in another cell.

That summer I was well enough to go with my two eldest sons to church camp. I wanted to savor what time I had left with them. One evening at campfire I closed my eyes and listened to the songs that took me back to my girlhood, when I was trusting and carefree. "Oh, how I love Jesus," we sang, and the words became my prayer. That's the last thing I remembered before I collapsed . . .

I see the sky, beyond the blue, out of reach of the stars. I see my younger brother, Rene. He died at 12, but here he's grown up. He smiles at me and sings. My mother too is here. The last time I saw her, her face and body showed the ravages of cancer, but now she is healthy and happy again. This is heaven. I hear the angels sing, a music more glorious than any I have ever heard before. I am so close to the angels I sing with them, "Oh, how I love Jesus."

Lying on the ground, I feel the hand of God touch the pit of my stomach and move up through my chest and neck with an intense heat. I hear God speak. "Be still," he says. "Now say, 'I am healed.'" I repeat those words, "I am healed. I am healed!" Then I get up and join the dance.

When I opened my eyes I was still on the ground. A friend was standing over me and I told her the good news: "I have seen heaven." I hadn't been praying for healing, I had just been concentrating on God and suddenly I had seen his realm. The door was opened to me and I had seen the beyond.

The first concrete evidence of my physical healing came in the fall when I went back to the OSU Medical Center to have my blood tested. My physician, Dr. Ernest Mazzaferri, was looking for a marker to see if cancer was present. The last time he had run the test, I had had a marker count of around 100. This time it was close to five—perfectly normal. "I couldn't believe it," Dr. Mazzaferri said. "I made the lab run the tests twice just to be sure there hadn't been any mistake."

For me the New Year of 1994 felt like the beginning of a new life. I could look ahead to the future with better expectations. But in February, when James Whitsett came up for parole again, I started to revert to that old familiar feeling—fear.

I had been so grateful for my healing, had felt so happy, had trusted God so completely, that I had almost forgotten my attacker. But now that man was back in my thoughts, spoiling my life. One night at dinner I announced, "I want to see James Whitsett."

Don nearly dropped his fork. "You can't," he said. "I won't let that man hurt you again."

"For as long as I harbor anger against him, I am hurting myself," I explained. "If I can trust God with my health, I have to trust God with this. I don't think I'll be completely well until I see James in person."

Don looked down at his plate, thinking. "Then I'm coming with you," he said.

After calls to the parole officer of the work-release program in Charleston, James agreed to see me, but the woman in charge was deeply suspicious of my motives. "If you attempt to intimidate him or retry him," she said, "the visit will be terminated."

We went into an office and waited. Then the door opened and in walked a thin man wearing a teal sports coat, black trousers and shined shoes. How different he was from the person I saw in my nightmares. He looked smaller, older, a little frightened.

"James," I said, "you look nice."

Self-conscious, he straightened his shirt collar and sat down across from us. "Thank you," he said softly.

Don squeezed my hand. Not sure of what more I was going to say, I leaned forward, looked James in the eye and asked, "Will you forgive me?"

James looked at Don, then back at me. "I tried to convince myself that I was justified in my anger at you," I said, "but it probably made me sick inside."

James listened while I told him about my cancer and the miracle of my cure. I could already see that another miracle was taking place in that room. It was as though the angels were back with me, showing me how to make my heaven here on earth.

James wanted to tell me more about himself, who he was before drugs and alcohol took hold of his life. He pulled two crumpled newspaper clippings from his pocket and handed them to me. I read about a star high school athlete destined for a great future, an All-American basketball player with college scholarship offers. "Kids used to ask me for my autograph," James said. "Then . . . " He fumbled for words. "I'm sorry I hurt you and your family."

We were both silent for a while. Then James said, "May I ask you something? Will God hear my prayers?"

"Absolutely. I believe that God can change you—has changed you. He sure changed me." My anger and fear were gone. I was free.

The next day I went to a bookstore and bought a Bible. I had *James Whitsett* inscribed in gold on the cover and mailed it to him with some highlighters and a note reading, "Mark whatever speaks to you. Make it personal."

That was two years ago. Today James is out of prison. He is dating a religious woman and has a good job at a Charleston restaurant. Most important, James has become a friend. We talk on the phone every few weeks and we exchange cards and letters. He's even had dinner at my home and traded sports stories with my sons.

That's how deep my healing has been. Nothing less than the power of God and his angels could have accomplished this. Nothing this side of heaven could have made me whole.

The Puzzling Power of Forgiveness

by John Plank, Waupun, Wisconsin

My wife was seven months pregnant with our seventh child. We lived in a modest four-bedroom home.

After 11 years as a vocational teacher at the State Reformatory in Green Bay, Wis., a vocational director's job opened at a nearby correctional institution, and I got that position.

I started in June. My new job was 90 miles from home. I rented a room during the week, and returned home on weekends. I had two months to find a place to live, sell our home, move our family, and get settled down. Five of our children would be starting school in September. My wife always delivered early and needed to be under a doctor's care.

I read want ads, made phone calls, talked with fellow employees, visited realtors, and prayed for guidance. Finally, I came across a contractor who was completing a duplex apartment he intended to rent. It would be completed by September 1. Though the place had only two bedrooms, I was certain it would be large enough.

I told the contractor I would rent one of the apartments, and offered to pay a security deposit and the first month's rent. He said that wouldn't be necessary; a handshake and a man's word were all he needed to seal the agreement.

Wow!

I had put our home up for sale, and soon we had a buyer. I lined up a mover, registered the kids in school, had our medical records transferred. It was still going to be a squeeze. Just one week left.

On Monday morning, I received a telephone call from the contractor. I was to meet him that night at his home. It was then that I received a real shock. We were not going to get the apartment.

Futilely, I mentioned kids starting school, pregnant wife, selling our house, handshakes, man's word. The contractor's wife said, "The place is too small for your family."

23

Stunned, I went back to my room and thought, *How can this be happening?* What really puzzled me was why I wasn't angry with the contractor and his wife. As a matter of fact, the more I wondered about it, the more I felt that I had to forgive them. I always felt that I was a Christian but, frankly, not that good a Christian. It is something that happened to me that I will never be able to fully understand.

I sat down at 11:30 p.m. and wrote a letter of forgiveness to the contractor and his wife. I mailed the letter that night.

The next morning, I went to my office. On my desk was a piece of paper about two inches square, with a penciled note. It said, "Call this number after five tonight."

At the time, there were only eleven other employees. I contacted all of them and asked if they had put the note on my desk. No one knew anything about it.

At 5 o'clock, I called the number. When I told the party my name, he said he hadn't called me. I asked him if he was planning to rent his house.

He said, "I'm moving to a new job right now and wanted to list my house, but I haven't even called the paper yet. How did you know?"

This beautiful home, in Waupun, had three bedrooms, was four blocks from school, and rented for less than the contractor's apartment.

Who wrote the note? I truly believe it came from God.

"Not As I Will"

by Shari Smyth

Therefore, rid yourselves of all malice...
—1 Peter 2:1 (NIV)

Just before my husband and I left for vacation, I learned of a betrayal by a friend that filled me with bitterness. I knew exactly how I would hurt her back. I carried my plan with me, thinking of it even as we lugged the suitcases into the hotel in Harper's Ferry, West Virginia, a small town carrying a burden of dark history dating to the Civil War.

The next morning, I got up early, leaving Whitney to breakfast and read the paper alone. I walked downhill to the foot of Harper's Ferry, where the Potomac and Shenandoah rivers merge together like old friends, and saw ugly stone stumps rising like tombs out of the water. Nearby, a uniformed guide was explaining to a group that they were once part of a railroad bridge. During the Civil War, it was blown up and rebuilt nine times by the North and the South. Both coveted the strategically located town where blood flowed, as first one side, then the other, conquered it. Loyalties were divided, families split.

"Now up there" (my gaze shifted as the guide swept his arm to a rocky summit far above on which a church stood alone, its cross piercing the sky), "is St. Peter's Roman Catholic Church. During the war it served as a hospital for both sides." When the war broke, the priest put aside his own loyalties and flew the British flag over the church, rendering it to a power that neither the North nor the South wanted to touch. Thus, St. Peter's survived the shelling and became a source of healing, both physical and spiritual.

I climbed the sixty-eight stone steps, worn smooth by time and tears, to the top of the summit, where the church stood larger than life, stronger than evil. I stepped inside the church's musty Gothic interior, eyes adjusting to the darkness, and moved up the bare wood aisle to kneel at the cross. Rendering myself to its healing power, I, too, found the church a hospital.

Back outside, I looked far down to where the river lapped at useless stone stumps and felt the start of a bridge in me. A bridge of forgiveness.

Heavenly Father, help us to pray the prayer of Your Son, when He conquered evil for the world: "Not as I will, but as thou wilt" (Matthew 26:39).

25

Children's Corner

Rocks in my Head

by Kathy Johnson Gale

"Look what I bought for you boys at the store today," Mom said proudly. She reached into the sack and pulled out two shiny new lunch boxes.

Oh, no! I thought to myself.

"Cool!" Jason cried, grabbing the one covered with brightly colored pictures of dinosaurs.

Mom said, "I picked this one for you, Eric, because I know how much you like outer space."

She handed me the lunch box decorated with rocket ships and planets. "Thanks, Mom," I managed.

I took the lunch box from her and stared at it. Flicking the latch with my thumb, I opened it up and looked at the chunky Thermos inside, galaxies spinning around it. How could I tell Mom that boys didn't take lunch boxes to school in the fourth grade unless they wanted to be called babies?

I smiled, but couldn't think of anything else to say. Mom had been so sad since the divorce, and she was just starting to be her old self again. I didn't want to say or do anything that would upset her.

I took the lunch box to my room and dropped it on the floor by my bed. I paced around my room a few times, thinking. Then, I picked up a shiny black igneous rock from the top of my bookshelf and started tossing it into the air and catching it.

I had the best rock collection of any kid in school. Mom was always bugging me about it, though. "When are you going to do something about all of these silly rocks, Eric?" she would ask. "I can't even dust your room."

I could see why it bothered her. There were rocks covering just about every surface in my room, including the windowsills. But no way could I part with them. Each one was special. I had several geodes with sparkling crystals inside, a quartz rock that my friend Tommy gave me, fossil rocks that I found at our old house before the divorce, a bunch of agates that my grandpa gave me and a real moon rock from Dad. At least, he said it was real. I began bouncing the igneous rock against my bed. What was I going to say to Mom? How could I tell her—without hurting her feelings—that I didn't want the lunch box?

By bedtime, I still hadn't thought of a way to tell Mom I didn't want a lunch box. Tomorrow was the first day of school, and my new clothes were laid out on a chair. The lunch box was still beside my bed, eating away at my self-confidence.

I fell back onto my pillow and stared out the window. Moonlight played softly on the rocks along my windowsill, *Only a kid with rocks in his head would carry a lunch box to school*, I thought. And then it hit me. The solution to my problem. It had been right under my nose all along.

Next morning, I found Mom in the kitchen cooking eggs.

"Hey, Mom," I said, holding the lunch box out for her to see. "This lunch box is great; it holds a lot of rocks."

She looked at the lunch box and then at me. "You put rocks in your new lunch box?"

I was talking fast now. "Sure. I can fit in all the ones that were on my windowsills and some from my desk too."

"But what are you going to take your lunch in?"

"I'll just take it in a paper sack," I said, pulling a small sack from the drawer. "That's what most of the guys, do anyway."

A slow smile came to Mom's face. "I see...well, hmm." She scooped the eggs onto my plate. "Rocks in your lunch box. Sounds like a good idea... especially if you'll wash off those windowsills when you get home." There was a mischievous light in her eyes that I hadn't seen for a long time.

"No problem," I said. And then I hugged her.

A guy would have to have rocks in his head not to love a mom like that.

Chapter Two

Finding Faith Again

Most merciful Lord,
Turn my lukewarmness
Into a fervent lover for You.
Most gentle Lord,
My prayer tends toward this—
That by remembering
and meditating
On the good things
You have done
I may be enkindled
With Your Love.

—Anselm
(1033 – 1109)

The Dazzling Darkness

by John Wren-Lewis, Sydney, Australia

My mother's admonition flashed through my mind when the man on the bus to Phuket, Thailand, dug two toffees from his pocket and offered them, smiling. But Mother died in 1940 when I was 16, and now, in 1983, after more than a decade traveling and working all over the world, I'd long since discounted her warning.

In fact, this well-dressed and well-spoken young man typified the hospitality my fellow researcher, psychologist Ann Faraday, and I had encountered during the past few weeks on the offshore islands of Thailand. We'd been enjoying a break from our fieldwork in neighboring Malaysia. We were grateful for the man's assistance in finding the bus, and his help in loading our luggage. We couldn't say no to his offer of candy. Neither of us suspected him of being a personification of the angel of death—and I mean angel in the full sense of Christian tradition, where the angel is a messenger from God.

Back then angels seemed like silly superstition to me. As a former mathematical physicist, I had little patience for things outside the realm of measurable human experience, even though I was a staunch Christian as far as ethics and social values were concerned.

I'd never really understood the lifelong interest in mysticism and religious experience that had been Ann's inspiration for turning her scientific abilities to the study of consciousness and dreams. For the past 15 years I had been a collaborator in her research, but mysticism still seemed to me like a neurotic escape from real life, perhaps even a symptom of grave mental disorder. I suppose, in retrospect, I was the perfect candidate for angelic attention.

"He must have had these in his pocket for a long time," Ann remarked, discreetly taking the toffee from her mouth and wrapping it in a tissue as we bounced along the road. I nodded, for mine too certainly had an odd, musty taste. But I didn't want to seem rude. The young man was concerned that Ann wasn't eating the candy, so he offered her another piece, which she politely declined. Then, at the first stop, he hastily got off.

Though still morning, the day was steamy and hot, and I began to feel drowsy. Sleep became irresistible. The last thing I remember is my chin hitting my chest.

I awoke in a hospital bed, with the sky darkening outside, an IV drip and an oxygen cylinder beside me. Ann was asleep in a camp bed on the far side of what appeared to be a small, private ward. A white-coated doctor stood over me. "We thought we'd lost you," he said. My first thought was that I must be dreaming, and it took some time for me to grasp the reality of what had happened.

"Thank goodness I trusted my taste buds, or we'd probably both be dead," Ann said later as a nurse served us supper. "The police think the young man was part of a gang who drugs tourists on buses and trains to rob them. This time he seems to have used an overdose—enough to kill, according to the doctors. He made himself scarce as soon as he saw that I wasn't eating the toffee."

Ann had understood immediately what had happened when my head slumped on my chest and I began to drool. She assumed it was simple knock-out drops and laid me out across the seat to sleep it off. But then I turned blue from lack of oxygen, and when she took my pulse, none was detectable.

She appealed to the bus driver, who at first thought I was drunk. When Ann convinced him it was an emergency, he reluctantly pulled over, helped her lay my comatose form on the grass at the roadside, then drove off, not about to let a thing like this upset his schedule. Only the good luck that a passing van carried a hitching policeman had enabled her to get me to a hospital in Surat Thani. There the staff struggled for four uncertain hours before reestablishing my vital signs.

For me, trying to take this all in, there was something else, something very strange, though I really didn't begin to focus on it until the hospital settled down for the night. I remained awake and astonished, for I felt as if I'd had enough sleep to last a lifetime. As I sat there propped up against the pillows, I began to realize that it had been no ordinary unconsciousness from which I had awakened.

Nor was it anything like those out-of-body experiences I'd read about from people who'd been close to death (experiences I'd dismissed with my usual skepticism). It was as if I'd emerged freshly made, with all my memories re-created, from a vast "dazzling darkness" where there had been nothing, yet everything, an unbelievable aliveness beyond space and time. It was like being reborn, and I remembered an old nursery rhyme:

"Where did you come from, baby dear? Out of everywhere into here."

That wonderful everywhere was right there with me in that hospital room, almost as if it were producing my consciousness by shining through the back of my head! It felt so palpably real that I put my hand up to the back of my skull, half wondering if the doctors had sawed part of it away. Yet it wasn't in the least a frightening feeling—more like the removal of a cataract from my soul, letting me see the world and myself properly for the first time. That dark lovely radiance seemed to reveal the essence of everything as holy—even the discolored sheets, the peeling paint, the smell from the bathroom, the coughs and groans from patients in adjoining rooms.

From the recesses of my memory emerged an image out of the Bible, of the whole universe coming into being from "the darkness upon the face of the deep," and the Creator finding it all, every bit of it, good. My scientist's mind immediately balked at the idea that I of all people might be having some kind of religious experience, and sought an alternative explanation. A lingering effect from the poison perhaps? But no, the doctor had said some hours back that the stuff had been metabolized out of my system. So was I just feeling extreme joy of living after surviving such a close brush with death?

At that point I got the biggest jolt yet, for I realized that were I told now that I was to die at any minute, that I would not survive the hour, I simply wouldn't mind! Somehow my fear of dying had been completely removed. It was as if the wonder of life was sufficient unto itself, moment by moment, no matter what the future might bring, in this world or any other.

The word *eternity* echoed through my head, and my mind finally surrendered to the idea of a mystical experience. I sensed something like a gentle chuckle in the dark, and I remembered Dante's famous vision of entering paradise and seeing "the smile of the universe." For the first time in my life I understood what he meant. How would I find words to tell Ann the next day?

I still wasn't contemplating the possibility that this wonderful consciousness had *come to stay*, and would be with me for the rest of my life.

Today, 11 years later, that sense of Presence is still with me. It's with me right now as I gaze out my window in Sydney at the cliffs and the ocean. It is with me as I type this, in the hardness of the chair that I am sitting on, and most astonishing of all, it is in the pain at the back of my neck, which warns me that I have been bending over too long and need a rest. For more than a decade, my colleague Ann has been able to study my ongoing religious experience. Perhaps most extraordinary has been the discovery that God can transform even the experience of pain. It's not easy to explain, but somehow I experience things like sore throats and stiff joints from inside, where pain isn't my enemy at all, but part of God's marvelous creation.

At an age when most people retire, I have been given a whole new life. I've read every book about mysticism I could lay my hands on, and am now convinced that the Presence is what faith is all about. For me the great discovery has been that Jesus was speaking the simple truth when he said the Kingdom of God is right here, in and amongst us, all the time.

Angels are any forces that God uses to wake us to the Kingdom's Presence. For me, closeness to death was just that, mediated by a would-be thief on a bus in Thailand.

Shortly after his return to Australia, John Wren-Lewis came across "The Night," a poem by the seventeenth-century Christian poet Henry Vaughan. The final stanza reads:

There is in God, some say,
A deep, but dazzling darkness;
*   as men here*
Say it is late and dusky, because
*   they*
See not all clear.
O for that night! where I in him
Might live invisible and dim.

"Nothing Can Separate Us..."

by Kelly Haugh Clem, Piedmont, Alabama

That March afternoon, the week before Palm Sunday, I picked up four-year-old Hannah at preschool and drove home through the Alabama countryside. She leaned against the car window, watching the sun blend into the horizon in a profusion of purple and pink— her favorite colors. "Look, Mommy!" she cried, bouncing up and down on the seat.

At times it seemed the word *exuberant* had been invented to describe Hannah. The smallest things exhilarated her—pinecones, rainbows, leaves with two different colors, the way an owl's head "turns all the way around." She never found a tree she didn't want to climb or a rock she didn't try to bring home. She was that kind of girl. An earth child, I called her.

I smiled at Hannah and her purple-pink sky, but my mind was elsewhere. For the last four years I had been the pastor of Goshen United Methodist Church, a small congregation in the farming and industrial community of Piedmont. We were planning a musical drama for Palm Sunday—one of the biggest productions we had taken on. Even the children would be singing. All week I had been preoccupied with the details. Now, as we pulled into the driveway of the parsonage, I glanced at the church door, reminding myself to check on the palm branches the children's choir would wave during the processional.

"Mommy?"

"Uh-huh," I said, figuring how many branches we would need.

"Will you, Daddy, Sarah and me all die at the same time?"

The question startled me. I turned and stared at her, wondering what had prompted it. Was it the tornado drill her school had gone through earlier that week?

"We may not die at the same time," I told her gently. "But I believe we'll all be together again."

She accepted this as a matter of fact. "When you die, you get buried," she said, nodding. "After that you go live with God."

"That's right, honey," I said.

As we climbed out of the car, the conversation hung in my thoughts like a cloud, but Hannah was already back to the splendors of being an earth child. "I'm going to pick up pinecones. I want to take a present to Rebecca and Katie," she said, referring to the girls next door. Hannah loved to give away treasures—the rocks in her pocket, leaves with two colors, the rainbows she painted in her room.

I walked with her next door, while she cradled two large pinecones against her T-shirt. On the way back I took her hand and squeezed it tight.

Palm Sunday morning I was at the church early for one last rehearsal. My husband, Dale, a Methodist campus minister at Jacksonville State University, had left the day before to take students on a mission trip to Oklahoma, so I had both of our girls in tow. I left two-year-old Sarah with the baby-sitter at the church and told Hannah she could come with me to rehearsal. Normally she would have been part of the children's choir, but she wasn't sure she wanted to sing. She didn't know all the words to the song; besides, she wasn't feeling well.

Inside the sanctuary the man playing the role of Jesus was practicing his walk down the aisle, dragging a wooden cross. Instead of live instrumentation we were using tape accompaniment, and Carol, the choir director, was trying to get the children to come in at the right time. "Why must the Little Lamb die?" they sang.

Hannah, in a pink dress and pink tights, climbed onto the altar rail to watch, unable to take her eyes off Jesus and his dramatic walk. "I want to sing too!" she told me when the rehearsal ended.

There weren't enough children's costumes, so we headed next door to the parsonage, where I found some blue-and-white-striped material and cut out a robe for her. On the way back to the church I looked up at the sky. It hung heavy and gray like a sodden quilt. The air was warm and still. *Strange*, I thought.

Inside the church a member was getting out candles in case of a thunderstorm. "We can't lose the electricity," I said, suddenly worried. "We'll have no music."

"Now, Kelly, we'll go on just fine—music or no music."

His words reassured me. As I stood behind the pulpit to open the service, I hardly noticed the sky rumbling outside. I had never seen a crowd this big at Goshen. The church was filled to capacity. A hundred and forty, I guessed.

As I took my place with the choir, I glanced over at Hannah to be sure she was in her seat. She sat quietly in the front pew with the other children, her Easter shoes sticking out beneath the blue-and-white-striped robe. I smiled at her. She grinned back.

As our musical drama began, the rain crashed down. Lightning and thunder cracked and shuddered. The lights flickered. I glanced up at them, feeling uneasy. The music halted, but we struggled on. "God has provided, praise his name forever," we sang.

As the next song began, two sisters performing a duet strained to lift their voices over the storm, but the wind and rain were intensifying, and by the time the song ended I could hear what sounded like hail hitting the south wall of the church. People turned and looked.

A pause of several seconds ensued, as if we sensed something was about to happen. I felt a change in air pressure. A baby near the back cried out. Then suddenly a stained-glass window on the south side shattered, spewing purple and white glass across the sanctuary.

"Get down!" someone screamed from the front of the church.

It was a tornado.

Pieces of the ceiling were starting to fall. *Hannah. I have to get to Hannah.* I was turning to run toward her when a brick hit me on the side of my head. I fell hard on my shoulder.

As I lay there, it seemed as though the world were exploding. Roaring, thunderous wind. The roof lifted off the building, then crashed down in the center aisle. The south wall toppled. Chunks of concrete and bricks were coming down everywhere. I threw my arms over my head.

When it was over, I looked up and saw the sky—clear, with a patch of blue. Everything was hushed, calm. No rain, no wind, no thunder, no voices. I pushed away bricks and managed to stand. The sanctuary appeared like the aftermath of a bomb blast—wall-to-wall concrete rubble, piles of bricks and cinder block, shattered glass, mangled pews, the roof looming up from the floor.

I saw arms and legs protruding from the debris. Several people were lying trapped and still, covered in white dust. "Oh, God, please help us," I prayed. In my whole life I had never prayed a prayer that was wrung from so deep a place.

Other survivors struggled to their feet, calling out to loved ones. *Hannah and Sarah. Where are my girls?* I looked toward the back of the church, where Sarah had been. That part was still standing, which gave me a surge of hope.

As I strained to lift beams and blocks to free those trapped around me, I realized my shoulder was injured worse than I had thought. I could barely use my arm. Still I kept trying to clear a path toward Hannah's pew, no more than eight feet away.

Someone at the back of the church held up Sarah, letting me know she was all right. Then another welcome sight—a rescue worker in a bright-yellow jacket picking his way through the ruins. "Down here," I shouted. "There are children down here."

Suddenly I saw Amy, who had been sitting beside Hannah. She leaned against the pew, her legs pinned, with no sign of life. As the rescue worker freed her, I looked down and saw a piece of blue-and-white-striped material protruding from a pile of bricks beneath the pew. *Hannah.*

As another rescue worker rushed outside with Amy, the man in yellow helped me move the bricks. He pulled Hannah out, laid her near the altar rail and began CPR. I touched her face and patted her arm, wishing she weren't so cold. "My Hannah," I said. "Mommy's here. Mommy's right here."

I thought she might be dead, but I couldn't absorb that. "My Hannah," I kept saying.

The man picked her up and rushed outside, stepping over what was left of the south wall. I struggled to keep up.

Outside, ambulance lights were churning in the grayness. Rescue workers scrambled in and out of the rubble, carrying equipment, bringing out victims. There was so much confusion, so much need. Sitting on the grass before me, a nine-year-old boy bent over his mother. "Don't die, Mommy," he pleaded. All I could think was how much I wanted to keep her alive, to keep this mother and child together. I felt for her pulse and began chest compressions.

Moments later when rescue workers took over, I stood up and looked around, but the man carrying Hannah was gone. I spotted Carol, the choir director, who was also a nurse, helping with the injured. "I've lost Hannah," I told her. "Did you see where they took her?"

"She was put in an ambulance. I think to Gadsden Hospital."

The hospital. Then maybe she was alive. I could still hope.

I found my other daughter sitting unhurt in the lap of a friend. "I'll take care of Sarah," she said, then took off her shoes and handed them to me. Somehow I had lost mine. I slipped the shoes on, then slowly turned to face the church. It was one of the grimmest moments of my life.

I saw a place filled with dead and injured. Less than an hour before, it had pulsed with songs of the Passion, with children gleefully waving palm branches. Now the building was a shell, completely devastated. In that moment I could not foresee our congregation going on. I imagined those who survived losing faith, losing the ability to worship again. *There'll be no more Goshen Church,* I thought. *It's gone.*

I looked down at my soiled white vestment, reminded suddenly that I was the minister, that this was my church and these were my people. A feeling of calmness came over me then, the sense of God's presence right there with me. I walked back toward the church.

For the next couple of hours I prayed with people, handed out supplies, tried to bring comfort. "My husband is dead," someone said, and I sat a while and held her hand. Everywhere I turned, I heard heart-wrenching words: "I can't find my little boy" or "My wife is trapped under the roof."

As the last of the people were brought out, a rescue worker noticed my bruised head and injured shoulder. He put a sling around my arm and directed me to the triage area that had been roped off on the front lawn. Soon after, I was driven to a hospital.

After X rays were taken of my shoulder, I lay on a stretcher in an overflow room. I asked every person I saw about Hannah, but no one knew anything. Finally I saw a nurse walking toward me. As she motioned for a minister, who was a friend of mine, my heart started to race. The two of them wheeled me to a secluded corridor, then stood beside me for a long, silent moment. My hands began to tremble. The minister held them. He said, "Kelly, I think you already know this, but Hannah died."

When my husband returned that evening, we fell into each other's arms.

Twenty people from the church died that morning and 86 were injured, many severely. As we moved through the days before Easter and as the funerals were held, I kept wondering if the church would go on. I wondered if I could go on. Stunned with grief and pain, I could not envision a future.

Then the phone began to ring. Church members wanted to know if we would be holding an Easter service. These were the same people who had lost loved ones, people who had been injured. I knew they were thinking about what happened to Jesus on the cross and what happened to our church, and they were longing for Easter.

Yes, I thought. *We'll have a sunrise service right on the lawn beside the church. We'll be out there at dawn waiting for Easter.*

On Thursday I woke with a piece of Scripture repeating in my head, and I knew God meant for me to read it to the people on Easter morning. I found my Bible, sat down at the kitchen table and read the whole passage:

"Who shall separate us from the love of Christ? Shall tribulation, or distress, or persecution, or famine, or nakedness, or peril, or sword?... No, in all these things we are more than conquerors through him who loved us. For I am sure that neither death, nor life... nor things present, nor things to come... nor anything else in all creation, will be able to separate us from the love of God in Christ Jesus our Lord" (Romans 8:35, 37-39, *Revised Standard Version*).

My heart was broken and my hope battered, but these words touched something deep inside me. I felt the strength of my faith.

On Easter morning I waited beside the church with 200 others in the cool predawn darkness. In the center of the ruins, where the altar had once been, someone had erected a large wooden cross. Then at exactly seven o'clock when I stood to begin the service, the sun spilled over the horizon in purple-pink colors Hannah would have loved. With my face swollen and my shoulder in a brace, I stepped up to the makeshift podium. "I can't think of any other place

I'd rather be," I said. "Can you?" Then I opened my Bible and read: "Who shall separate us from the love of Christ?… "

When I looked up, I saw people nodding with tears in their eyes. Their faces told me we would go on.

In July, four months after that Palm Sunday, Dale and I celebrated Hannah's birthday. She would have been five years old. We stood in the backyard on the stump of a tree that had been destroyed by the tornado. We held seven helium-filled balloons, each a different color of the rainbow. As we let them go one by one, we celebrated something about Hannah's life.

We remembered her exuberance, her delight in small things, the way she gathered all the living she could. We remembered the love that compelled her to give away her treasures. We recalled her words about death in the car a few days before she died, and her simple faith that God is good and life follows death.

As the balloons sailed away, I felt Hannah was teaching me the things I needed in order to go on. It was as if God was reminding me through Hannah's life to live deep, to love much and to have faith.

Almost a year after the tornado, our congregation gathered in a field and broke ground for a new church, which would be built in the shape of a butterfly, a symbol of rebirth. As I watched the children pushing shovels into the ground, I thought about the difficult months of trying every day to live deep, love much and have faith. People often asked Dale and me how we could go on having faith after this.

"You don't need faith for things you understand," Dale told them, "but for the things you don't."

That's why I needed Hannah's childlike faith. I didn't understand why death and tragedy came. I only knew they are part of life, part of a natural world. Storms can't be avoided—even Jesus wasn't spared—but without a doubt God is with us in our suffering. For in the end nothing can separate us from God's love, Not tornadoes. Not anything.

My thoughts were interrupted as people came forward carrying cups of dirt from the old church site and emptied them onto the soil the shovels had dug, blending old and new. I looked at Sarah, at the circles left on her knees from kneeling in the dirt. I looked at my husband; at the good, sturdy faces all around; at the sun glistening on this field that would one day be our church home. I felt my heart grow large with thanksgiving. In spite of everything, Easter had come to Piedmont, Alabama.

Thanksgiving with the Homeless

by Linda Neukrug, Walnut Creek, California

This seemed more like April Fools' Day than Thanksgiving—I was right in the middle of the kind of bizarre mix-up that could only happen to me.

Just a few hours earlier I had been pretty smug about my Thanksgiving plans. Originally I had had nowhere to go—my family was 3000 miles away and I hadn't made any friends yet here in San Francisco—but then I had my bright idea. A quick phone call to a downtown soup kitchen, and suddenly I had something important and useful to do. More than useful—*noble*.

When a coworker extended an invitation for me to dine with her family, I didn't succeed at keeping smugness out of my voice as I said, "No, I decided to do something useful this year." After I explained, she seemed impressed. *As she should*, I thought. I was pretty impressed myself.

I awoke at six o'clock on Thanksgiving morning, eager to get to the city. I didn't envy the families I rode on the train with, who were chattering and admiring one another's color-coordinated outfits. One day I would have friends here too, but this year my jeans and T-shirt were appropriate. After all, I was on my way to do good work, not enjoy a party.

When I arrived at the shelter, I wasn't surprised by all the people lined up. Year after year, safe in the cozy confines of my family's living room, I had seen the pictures on the TV news: hordes of people at long tables, squalling children, toothless old men. I looked around to see where I was supposed to go.

In the alley, scores of people were standing in clusters under an oaktag sign reading, "Volunteers Pls. Wait Here." I made my way over, alongside other volunteers, surprised so many were willing to do a good turn. Apparently the man holding the clipboard was surprised too, for he stumbled over his words as he said, "I'm Ed. Er, folks… this has never happened before, but we have way too many volunteers. We usually never get the fifty we need, so we had all the radio stations mention it this year. Now we have two hundred, and no place to put you all, even in double shifts." He grinned. "Just to remind you, we could sorely use your help the rest of the year." Then Ed added, "But today you good people get a reprieve. So we would like to thank you all for coming and wish you a happy Thanksgiving. God bless you."

A surprised murmur ran through the crowd; everyone besides me seemed delighted to be able to leave. "That's great news," the red-cheeked man in front of me said to his pal. "Now I can go over to my sister's. Vicki's always claiming she doesn't see enough of me."

A woman was thrilled to be going to her cousin's. "Sarah told me to drop in any time. The kids'll be tickled by my surprise visit."

My stomach felt hollow as I realized I didn't know anyone in town well enough to show up at the last minute saying, "Here I am after all!"

Just then Ed called out, "All you volunteers are welcome to join us for lunch, of course."

I shuddered as the others left. Obviously he had meant it as a joke, but to me it wasn't funny. The only contact I had ever had with homeless people was when I had occasionally—and gingerly—handed one a quarter on the street. And I had no desire to deal with them without that plastic barrier—the one that separated me and the food from them—between us.

But when I finally turned to leave, I couldn't. I had waited too long. When Ed opened the gates, people swarmed in through the narrow corridor. The line surged forward and turned into a crowd, with me somehow in the midst of it. I was carried inside. "I don't belong here," I cried out to the burly man behind me.

He shrugged. "Who does?"

"No," I insisted. "I've got to get out." But all I succeeded in doing was moving back about a dozen feet. The line just kept on coming, taking up every available inch in that corridor. Eventually, I was swept up to the counter where the food was being served.

"I'm a volunteer too," I said as I accepted two slices of turkey from the woman behind the Plexiglas partition separating me from the food. "I mean, I don't belong on this line. They had too many of us."

She merely dumped a dollop of sweet potatoes and a tiny pleated cup of cranberry jelly on my paper plate. "Happy Thanksgiving. Next!" she barked. I moved along.

"I'm a volunteer too," I told the man behind the counter as he handed me a plastic cup of apple juice and a corn muffin.

"Happy Thanksgiving and God bless you, darling," he said.

Defeated, I slowly made my way toward a long aluminum table covered with a thin paper tablecloth. I settled into one of the empty seats, too tired and discouraged to leave but not wanting to have any of these people get too close. A man sat down opposite me. He stuck out his hand and shook mine. "I'm Fred," he told me. "I'm an alcoholic," he added, going on to say that he was now "on the road back."

"That's nice," I said. "I was supposed to volunteer here."

"Oh." His face fell and he turned to the man next to him.

A pregnant woman, somehow managing to hold a toddler as well as two plates of food, slid into the end seat and smiled at me warmly. "It's nice to sit down," she said. "You know how it is—this is the first time I've been able to eat in peace in days!"

"I'll feed your son," I offered.

"Oh, would you? That's so kind."

"Well, actually, I'm a volunteer. It's kind of my job… "

"Oh." Her face clouded, and she ate quietly, not saying anything else.

The only other people at the table were a father and son—a man in a tank top with a rip in the side, along with a boy with a blond cowlick and a missing front tooth. They bowed their heads briefly and I averted my eyes. I watched them as I picked at my crumbling corn muffin. The turkey was dry, and the room smelled terrible—like my junior high lunchroom.

I heard the boy say, "Daddy! Mmmm! I like this food!"

The father smiled at his son's exuberance. "Don't eat too fast, Son." He turned toward me and said in explanation, "It's been a while since I could afford to give them a good meal like this one. You know?"

"I'm a volunteer," I said quickly.

The father's face went bright-red, and there was an awkwardness in the air. Unaware of it, the boy chimed in helpfully, "We got a volunteer in our class at school. She sits right down at our table with us in school. You know, she teaches us better than our teacher—'cause she's right at the same table," he repeated, "not way up in front of the room." He smiled, then jabbed his plastic fork into the sweet potatoes and ate them with gusto.

I stared at the boy, amazed that he had put his finger right on the heart of the matter. I had been so busy looking for differences between me and everyone else that I was acting as if they were a separate species! But were they so different? Hadn't I had bad relationships? Hadn't I had job problems? Didn't I have friends who were recovering alcoholics? And what about my 20-year-old niece, who was already the parent of a toddler and an infant? Was this woman in the shelter less worthy just because she didn't live in a suburban home? Thoughtfully I finished the corn muffin.

By the time I left, I had spoken with Fred, Dave and Ella (my tablemates), along with Donald and Fredda (the children). By then the crowd had thinned considerably, and I was able to make my way through the hall easily. Once outside, I blinked in the bright sun—then cringed when I saw a TV newscaster poking his microphone in the faces of several of the people on line. *What do they think these people are—animals in a zoo?*

I stopped dead in my tracks then, having to smile at my own indignation. I had been feeling superior too, believing I was better than the people I was volunteering to help. Then I had been thrust into this odd situation of having lunch with them—only to discover we weren't so different after all! The only barrier separating us had been one I had erected myself—my unwillingness to see these people as what they were: people.

That was when, caught deep in thought, I bumped directly into one of the newspaper reporters! Holding a pen over his notepad, the man asked me: "How was your meal?"

I considered the question, then surprised myself with my answer. "The food was a traditional Thanksgiving dinner," I said, "but the best part of the meal was talking to the really nice people I shared it with."

What Happens When Love Fails?

*by Hannah Pierson**

My sister, Katie, and I are trapped in the pantry with our mother. She is giving us shots of blood-red vinegar. Even if I swallow quickly, the sharply acidic taste remains in my mouth. She holds my face toward her as her thumb pushes in under my jaw-bone. I used to admire the crystal shot glasses kept in Gram's cabinet, but now the glass is thick and cold as my mother forces the caustic punishment down my throat.

It is a few years later. I am eight. I am sitting at the dining room table with *Strong's Exhaustive Concordance of the Bible.* It is an immense book with tiny type. There are no sentences, only phrases, abbreviations and reference numbers. I love to read; I have a list of the books I have read this year, but *Strong's* does not have stories in it. The leather-bound King James Bible has stories in it, but my task is to find all of the verses under the bold heading that reads "tale-bearer"; after that, "liar." Then I write out the relevant Bible passages in their entirety. My only recourse is to do as I am told, so that maybe this will not hap-pen again. It starts to get dark. My fingers hurt and I get thirsty, but I stay at the table until I am all done.

I accept these "disciplinary measures." They are not painful like the under-the-chin punches that do not leave much of a visible mark. As I get older the injustice strikes me harder. Words cause me the most pain. The words last much longer than the bruises. My mother wishes out loud that I had never been born. She destroys my self-confidence. I have developed a sort of cynicism—I doubt that people could honestly be good to *me*, that they could like *me*.

I have no sense of security or trust. I find a kitchen knife on the floor in my room and wonder what was contemplated while I slept. Sometimes I try to hide, alone and scared, in a dark, cold cellar or garage. Sometimes we fight all night. I struggle to get away until she becomes bored or tired. It is futile for a

60-pound child to try to escape from the bathroom when a large and strong woman blocks the door. Grandpa threatens to call the police, but he never does. He is afraid of her too. My head aches. Welts rise on my arms. Blood rushes to my face as I feel my cheek grow warm under her handprint. Her anger comes from something other than my failings. Something else sets her off, but she attacks Katie, Gram and me. I am the strongest, the angriest, and I fight back. I do things to distract her from them, like throw her diet soda on her worn blue bathrobe; then her hatred is turned to me. But I am only a weak child, and I cannot do anything to make it all stop.

Sometimes my mother speaks with no emotion, no expression on her face. It scares me when she is hollow like this, because I know she is agitated, perhaps on the verge of an explosive wrath. I do not want to upset her. I am afraid of messing up. I am always treading on thin ice. My efforts to avoid confrontation by careful obedience are doomed to fail. I have become a meticulous perfectionist, a neat child to those who do not know. People think I have good manners. I am unheard and unseen; I just watch. I have plenty of time to study my family members because I am observant and am sensitive to what the people in my house are feeling and thinking. It is like keeping track of the pieces on a chessboard. It is necessary that I know how each piece moves and how the opponent will react. I do not worry about winning, just keeping myself out of check.

I start sixth grade at a new school. Katie goes too. I try not to be noticed. This is difficult because my class is small and other kids are nice to me. I go to their birthday parties and eat dinner at their houses; maybe they like me a little. Their moms seem nice, but my mom can seem nice too. My teacher is more than just nice; she understands. Mrs. Hoffman must remember what it was like to be a kid.

I work hard in school. If I do really well, my mom might not get so angry with me. Dad might notice that I exist. He might listen. He might be around more. He spends plenty of time with other kids; he directs the youth group at church. I bring home almost perfect report cards, but he does not say "Good job." I work hard anyway because I am learning. I am learning that there is much more that I want to know.

Dad comes home late at night, wearing his leather jacket, after youth group. He smells like bowling alleys and pizza. He sits on the edge of the bed. Dad says that Mom might have to go away for a while to get some help. Instead of this sudden information solving my problems, it adds to them. Information preceded by "Don't let your mother know" is dangerous. If my collusion is discovered later, the consequences will be severe. Katie is worried, and I try to comfort her.

Mrs. Hoffman can tell that I haven't slept. She does not know that my mother had her hands around my throat last night. I talk to her. I tell her some of what is going on. She goes with me to the headmaster. I cry because I know it may only get worse from here. They give me dry, papery Kleenex. When my dad picks Katie and me up from school, we cannot go home. Katie cries, she does not want to leave Mom. My dad says he is taking us away. We end up at a foster home in the next state. It is a Christian family, and they pray for us. The family already has plenty of kids. Eventually, Dad, Katie and I move back together without Mom.

The next years are filled with lawyers and social workers. A psychiatrist evaluates us. He says my sister and I are okay. I think Katie and I have learned to cope with a lot. I have to go to court. One of my teachers gives me an index card with verses on it to give me courage. These are kind verses from the Bible, not a punishment or condemnation. They are not about talebearers. God says he will be there even when your father and mother forsake you.

I have not had a mother in an emotional sense; now I do not even have one physically present. I am the oldest. I am independent and responsible; I have to be. Some of my friends have moms who wrap sandwiches in wax paper for brown-bag lunches. Their mothers do their laundry for them, come to their eighth-grade graduations, and make sure their dresses fit. I buy the fabric for my dress with my own money, and I sew it myself.

I still have my dad, but he cannot fill the void where two parents should be. He is still the same. A woman who is also a youth group leader is my father's wife now.

My mother still haunts my daily existence. She calls my school, my house, my friends' mothers. She shows up at my church. She follows me and makes threats. She tells people that I am a terrible person. She throws the red punch that they serve after church onto our car. Restraining orders are only pieces of paper. When she is committed to a hospital, it just makes her more angry. Gram insists she is sick, that I should not hold it against her. Christ commanded us to love everyone. I go to visit my mother. She is with the insane people on the tenth floor. I appease Gram. I should forgive. Later, I think I do.

It is difficult for me to love. I have started with accepting myself. Even though my mom wished I had not been born, I could not be happier to be alive. I have found that there are people who really do love me for who I am. To really love, I have to trust first. My trust is hard to earn because I have lost a lot by trusting a little. Maybe I am not emotional because I do not find love quickly, but I am emotional in the sense that I value love more because I perceive it as rare. God's love is abundant, yet rare in its perfection. I have been looking for faithfulness and unconditional love among my fellow imperfect human beings. Now as I face questions about my future, I can look back and see how God has carried me through. He has been faithful. As I fall away, he calls me back. Sometimes I think I have to study, to search for God or receive a sign. When I stop searching and just think about all that he has done for me, faith, trust and love become so simple.

God for the good day,
    God for the bad day,
God for the pleasure,
    God for the pain,
God for the rain,
    God when our barns are empty,
God when they're full again.

              Irish blessing

I Promised Mama

by Nissan Krakinowski, Brooklyn, New York

I t was in a Nazi concentration camp in Stutthof, in the Danzig region, that I promised my mother, Pesah, I would look after my brother, Chaim. Though I was still young myself, I think Mama saw that I was the one with chutzpah, already wise to the ways of the world.

But the world's ways in those awful days were inspired by the spirit of evil, I believe. In June of 1941 my family had lived in Kaunas, Lithuania. One day at midnight a friend frantically beat on our door to warn us of what the invading Nazis would do to us Jews. But Papa, a highly respected tailor, could not believe him. My father, Shimon, was one of the first Jews to be shot in Kaunas.

Mama, Chaim and I were forced to live in the Kaunas ghetto, and to labor on the local military airport. Mama helped keep us alive. One slice of moldy bread washed down with a watery soup was our only daily meal. She would always break her bread in half and give each of us a quarter.

"Mama, what are you *doing*?" I'd scold.

"Shhhh," she would whisper, looking around. "I don't need so much. It's better you two should have it."

It hurt me to see Mama wasting away, but she would not have had it otherwise.

She reminded me that we do not live by bread alone, but by every word that comes from G-d,* a reference to Deuteronomy 8:3. "Keep your mind on him, my sons, for what the dwellers of Gehenna are trying to do here won't last. Always have faith," she emphasized, "and he will watch over you."

I needed him more than ever that terrible day in 1944 when Chaim and I were herded into a line to be sent to a camp in Kaufering, Bavaria. The Nazis had chosen only those who could work. It was obvious what would happen to the ones left behind.

* A spelling used by the author and many other Jews who, out of reverence, do not write the full word when referring to the Lord.

We had only a moment to say good-bye. Mama held us close to her bony body, her dark-brown eyes full of tears. Then as we turned to go, she held me back a moment. "Listen, my son," she whispered, "you should always keep an eye on your brother. I feel if you survive, he will survive. Stay with him always."

"Yes, Mama," I choked.

"Promise?"

"I promise."

That was the last I ever saw of my mother.

When we stumbled out of the boxcar at the new camp, we were so stiff we could hardly walk. A guard began beating me for not moving fast enough. As his truncheon slammed my head, all went black. I regained consciousness, my face in the cold mud, tasting salty blood. I was glad Mama was not in this place.

She would have been overcome on seeing the decline of Chaim, who became more frail every day. He had been bruised on his right leg, making it difficult to walk. Then came the day they lined us all into two columns, facing each other. Those able to work, including me, stood in one formation. Chaim and the rest of the sick ones made up the other. Guards stood ready with rifles. I saw Chaim's eyes filled with fear and tears. Heartsick, I wondered, *Should I run to his line?* Finally, in desperation, I took a terrible chance and motioned Chaim to join me. He suddenly left his line and limped toward me. I held my breath, praying for his safety. Everyone saw but no one stopped him. They thought, I assumed, someone had given permission. I knew it was a miracle.

Though Chaim remained among us living, he slipped lower. Gangrene had blackened his leg and he could not walk. I tried to cover for him as much as possible. And the guards were not so strict when rumors circulated that the Allies were approaching. I wished they would obliterate the camp and put us out of our misery.

Then on the morning of April 27, 1945, the Nazi commandant issued a proclamation. All prisoners were to leave the camp at noon to go deeper into Germany, after which the premises would be dynamited to the ground. We knew this was to eliminate evidence of the atrocities.

But what about Chaim and the others who were unable to walk? I worried. By now everyone else was leaving the barracks. I sat with Chaim and looked into his eyes. "Chaim," I pleaded, "you *have* to walk. Look, I can help you."

"No, Nissan," he moaned, "I can't move." His thin hand pressed mine. "Go," he pleaded. "I'll be all right. Go yourself."

The barracks had become quiet as the others were lining up at the gate. Just to be outside this place, no matter where, would be heaven. Thoughts raged within me. *Your mother will never know. Your brother is close to death anyway. Don't be a fool. Go!*

49

But I also remembered Mama's hand on my arm and her pleading: *"Stay with him always."*

I promise, Mama.

I leaned down and put my arms around my brother's skeletal body. "No, Chaim. I stay no matter what."

We heard soldiers hurriedly laying dynamite, others stringing wires. At this point I committed us into the arms of G-d.

By noon only a few of us remained in the barracks. A low chanting of prayers began. I joined in with Chaim, praying that death would be quick…

Then, a distant rumble. It came closer, the groaning of tanks. It had to be our liberators. Within an hour American soldiers poured through the gate. The dynamiting never came. Who knows what happened?

The soldiers were so kind, so good-natured. They gave us chocolate bars and food. I ate so much so fast, I became ill. Chaim was given medical treatment and recovered soon after.

Later I learned terrible news. I happened to meet a fellow inmate who had left with the others that April morning. He supported himself on crutches. "We were all walking along the road when fighter planes roared down and strafed us with their machine guns," he said. "It was dusk and they must have thought we were enemy troops." He stared into the distance. "Many were killed." He looked at me and said, "You were very lucky." As he limped slowly away, I thought, *Lucky? No. Obedient.*

Discover the Amazing Power of Prayer

by Norman Vincent Peale, Pawling, New York

I n a business office, two men were having a serious conversation. One, heavily troubled by a business and personal crisis, paced the floor restlessly. "I guess no power on earth can save me," he sighed in desperation.

The other reflected for a moment, then spoke. "I have found that there is an answer to every problem. There is a power that can help you." Then slowly, he asked the man, "Why not try prayer power?"

Somewhat surprised, the discouraged man said, "I never thought of it that way, but I'm willing to try prayer if you will show me how."

He did apply practical prayer techniques, and matters ultimately turned out satisfactorily. That is not to say he did not have difficulties, but ultimately he worked out of this trouble. Now he believes in prayer power so enthusiastically that I recently heard him say, "Every problem can be solved and solved right, if you pray."

A famous psychologist said, "Prayer is the greatest power available to solving personal problems. Its power astonishes me."

Prayer releases spiritual energy, and seems able even to normalize the aging process. It is not necessary to allow your spirit to sag or grow stale or dull. Prayer can freshen you up every evening and send you out renewed each morning. You can receive guidance in problems if prayer is allowed to permeate your subconscious mind. It also has the power to keep your reactions correct and sound. Prayer releases and keeps power flowing freely.

You are dealing with the most tremendous power in the world when you pray. If you have not experienced this power, perhaps you need to learn new techniques. The secret is to find the process that will most effectively open your mind humbly to God. Any method through which you can stimulate the power of God to flow into your mind is legitimate.

A man opened a small business in New York City many years ago—"a little hole in the wall," as he called it. He started with one employee. In a few years, they moved into extensive quarters, and the business became very successful.

This man's method of business, as he described it, was "to fill the little hole in the wall with optimistic prayers and thoughts." He declared that hard work, positive thinking, fair dealing, right treatment of people, and praying always get results. This man worked out his own simple formula for solving his problems through prayer power. I have practiced it and know that it works.

The formula is: 1) Prayerize, 2) Picturize, 3) Actualize.

By "prayerize," my friend meant a daily system of creative prayer. When a problem arose, he talked it over with God simply and directly in prayer. He conceived of God as always being with him as a partner.

He took seriously the biblical injunction to "pray without ceasing." Every day, he discussed with God the questions that had to be dealt with. The Presence came finally to dominate his conscious, and ultimately his subconscious, thinking. He "prayerized" his daily life.

The second point in his formula is to "picturize." The basic factor in psychology is the realizable wish. This simply means that the man who assumes success tends already to have success and that people who assume failure tend to have failure. When either failure or success is picturized, it tends to actualize.

To assure something worthwhile happening, first pray about it and test it according to God's will; then print a picture of it on your mind as happening, holding the picture firmly in consciousness. Continue to surrender the picture to God's will—that is to say, put the matter in His hands—and follow God's guidance. Work hard and intelligently, thus doing your part to achieve success. Do this, and you will be astonished at the strange ways in which the picturization comes to pass.

In this manner, the picture "actualizes." That which you have "prayerized" and "picturized" "actualizes." It does so according to the pattern of your basic realizable wish, when conditioned by invoking God's power upon it—if you give fully of yourself to its realization.

I know many people who have successfully applied this three-point technique, not only to personal affairs but to business matters as well. When sincerely and intelligently brought into situations, the results have been so excellent that this must be regarded as an extraordinarily efficient method of prayer. People who use this method get astonishing results.

I believe that prayer is a sending out of vibrations from one person to another and to God. Molecules of a table vibrate, as does the air, as do reactions between people. All of the universe is in vibration. When you pray for another person, you employ the force inherent in a spiritual universe. You transport from yourself to the other person a sense of love, and you awaken vibrations in the universe through which God brings to pass the good objectives prayed for. Experiment with this principle, and you will discover its amazing results.

For example, I often pray for people I pass. On a train traveling through West Virginia, I began praying for people I saw as the train passed. First, I prayed for a man plowing the field and asked the Lord to give him a good crop that year.

I saw a mother hanging up clothes. I prayed that she would have a happy life, that her husband would always be true to her and that she would be true to him. I prayed that they might be a religious family and that the children would grow up strong, honorable young people.

Prayer is also a stimulus to creative ideas. Within the mind are all of the resources needed for successful living. Ideas are present in consciousness which, when released and given scope, together with proper implementation, can lead to the successful operation of any undertaking.

When the New Testament says, "The kingdom of God is within you" (Luke 17:21), it is informing us that God our Creator has laid up, within our minds and personalities, all the potential powers and ability we need for constructive living. It remains for us to tap and develop these powers.

Alert people everywhere are finding that by trying prayer power they feel better, work better, do better, sleep better, are better.

Experts in physical health often utilize prayer in their therapy. Disability, tension and kindred troubles may result from a lack of inner harmony. It is remarkable how prayer restores the harmonious functioning of body and soul. Prayer also adds to personal efficiency, helping people tap forces not otherwise available.

One of my friends likes to fall asleep while praying, for he believes that his subconscious is most relaxed at that time. It is in the subconscious that our life is largely governed. If you drop a prayer into the subconscious at that moment of the mind's greatest relaxation, the prayer has a powerful effect. My friend chuckled as he said, "Once it worried me because I would fall asleep while praying. Now I actually try to have it so."

Frank Laubach, author of *Prayer, the Mightiest Power in the World*, believed that actual power is generated by prayer. When he bombarded passersby with prayers, sending out thoughts of love, he was convinced that they felt the emanation of a power like electrical energy. He was right.

Once in a dining car, I encountered a half-intoxicated man who was quite boorish and rude. I felt that everyone in the car took a dislike to him. I determined to try Laubach's method. So I prayed for him, meanwhile visualizing his better self and sending out thoughts of good will.

Presently, for no seemingly apparent reason, the man turned in my direction, gave me a most disarming smile, and raised his hand in the gesture of salute. His attitude changed and he became quiet. I have every reason to believe that my prayer effectively reached him.

A young married woman admitted that she was filled with hate, jealousy and resentment toward friends. She was also apprehensive, worrying about her children. Her life was a pathetic mixture of dissatisfaction, fear, hate and unhappiness. I asked her if she ever prayed. "Only when I am desperate," she replied.

I suggested that the practice of real prayer could change her life, and I gave her instructions in sending out love thoughts instead of hate thoughts, and confident thoughts instead of fear thoughts. This revamped her life, as is illustrated by this letter:

"I have made wonderful progress, from the night you told me, 'Every day is a good day if you pray.' I began to affirm that this would be a good day the minute I woke up, and I have not had a bad day in the six weeks since. My days haven't been any smoother than they were, but they don't seem to have the power to upset me anymore. Every night I begin my prayers by listing all the things for which I am grateful, little things that added to the happiness of my day. This habit has geared my mind to pick out the nice things and forget the unpleasant ones."

She discovered amazing power in prayer. You can do the same.

"Don't Expect Anything for Christmas"

by Myrtle Archer, Castro Valley, California

I n 1934, our family was living in a ranch house in the Rockies, an eagle's short flight from Canada. As my eighth Christmas approached, the air snapped with cold; icicles hanging from the roof pierced the snowbanks. Only a door and a path toward the barns indicated where the house lay snuggled under all that snow.

"We ought to cut the fir by the river for our Christmas tree," Don, my 12-year-old brother said, as he unfastened his homemade wooden skis.

"Let's cut the one by the old barn," Vere, another brother, said. "It's more rounded."

For months, we three eldest of seven children had studied just about every suitable tree on our wooded 250 acres.

As I set a pail of snow, to be melted for water, on the counter in the kitchen, I heard Dad say, "There'll be no presents for Christmas."

Tears welled up in my eyes, as they always did when he pronounced those words.

"I don't believe in Christmas as it's celebrated," he said. "All those presents."

I knew that poverty had forced Dad and Mama to abandon gift-giving. Our Christmas would be whatever we could struggle to make it. The first school day after Christmas every pupil would bring his presents to the schoolhouse. I would have nothing to show. Nor would Don, Vere, Fay, or my other school-age siblings. What would be the use of appealing to Dad, or to Mama, with a new baby to tend, meals to cook and with little food in the pantry and root cellar?

"There is no Santa Claus," Dad said as he punched a hole in a harness with his awl. "And it's vicious to say that Santa will reward children with presents if they've been good and punish them with nothing if they've been bad!"

I had been a good child, but of course, good had nothing to do with presents.

It was money that bought presents. But my desperate hope for a present felt more like a sob stuck in my mouth.

Still, I would enjoy our freshly-cut tree, and our singing round it "Adeste Fideles" and "It Came Upon the Midnight Clear" and our reading aloud and our story-telling. Most of me turned warmly happy just thinking about it.

In the nearby one-room schoolhouse, the teacher said, "For our craft project, we'll make clay presents for your parents."

Carefully, I worried half of my hunk of clay into the shape of a four-inch vase. In the spring, I could fill the baked vase with Johnny-jump-ups for Mama. Wild roses would brighten it in summer, and in the fall, everlasting and goldenrod. For Dad, I made a handprint ashtray, though he never smoked. Maybe he could use it for something else.

Four days before Christmas, Don announced, "It's time."

We all followed Vere as he headed out toward the East River. In summer, we caught rainbow trout here; mink and beaver frequented its edges. Seven feet high, the fir looked glorious, and fragrance spilled from it, and, under the snow, replacing seedlings grew thick. "This is the one," Don said.

With chips flying, Vere brought the tree down. He and Don grabbed hold of it and tugged it toward the far-off plume of smoke from the house.

Vere nailed the fir, already spouting pitch from its cut, onto our old wooden stand. He and Don carried it into the cold front room and stood it up in a corner, against the calcimined walls.

"It looks good." Mama balanced baby Garner on her hip. "I used to enjoy Christmas, but it seems I just don't care for it any longer. Nor does your father." Garner let out a cry and Mama carried him back into the warmth of the kitchen.

I'd read of cranberries being strung to make decorations, but we had no cranberries. I had never even seen a cranberry, though they might be like our gooseberries, only red. The gooseberries were long gone into sauce. I'd heard of popcorn decorations, but I'd never seen popcorn either. Our food was the deer, the grouse, the bear of the forest, the fish and whatever Dad could grow from May to October.

At the kitchen table, out of red and green construction paper, leftover from a school project, we cut and pasted rings, then strung them together for decorations.

"I'd get you presents if I could." Mama rocked in the creaky, wooden rocker and nursed Garner. "But we need every penny for the taxes on this place, and for sugar and salt and such. And we haven't time to make presents."

I nodded. Dad said, "Plenty of ranchers can't even pay the taxes on their places and are losing them."

I'd never want to lose our ranch! I thought.

After swirling our decorations about the fir, we attached tin candleholders, from some more abundant past, to its green limbs. We had no candles, but what of that?

As the days inched toward Christmas, every day Dad repeated his words to us, "Don't expect anything for Christmas."

Christmas Eve, before the tree, we sang, "Joy to the World," "Oh Little Town of Bethelehem," "The First Noel" and "Up on the Rooftop, Click, Click, Click."

Christmas morning dawned. I jumped out of my crowded bed. Christmas! Even the word rang with joy. I rushed to the fragrance of our tree. Eight packages, wrapped in newspaper, waited under it, beside the presents we'd made for Dad and Mama.

We had Christmas presents after all! I grabbed up the one marked *Myrtle* and tore into the kitchen. Dad, bent over the galvanized iron washbasin, splashed water onto his cheeks, and Mama stirred sliced potatoes in the blackened skillet on the wood stove.

I hugged my package and savored its mystery, its wonder.

With my stomach nearly dropping out of me, I inched the wrapping off my package. Amongst crumpled, torn newspaper lay a pencil—long, yellow and marked *Ticonderoga*. The pencil was not even sharpened! I owned the full-length of a pencil for once in my life, a pencil all my own!

Don unwrapped a calendar from Hudson Bay Fur Company; Vere, a 1929 license plate last seen nailed onto the barn; Fay, a scrap of pink gingham that would make a dress for her clay doll; Percy, an oversized pine cone, and Phyllis, a smoked whitefish. Baby Garner's present turned out to be sugar tied into a square of white cotton cloth. Most likely, our presents would have been scorned by other children, but what of that? At school, I could display a story I'd written with my brand-new pencil.

"I thought it wouldn't hurt to give you a wee bit of something," said Dad as he picked up a thick white cup, with his morning coffee steaming from it.

When grown, I poured words onto paper and eventually sold them. I believe that gift of a pencil all my own, a present from a father who had done all he could for me, opened up a world filled with opportunity.

"Finding My Way"

by Oscar Greene

He was lost, and is found....
—Luke 15:24

In 1946, my spiritual life crumbled. The downside began during a fifteen-day downpour in poverty-stricken, war-torn Korea. Everything seemed in conflict with the Ten Commandments, the Sermon on the Mount and the Golden Rule. People were suffering, and the children were ill-clad and underfed. Then, my possessions were stolen, along with my *Book of Common Prayer* received at Confirmation in 1932. My faith vanished. I no longer believed in God.

After leaving the Army, I avoided church. My working hours were three until eleven, six evenings a week. Sunday was my day, and I pretended not to hear the tears in my wife Ruby's voice as she begged me to go to church. Even though the church bells left me feeling isolated, I held firm. I clung to wartime memories, and I struggled with disruptive dreams.

In September 1954, nine-year-old Oscar, Jr., pleaded with me to attend church. "All the daddies will be there," he said. I shook my head. Why should I pretend?

That evening another nightmare struck: I was back in Korea trudging that mud-filled path. A child was there, huddled, shivering and crying. As I knelt, the child looked up. It was our son! I awakened shaken and weeping.

War had deprived those children, but wasn't I waging a war of my own? Weren't Ruby and Oscar, Jr. victims seeking my understanding, cooperation and love? Wasn't I using the war, my working hours and twisted reason to get my own way?

Hesitantly, I entered church the next Sunday. Ruby smiled from the choir loft, and our son clapped. I returned the following Sunday and the next. Gradually, I learned there was a spiritual family waiting to welcome me and to lessen the trauma I had suffered in Korea. My nightmares melted into dreams.

Risen Lord, I lost my way. Thank you for using loved ones
to help me return to You.

Making Change

by Dennis Pieper, Jackson, Michigan

I remember one Sunday when I was 17. 1 was working part-time and tithing my money. I had learned in church that ten cents of every dollar I made belonged to the Lord. So that morning I was supposed to put in $17. All I had, though, was a $20 dollar bill. As I placed the $20 bill into the offering plate, I said silently, "Well, Lord, I'm really only supposed to offer seventeen. But You can keep the change. After all, 1 guess You can't make change for a twenty."

Then, I heard a still voice say, "I can do anything. All you have to do is ask." Surprised, I replied, "No, Lord, it's Yours. Put it to good use."

And again the voice came: "I can do anything."

Finally I said, "Okay, Lord, I have to admit my finances are awfully tight. I need every penny for college savings. If you could give me my three dollars in change that would be great."

As I left the service I couldn't help laughing to myself. How would the Lord ever fulfill this one?

Sunday passed by, as did Monday and Tuesday. I was ready to forget my three-dollar conversation with God. But on Wednesday the manager of the restaurant where I worked came to me and said, "Here's a small bonus. Last month's sales exceeded our projections."

Into my hand the manager placed three crisp one-dollar bills.

I offered my silent thanks and then sat widely, thinking, *If the Lord can make change for a twenty, He can certainly change my life.*

And He has—all for the better!

Chapter Three

Help in Desperate C

cumstances

We shall steer safely through every storm,
so long as our heart is right,
our intention fervent, our courage steadfast,
and our trust fixed on God.
— **St. Francis de Sales**
(1567 – 1622)

Leap
of Faith

by David Michael Yoder III, Mobile, Alabama

T he windows of the base operations room at the U.S. Coast Guard Air Station, Elizabeth City, N.C., rattled as 60-mph gusts from the worst storm of the year lashed the base. Staring silently into the rain-slashed blackness I was despondent—a feeling shared by the three other crewmen of our H-60 rescue helicopter.

We had just received word that three exhausted men were about to abandon hope as fierce Atlantic seas battered their disabled 41-foot ketch, the *Malachite*. This was what we were trained for, why our unit existed. But we couldn't help. The men were beyond our reach. The H-60 had a 300-mile operating radius and the sailboat was about 400 miles offshore. We could get there, but we would never make it back. The nearest ship was 10 hours from the sailors' position, and they wouldn't last that long.

I clenched my fists in frustration. This would have been my first offshore rescue mission. I had joined the Coast Guard because I wanted to save lives. But in my gut I felt the churning grasp of fear. Would I have been able to do it? As an aviation survivalman, I was trained to assist shipwreck victims. But I was a greenhorn. Lives could depend on me—and I was terrified that I would fail.

Then Lieutenant Bruce Jones, our pilot, broke the silence. "Bermuda," he said.

Our heads snapped up.

"If we continued on to Bermuda we might make it," he said, excitement in his voice.

Bermuda was 620 miles from the base—the extreme limit of our helicopter's range. Even under ideal conditions, no H-60 had ever flown to Bermuda from the States. In the midst of a storm and stopping to hoist the sailors aboard, it would be touch and go.

After calculating our fuel reserve, we figured we would have 30 minutes to save the men. The H-60 couldn't land in the water. I would have to be lowered onto the deck of the sailboat and help the sailors into a rescue basket.

My heart pounded with excitement—and apprehension—as we took off into a raging blackness punctuated by jagged flashes of lightning. For two and a half hours the H-60 shuddered and pitched as the storm-fed gusts slammed into it. I could hear Lieutenant Jones and copilot LTJG Randy Watson over the intercom refiguring the distance and fuel calculation. They were convinced that our safety margin was narrowing. The winds and bone-rattling turbulence were even stronger than the forecast. But I was alone with my thoughts. *How can that boat survive this? Will I be able to get aboard to help them? Will it be afloat when we get there?* Below, like angry slashes in the blackness, were towering white-flecked waves. I thought of the worst scenario: The crew would already be in the water and I would have to go in after them. *Can I do it? Will I jump into those seas?* I felt cold sweat on my body.

Then we saw the boat. Illuminated in the beam of our searchlight was the *Malachite.* Shreds of her sails streamed in the intense wind. The boat hurtled down immense waves that loomed over her masts, which whipped back and forth. The crew radioed that they were taking on water. They wouldn't be able to stay afloat much longer.

As I sat in the yawning side hatch of the helicopter with my feet dangling over the side, my worst fears were realized. There was no way I could be lowered onto the boat's deck—not the way those masts were whipping. My fingers hurt from clutching the sill of the hatch. For the men to be rescued, they would have to jump into the ocean—and I would have to go in after them. Lieutenant Jones's voice crackled through the headphones in my helmet. "The boat's sinking, Dave. They want to go in. Will you do it?"

I hesitated. I didn't have to go and nobody would blame me if I decided not to. The blackness below terrified me. Cold sweat poured under my diver's dry suit.

The earphones crackled again. "I have to know now, Dave."

I looked down into the raging blackness. *God, what should I do?* I silently prayed. And the answer was immediate. I had a choice. Those men below had no options. I had always professed my belief in God. But I never had to prove it. This would be my leap of faith. I turned to flight mechanic Dave Barber and nodded.

My headset crackled once more. "Thirty minutes, Dave. That's all the time we have."

I didn't need further explanation. The copter would leave in 30 minutes whether I was aboard or not. The rest of the crew couldn't be jeopardized for one man. My stomach was in knots, but I made my choice. I rode down in a sling and jumped.

As soon as I touched the water, the force of the sea tore me from the cable.

While rising on the crest of each wave I frantically searched for the boat, hoping the survivors would be nearby. But the boat was gone.

Finally, in the glare of the chopper's searchlight, I spotted one man. We had wanted them to stay together, but the sea had torn them from one another. I figured I would never be able to reach all of them in time. But if I could save one, maybe two…

I fought to keep from becoming disoriented. Sky and sea seemed to merge, and at times I couldn't tell up from down. I struggled to the first man, then held onto him and snagged the rescue basket as it danced wildly at the end of its tether. After helping him in and giving the signal to hoist, I checked my watch. I had been down 15 minutes. There was still time.

Then I was tossed to the crest of another gigantic wave—and spotted a second man. *Just a few minutes left, Lord. Give me the strength to get this one too.* I was tiring, and the sailor, in his weakened state, couldn't help much. I struggled to lift him into the basket. When he made it, I took a deep breath and tried to still my trembling hands.

I looked for the third man, but all I could see were whitecaps. *That's it,* I thought. *We were fortunate to get two.*

Suddenly the searchlight flashed through the flying spray. There was the third man! Although exhausted, I began swimming, feeling my remaining strength drain. Could I get him into the basket when I reached him? As I got closer, I wondered if he was even alive. Suspended in his lifejacket, he was bobbing in the waves. Then he rolled his head up and, with a haunted expression, looked me in the eye. My heart jumped.

I tried to lift him into the basket, but each time, I couldn't make it the last few inches, and we both splashed back into the water. Finally, with strength that was outside my own, I gave one last heave and he was in.

I had done it. *Thank you, God.* I thought the worst was over.

I glanced at my watch—five minutes to go. I signaled for the cable to come down without the basket. The way the basket had been flailing, it would be quicker for me just to ride the cable back up.

With two minutes to spare, I grabbed the end of the cable. But as I was about to be hoisted, a monstrous wave flipped me high in the air and spun me upside down. The cable snapped taut, leaving me entangled and underwater. For an instant I didn't think I would come back up.

But the fear was gone. I had made my leap of faith and had put myself in God's hands. *If you want me now, Lord, I'm ready,* I prayed.

Then the cable jerked, and I was out of the water and being cranked up toward the helicopter. Yet I was still not out of danger. As I watched helplessly, I saw the cable fray and unravel, until only one of the three strands remained intact. I was swinging wildly at the end of the tether, still 20 feet from the chopper, and 30 feet above the waves. If that third strand broke, I would be lost. There would be no way for the chopper to pick me up, even if I survived the fall.

But Dave Barber worked the frayed cable up to the door and wrestled me in. Relief washed over me as I settled back inside the helicopter.

"Great job, Dave," Lieutenant Jones's voice crackled in my headset. "Not bad for a first rescue."

After more than five hours in the air, we landed in Bermuda and still had 50 minutes of fuel left, thanks to a strong tailwind. When it was all over, we watched the video of our mission, and the scenes of those mountainous waves showed us just how big a miracle had occurred. The rescue operation had been beyond the ordinary human and mechanical abilities of our helicopter and crew. God had definitely been watching out for us and those men. And even though I had always believed in God, this really put the lid on it for me.

That meant I was a greenhorn no longer—in more ways than one.

Wrong Number, Right Answer

by Jessie McGinnis Jones, Forest City, North Carolina

That morning, February 28, 1992, my granddaughter Melissa fixed my hair at the beauty parlor where she works while I caught up on the local news I had missed during my recent hospital stay. On Valentine's Day, after a spell with my heart, I had had a pacemaker put in. I felt good now and I was glad to be away from all those doctors and nurses constantly fussing at me.

My daughter Rita picked me up at 11:30 and ran me back to my trailer. "Mama," she said on the way, "why don't you come over to my place and I'll fix you a sandwich and—"

"No, uh-uh," I interrupted her. "You already do too much for me. Thank you, I'm fine." Rita was always trying to keep an eye on me, especially since my heart spell. I didn't want to be rude, but I thought I could look after myself. I wanted to convince my six kids of that. It had been a battle just to stay in my trailer. Fact is, at age 80, the more independent I felt, the happier I was. I had been strong all my life. If anything serious happened, Carolyn, another daughter, lived right next door to me. I loved my kids but I didn't understand what they were all so doggone worried about. I would let them know if I needed something.

I said so long to Rita and thanked her again for her offer of lunch and the ride home. "I'll call you later, Mama," she said, pulling her car away. I shrugged and went inside, latching the chain on the door behind me. I wanted to get a little work done around the trailer but first I had to get out of my blouse; some hair clippings had caught under the collar and were itching like crazy. I sat down on my bed and pulled my left arm out of the sleeve. Then the right. But something was wrong. *My arm is stuck.* I tried again but my right arm wouldn't move. It was just hanging there. I realized with a shock that the whole right side of my body was limp. *My Lord, am I having a stroke?*

I reached for the phone on the table near the bed. I couldn't coordinate my movements. It was the most frightening sensation. I was helpless, alone. Carolyn had her grandson for the day and probably wouldn't check on me, especially the way I had been carrying on lately.

I managed to slide down onto the floor and tried to kick the table to knock the phone over, but my legs thrashed around uselessly. I finally hooked my left foot around one leg of the table. I gave it a jerk and the phone moved a few inches. I jerked again. A few more inches. Still a long way to go. Again. Getting closer. My strength was failing. Just as I got the phone poised to go over the edge of the table, it rang.

Carolyn? Rita? Oh, God, let it be one of the kids! Two rings, three, four... I struggled desperately to topple the phone. *Don't let her hang up. Please don't let her hang up.* I let out a weak cry as I made one last lunge for the table and the phone thudded over on the carpet, the receiver landing just inches from my reach.

My trembling left hand crept toward the receiver, closer. At last I held the cool plastic to my ear. "Help," I gasped. "Help me."

There was a silent pause, then a man's voice hesitantly came from the receiver: "Wha—what?"

"Help! Please, I need help!" I screamed. But this time I heard myself. My words were a horrible, slurred garble. With fear and frustration storming through my head, I tried it again. "Aaarghhar..."

"I'm sorry, I can't understand you. Who is this?" the stranger asked.

I clutched the phone like a lifeline. *Please don't hang up. I need you.*

"Are you hurt? Are you sick?"

Yes, yes! my mind screamed. Then he talked to someone on the other end and a woman's voice came on. "Hello?" she said. "Can we help you?" Again the horrible sounds came out of my mouth and I was so angry I wanted to throw the phone aside, yet I knew these people were my only hope. *God, help them to help me.*

The voices conferred again, then the woman said, "We've dialed the wrong number but you obviously need help. We're going to hang up and call the police..."

"Naahrga..." *Don't hang up!*

"Listen, please try not to worry. I promise we'll get help for you."

Then the line went dead. I felt tears rolling down my cheeks as I pushed the receiver back into its cradle. A terrible silence fell over my trailer. Was this how I was going to die? All alone, begging strangers for help? How would they ever find me?

In my living room there is a montage of snapshots I've put together over the years in a big, overflowing frame. Two loving husbands, both of whom God called home. My six children and all their children. Weddings. Graduations. Births. I wanted to crawl there now so I would be close to them if my time was at hand. Instead, gasping for breath, I rolled back against the bed and berated myself for being so stubborn and foolhardy. *All they wanted to do was help.*

My thoughts began to swim and swirl. The shrill ringing of the phone snatched me back to reality. Grappling with the receiver, I finally got the mouthpiece close and made a croaking sound. A woman's voice answered back, "This is 911. Thank goodness we reached you! Now I need your help. I'm going to ask you some questions. Make a sound only when I'm right. We're going to start with the kind of house you live in."

She ran through a list of descriptions: Red, blue, yellow. Big, small, ranch, Colonial. *No... no, not a house!* I struggled not to cry out in despair. I tried to send the image over the line to her, forcing myself to concentrate. Finally there was a pause. "I know!" she cried. "You live in a trailer!" *Yes!*

We went through the same process of elimination for the part of town I live in, my street, what side of the street. I could hear people in the background rustling through maps and the phone book. Finally came the one question I was waiting to answer. "Are you Mrs. Jones on Mount Pleasant Church Road?"

Thank you, God! Thank you.

In a matter of minutes Carolyn was talking to me through a window while firemen broke open my door. A short time later at the hospital, doctors confirmed that I had indeed suffered a minor stroke. This time I didn't mind them fussing over me so much and I couldn't have been happier to see all my children and grandchildren fussing over me too during the next few days. I bounced right back and was out of the hospital inside of a week.

The couple who had dialed my number, Mike and Paula Pruitt, had called the police after hanging up with me. They had an idea about how they might have misdialed, and 911 took it from there, frantically trying combinations of numbers until they got through to me.

Today I'm back to normal and enjoying my independence again, but I'm not as sensitive as I was about my family looking in on me. They're not trying to run my life; they never were. They just love me and want to keep me around for a while. I've set up an intercom system from my trailer to Carolyn's, and everyone has keys to my place.

We all need one another. Kinfolk especially should stick close. Sometimes it might feel like we're stuffed together in one big clan, knocking elbows and knees and pushing for space like the pictures in my frame. But we are held together by love, and by a God who can turn a wrong number into a right one.

The Magic Violin

by Shony Alex Braun, Los Angeles, California

I'm a concert violinist, yet I find it strange that the instrument I play for people's enjoyment also figured in the two most horrific times of my life.

The first happened when I was four. Our family lived in a small town in the Romanian province of Transylvania. Papa was a jeweler, a deeply devout man who carried on his father's rabbinical traditions. Mama kept the Sabbath, lit candles when she prayed, and nurtured us six children in our faith.

One day while Mama was busy cooking, my young nursemaid walked me near the thick woods outside of town. However, in rendezvousing with her sweetheart, she forgot about me. Intrigued by the trilling of birds, I wandered into the forest. Soon I was lost. Amid towering dark trees, my fascination turned to terror. Crying hysterically, I pushed through brush and brambles to find myself in a clearing. It was a Gypsy encampment of wagons and brightly painted caravans. Smoke rose from cooking fires tended by women in long, billowing dresses. One of them saw me, came over and knelt before me. "Where are you from, little one?" she asked. I cried harder.

She called to a swarthy man with a dangling gold earring. He came over carrying a violin. Lifting it to his chin, he said: "Watch now. There's a birdie inside that will hop out when I play."

As if by magic, beautiful birdsongs sounded from the violin. My tears dried. For the brief time I was with the Gypsies, I was enthralled by their music.

After being delivered home, I was consumed with a passion to play the violin. Papa found a child-size instrument and I practiced for hours every day. At age 10 I played on Radio Bucharest and at 13 was accepted to study at the Budapest Academy of Music. Then, just when life seemed most glorious, Nazi troops marched into Hungary, which had been ruling northern Transylvania. The Csendorok, local police who worked with the Nazis, rounded us Jews up in carts. Cattle cars transported us to Auschwitz, and our nightmare began.

I last saw my mother holding my nine-year-old sister's hand as they walked to the gas chambers, which were disguised as showers. And there in Auschwitz I learned to shrink from the dreaded Kapos. These were vicious, hard-core convicts appointed by the SS to head work gangs. Though still prisoners, they were free to brutalize us.

We were moved from one concentration camp to another, losing loved ones along the way. By the time we were enslaved in the Kochendorf salt mines only Papa, my brother Zoltan and I were left. My sister Violet and brothers Emil and Adolf had been shipped elsewhere. But my father, a shining example of love and goodness, would not speak ill of the Nazis. "Never be hateful toward *anyone*," he admonished us.

Hunger had reduced us to near animals. A Kapo eating an apple was watched fiercely. The instant he tossed away the core, a horde of inmates flew at it. Finally, I could not take the beatings and cruelties any longer. I was 14 years old and I wanted to die. I looked at my father laboring next to me and staggered toward the electrified fence. Knowing my thoughts, Papa gently took my arm. "Son, did you practice the Brahms violin concerto and the Kreisler composition today?"

I shook my head.

"God has given you a wonderful talent and you want to throw it away?"

Reluctantly I turned back. While swinging my hammer at the iron-hard salt, I played the music in my mind, as Papa had me do every day. When I finished, I didn't want to die.

One cold morning, my dear papa did not show up for roll call. "Find him!" roared an officer. Worn from hunger and hard work, he had overslept. As he was dragged before us, the officer bellowed: "It took ten minutes to find this dirty Jewish dog. That was ten extra minutes Germany was kept from victory!"

Zoltan and I were forced to watch while guards ferociously kicked and bludgeoned our father. I pleaded for God to save him. But Papa crumpled into the snow, blood streaming from his mouth. His lips were moving and I leaned closer to hear his dying gasp: *"Shema Yisroel Adonai elohainu Adonai echod."* ("Hear, O Israel, the Lord our God, the Lord is one.")

All Zoltan and I could do was wail in anguish. Then my agony turned to anger at God. How could he allow this to happen to such a saintly man? We trudged to the mines, and I decided there was no God.

That night as I slept on vermin-infested straw, Papa came to me in a dream. "Yitzhak," he said, using my Hebrew name, "God is *real*. Have faith, trust in him, and you will survive!"

I awakened comforted. I knew Papa was right. But I wondered about his promise of my survival after we were moved to Dachau. Evil hung over it like a turbid cloud.

One evening an SS officer strode into our barracks holding a violin. I hadn't seen a violin in so long. "Anyone who can play will be given food," he promised. Three hands shot up, including mine. The others were older men, one in his 40s, the other about 25.

We were hustled to a large room and pushed before the SS commandant. A tall, steel-eyed man in jackboots slouched in a chair. A menacing attack dog sat at his side. Three hulking Kapos, each one gripping an iron pipe, stood nearby. The commandant pointed his stick at the oldest prisoner, who was handed the violin.

"Play something," the commandant ordered in a bored tone.

The man tuned the instrument and began to play. His first notes were shaky, but soon he was playing Bach's *Chaconne, Sonata No. 6* beautifully. When the final note died, the SS man barked, *"Scheusslich!"* ("Awful!") He waved at one of the Kapos, who lunged forward and viciously brought the pipe down on the violinist's head. I realized we were there for sadistic entertainment.

The body was dragged away and the second prisoner shoved forward. His face was ashen and the violin shook so in his hands that he could not play a straight note. The SS officer sneered, "You want me to give you food for *that*?" He motioned and two Kapos began kicking and beating him to death. In the commotion I bolted for the door, but another guard caught me and thrust the violin into my arms. I had never played a full-size instrument before. Trembling, I tried to focus. I had planned to play a sonatina by Dvořák or a composition by Kreisler. But my mind went blank.

"Spiel!" said the SS man, ordering me to play.

I lifted the violin to my chin, praying: *Oh God, how does the sonatina start? How does the Kreisler piece begin?*

"Play, *Schweinhund!*"

My fingers were so weakened by starvation I could barely curve them around the fingerboard, much less press the strings. My body turned to water as one of the Kapos eagerly advanced, raising his iron pipe.

As I stood there waiting for the pipe to strike my skull, a powerful force took hold of me. My right and left hands began to move in perfect unison without conscious effort on my part. Beautiful music poured out of my violin, like the birds that had flown out of the Gypsy's that day long ago. I was playing Johann Strauss's *Blue Danube Waltz*. The idea of playing that piece had not entered my mind. I had never played it before, nor had I ever seen the music. I knew immediately God was protecting me; his angel was guiding my hands.

I continued playing. All eyes were on the SS officer. But instead of signaling to the Kapo, he began humming the melody and tapping its rhythm with his fingers. When my bow swept out the last note, the commandant growled: *"Sehr gut!"* Give him the food."

But I had already gained my reward: The strong certainty that whether I survived Dachau or not, God would always be with me, his angels guiding me.

Just before the American liberation of Dachau in April 1945, Shony Alex Braun was shot by camp guards attempting to destroy evidence of Nazi atrocities. While recuperating in an Allied hospital he played his violin in bed. Another patient, Shári Mendelovits, heard his music. Today Shári, a survivor of Auschwitz, is his wife, and they have a son and daughter. After the war, Shony studied at music conservatories in Augsburg and Munich and graduated with honors from the famous Mozarteum in Salzburg. On coming to the U.S., he studied with the distinguished Josef Gingold. He is also a prolific composer, and in 1994 he was nominated for a Pulitzer prize for his Symphony of the Holocaust.

Tight
Squeeze

by Michael Ulrich, North Royalton, Ohio

"That boy is still trapped!" Dad said. "Gerry, get dressed. You too, Mike. Maybe we can help." It was 6:30 in the morning, but right away Gerry and I knew which boy he was talking about. It had been the top news story on radio and TV the night before.

It was 1965 and three teachers and 16 boys from the Methodist Children's Home in Berea, Ohio, had gone on an outing. The van carrying them had broken down shortly before noon. While it was being repaired, three of the young guys spotted a cave and decided to do a little exploring. One of them the same age as me—15—crawled through a narrow opening in the cave's interior, then became disoriented and slid headfirst about 10 sloping feet into a V-shaped crevice. He was stuck fast.

By mid-afternoon newscasters had put out a call for help. Volunteers needed to be strong yet small enough to squeeze into the narrow passage where the boy was trapped.

That night after hearing the news Dad had seemed especially serious. His eyes scanned us eight boys gathered around the supper table, and I wasn't surprised when he said, "We ought to do something."

"They've got plenty of experts and gear," Mother said. "You'd only get in their way."

Dad said nothing more about it—until the next morning when he headed for work and heard on his car radio that after 18 hours, the boy, Morris, was still wedged head-down in the cave.

Rescuers had been working all night. An 85-pound nurse from Akron, with ropes tied around her waist, had slithered through the opening and managed to wriggle within two feet of the victim. But she panicked in the cramped quarters and had to be pulled out.

Ohio's governor had contacted expert spelunker William Karras, flying him and his crew in from Washington, D.C., in an Air Force jet. But even Mr. Karras—135 pounds and skinny as a piece of spaghetti—wasn't thin enough to get through to hook rescue gear onto Morris.

A rig was being brought to drill down a hundred feet from the top of the overlying cliff. It was a dangerous move; the whole cave might collapse. But all other efforts had failed.

That's when Dad pulled up to a phone booth and reported he wouldn't be at work. And he turned around and came back home to get us kids.

An hour later, he and Gerry and I had driven the 20 miles to Wildcat Cave. You would have thought a county fair was going on. Reporters. Cars. People. Generators to keep the lights and equipment going.

The opening of the cave itself stared out like a huge dark eyeball.

Dad asked to see someone in charge; said maybe we could help. But so many others had volunteered that no one paid much attention to us.

Mr. Karras was pacing and running his fingers through his hair. Dad looked at us and when we nodded our okay, he tapped Mr. Karras's shoulder. "I'm sure my boys can squeeze through. They're small, but they're tough."

Mr. Karras studied us. You could tell he was desperate. Finally he said, "You'll have to sign a liability release." Dad hesitated, swallowed, then uncapped his pen.

Gerry was 12 and weighed only 82 pounds. Mr. Karras attached two ropes to my brother, gave him a light and plenty of instructions. Morris was trapped about 10 feet down in a crack about 18 inches wide at the top and nine inches at the bottom.

We watched Gerry wiggle through a slit in one of the cave's inside walls. Almost right away he yelled he wanted out and was hauled back. "Did you get to him?" we shouted.

"Almost." Gerry was pale. "But I can't do it!" He bent over. Sick.

"It's okay, son," Dad said, hugging Gerry. "Mike… your turn."

My usual weight was 135, but I had trained down to 120 to get on the wrestling team at high school. Dad also told Mr. Karras about my first-aid training as an Eagle Scout.

I worked my way through the darkness like a crab. While the others shone lights in behind me, I eased into the fissure headfirst, wriggling downward in a weird kind of swim. The passageway was so tight I had to exhale in order to inch myself ahead. Every time I took a breath I was locked tight against the wall.

Ten minutes later I had squirmed my way only eight feet. No wonder the kid got stuck in here. I could get caught myself!

When I finally got close to Morris, I understood why my brother had gotten sick. Morris smelled like a rotten fish. He had been pinned in for 20 hours by then. The odor turned my stomach too.

Rescuers above were poking lights in as far as they could. But I was in my own shadow. Couldn't use my right hand, either. I needed it to brace myself to keep from sliding in on top of Morris.

"Get me out!" I heard his muffled voice. *"Please."* He couldn't help me; one arm was wedged beneath him. Worse, he was slipping in and out of consciousness.

Mr. Karras's voice echoed through the opening. He was yelling at Morris about how stupid he was to have gone in the cave in the first place. It was a smart tactic. It roused the trapped boy, making him mad enough to answer, "When I get out of here, I'm going to beat you up." Anger made his blood stir, keeping him alert.

With my left hand I worked a strap around one of his knees. The hardest part was getting it through the buckle using only one hand.

Sucking in my breath, I wriggled back out. Mr. Karras and the other rescuers cheered and grabbed the ropes to pull at Morris's body.

My limbs felt as if they were full of hot needles. I rubbed them to get feeling back. Wrestling had never taken strength like that! It was good to see daylight again. To breathe in fresh air instead of a stale cave and a kid who smelled like an outhouse.

The cheering stopped. It turned out the pulling had merely wedged Morris tighter.

"Not enough lift," Mr. Karras announced. He looked at me, still sprawled on the ground. "You're the boy's only hope," he said. "I hate to ask you, but could you go in again?"

When he said that, the story of David and Goliath flashed across my mind. This was a challenge that sure seemed as big as any Goliath. David had been a young guy like me. And he had been given strength to conquer his giant. With God's help, I would too.

It was even harder the second trip in. But at least I had been given more directions about what to do.

Another strap, but now around both of Morris's legs. Next, groping the rocks to find someplace to hook on a second rope. A doorknob-sized stone jutting out might work. With my left hand—and my teeth—I managed to fasten a loop around the rock to pass the first rope through. Like a pulley to give lift.

When I finally got out, I couldn't stand without help. The men hauled on the rope. "It's working!"

Then groans again. Only the bottom half of Morris was moving. His upper half was still stuck fast.

Nobody said anything. Mr. Karras's eyes were moist as he came toward me again. *I shouldn't be asked to make another trip into that pit.*

David. I bet he felt weak. Scared. Not up to it. And in the Bible story he had carried five stones—not just one or two—when he went to face Goliath. As I saw it, he had intended to persevere, not just turn and run if his first attempt didn't hit its mark. He had a job to do and he did it.

I began my third trip into that cold, dark dungeon.

Once again I made a loop of rope with my left hand and teeth. Morris was barely conscious. "You've got to help me or you'll never be able to get out and beat up Mr. Karras," I told him. That roused him and finally, between us, we worked the rope around and beneath his shoulders.

I secured the ropes and straps… for the last time, I hoped. Then I slowly shimmied back out again.

This time the rescue team had rigged up a long pole with a hose attached. They shoved it into the crack, then poured a gallon of glycerin into the hose. Morris was greased like a pig to help slide him out.

The men pulled. Morris moved. He was emerging!

At 1:30 that afternoon I got my first real look at the boy I had helped save. Bruises covered his face. Morris was carried to a waiting ambulance. After twenty-five and a half hours of being trapped, he was free. "He'll be fine in a few days," doctors said.

Suddenly I was no longer tired. I felt *good*.

Sometimes the tasks or circumstances we face seem like Goliaths. They appear to be impossible. But when you confront them, you'll be given the strength to carry on, overcome—and maybe even help somebody else along the way.

Breaking the Cycle of Abuse

by Robert Plummer, Marietta, Georgia

There was once a boy who loved the things 10-year-old boys in the 1940s loved: ice cream, *Jack Armstrong* on the radio, Sunday school, cowboys and Indians—especially Indians. But this boy had a terrible secret. He lived in dread of his father, a dread that made him feel he was never safe.

That boy growing up in Columbus, Ohio, was me. I tried to love my father because I did not know other boys weren't beaten when they spilled a glass or broke a toy. But mostly I feared him. I feared his very shadow.

He was a stocky, muscular man whose roaring voice gave an extra dimension of profanity to the curses he spewed when he had been drinking, which was often. He liked to use a leather strap, cracking it like a lion tamer. A lion tamer rarely lets his whip touch the animals. On me, Dad's strap always left a reminder of his untamable fury. I wondered why my father was so full of anger, and if it was my fault.

When my mother tried to stop him she learned soon enough that any intervention on her part only provoked greater punishment for us both. We simply tried not to upset him, especially when he was drunk.

One pleasure my mother and I enjoyed together, though, was church. I especially loved Sunday school, where I discovered a father who was not frightening but all-loving and all-forgiving, who had creatures at his command called angels. We were taught he would send them to us in times of need. I thought a lot about angels and what they looked like, and I prayed I would not be frightened if I ever did see one. I spent so much of my boyhood in fear.

I loved to sing in church. At school I could hardly wait until music period so I could throw myself into "God Bless America" and "Battle Hymn of the Republic." I had a strong voice too. If someone had asked me my greatest ambition,

I would have answered without missing a beat: "Traveling the world, singing with an orchestra like Lawrence Welk's!" When I sang, I felt free from fear.

Though my father held a steady job in sales, we were not well-off due to his carousing, and he often used debts and the hard hours at work as excuses for his drinking. One September day it all came together in an explosion of rage.

That morning my father reminded me to do my chores—not that I ever needed reminding. There was the devil to pay if I forgot. After school I cleaned the house and settled into the den to listen to *The Lone Ranger* on the radio. Transported by the sounds of galloping hooves and ricocheting gunshots, I barely noticed my father come home until I heard him bellow, "Bob, did you do your work?"

"Yes, Pa," I answered.

I hoped he would go upstairs and sleep, but instead I heard his lurching footsteps heading for the living room, followed by muttered curses and something crashing to the floor. My whole body began to quake.

"Get in here, boy!" he roared.

I snapped off the radio, my mouth as dry as dust, and went to my father. His face was flushed and his eyes smoldered ominously.

"You telling me you cleaned this room?"

"Yes, Pa . . . . "

"Liar!" He kicked the scattered pieces of a broken lamp across the floor. "What about that mess?" He began to loosen his necktie, a bad sign.

I knew better than to argue. He grabbed me by the collar and dragged me toward the basement door. In one swift movement he reached behind it, snatched his old, heavy leather belt and pulled me down the stairs, my heels clattering on the steps. I was so scared I could hardly breathe. He yanked on the light chain. The suspended bulb swung crazily and shadows convulsed on the walls. A small length of clothesline hung from a pipe running along the ceiling; my father used it to tie my hands to the pipe so that my feet dangled above the floor. He jerked the back of my shirt up over my shoulders.

"Now," he snarled, snapping the leather belt, "I'll teach you!"

I closed my eyes and braced myself for three nightmare impressions: the crack of the belt as it struck through the air, its flaming sting on my flesh, and the smell of alcohol as my father expelled a grunting breath with each furious effort. *Please, dear God,* I prayed, *please save me.*

It was then he came, appearing silently and fully to me—a tall, broad-shouldered, unmistakable American Indian, hair the color of shiny coal hanging down his back over a blue-beaded vest. Everything about him spoke reassurance and peace. I knew God had sent him, and I wasn't frightened. His deep, scintillating eyes searched mine for an instant, then turned piercingly on my father who was at the point of whipping me. I heard a gasp and the belt fell to the floor, its brass buckle rattling on the cement. I turned to see my father cover his face with trembling hands and then stagger up the stairs.

When I turned back, the Indian was gone. But I knew for certain that in one form or another that noble angel would always be there for me.

I don't know if my father saw the same angel I did, or if he saw anything at all. When he came down a few minutes later to untie my hands, he was silent. He never spoke of the incident. And he never laid a hand on me again.

Something happened that night that seemed to open up my life to all the possibilities of God's world. I felt I had been given a measure of confidence I had always lacked, except when I sang. The next morning at school my teacher surprised me with an announcement. "Bob," she said after homeroom, "we've picked you to audition for the Columbus boys' choir this afternoon. Only a few boys get selected. Do your best."

I drew in my breath. The Columbus boys' choir was a local group that had gained national fame. I never dared dream I was good enough to join.

After lunch, I dashed home, put on a tie and hopped a streetcar to the school where auditions were being held. The headmaster, Mr. Hoffman, patted my shoulder and straightened my tie. "Show us what you've got, Bob," he said.

In a bright soprano voice I sang my heart out, a Mexican song about a youth who escapes home through a window to find his lady love. A few days later I got the news: I was chosen. I had never known such happiness. For the next five exhilarating years I lived and traveled the world with the choir. We had our own school and held class on a bus when we were on the road. It was during those five years that I began to grow into a man, one who would be different from my father.

Dad died four years ago, and I pray that he made his peace with God. I don't know if I could have ever fully loved my father, but I have forgiven him, and sometimes that is the only love we can give. I understand him better now, knowing he himself had been horribly abused as a child. What he did to me was what had been done to him.

But it was not what I would do to my two sons. That terrible cycle of violence was finally broken one night when I was ten years old and one of God's angels stepped between me and a leather strap, banishing my fear, giving me reassurance.

The Cross That Came Back

by Rear Admiral Jeremiah A. Denton Jr. (Retired), Mobile, Alabama

I t's very easy to despise our adversaries and condemn them all, without exception. Whenever I'm tempted to do that, I remember something that happened years ago when I was a prisoner of war in North Vietnam.

In the fortress-prison where I was confined, the most reliable way we prisoners could communicate was by tapping in code to neighboring cells. Each covert "conversation" ended with a tapped "GBU" (God Bless You). But our requests for church services were denied, and every sign of religion was ruthlessly destroyed.

I had a small cross that meant a lot to me. It had been made by a fellow POW out of bamboo strands. Making it had been a great risk for him; getting it to me was a great risk to both of us.

I knew the guards would never let me keep the cross, so I hid it in a propaganda pamphlet, along with a list of other prisoners in the camp. By day, the pamphlet was under my pallet. But at night, I took it out and held the cross in my hand as I prayed. There was great spiritual comfort in it for me.

I'd had the cross several months when I was told that a North Vietnamese work crew was making its way through the camp, cutting down the ventilation openings in each cell by adding bricks. When my turn came, I was ordered outside while a guard made a search of my cell. In a few minutes, I heard his grunt of triumph. He had found the cross.

Coming out, he stood glaring at me as he broke the cross into bits and threw the pieces into an open sewer. I was furious. And helpless.

The work crew had been standing by, watching, five or six very old Vietnamese men and women, too old for any other kind of work. They were ordered into my cell to do their job. A half hour passed before they came out and I was allowed to return.

Immediately I reached under the pallet and found the pamphlet. The list of prisoners was gone. Still angry, I began tearing the pamphlet apart. Then I felt a bulge among the pages.

There was a cross. A new one, carefully and beautifully woven from the straw strands of a broom. Obviously the work crew had made it. I shuddered at the thought of the punishment they would have suffered had they been caught.

Then I realized something, something that gave me even more spiritual comfort and hope for the future as I prayed with the new cross. Despite the deeds of men that can make enemies out of strangers, the love of God can still reach down and make men brothers.

The Only Explanation

by Sara Davis, Reneé Wilkins and Myers Bruso,
Atmore, Alabama

SARA DAVIS: At First Assembly of God Church in Atmore, Alabama, the time after evening services is an opportunity for parishioners to talk and visit. But one night last year a mysterious series of events unfolded. It wasn't until afterward that several of us pieced our separate stories together, and reached a startling but inescapable conclusion.

On Sunday, March 5, 1995, church was over a little after 8:00 P.M. My three-year-old daughter, Sara Beth, quickly found her playmates, Cameron McGhee and Brett Wilkins. Reneé Wilkins was holding Brett. He wiggled and begged, "Please, Mommy! Put me down." "Okay," she answered, smoothing his thick blond hair, "but I'll hold your toy fishing pole. You might hit someone with it." The children then began their usual game of climbing the three steps to the altar platform and jumping bravely back down; they never seemed to tire of this game.

I was standing at the back of the sanctuary, chatting with Cameron's mother, Cyndi, when Sara Beth and Cameron came racing toward us. Sara Beth's blue eyes were wide as saucers as she cried, "Mommy, Mommy!"

"Just a minute, Sara Beth," I said. "We're talking."

Sara Beth waited eagerly, but Cameron arrived close behind her, too excited to be put off.

"We just saw Jesus' angels!" he sang out boldly.

"Where?" Cyndi asked.

"Up there, in that choir booth."

Sara Beth nodded vigorously. Cyndi and I looked at each other, then at where the children were pointing.

Our church is designed like a tiered fan, with the pews facing the front altar platform, and the choir loft and baptistery behind it. Fresh green ferns frame the baptistery glass, through which the congregation can watch my husband,

Don, the pastor, perform baptisms. From out front, you can't see the five-foot-deep tank, or the stairs leading to it behind the sanctuary wall. In fact, there had been a baptism during that evening's service, so the baptistery was full of water. "Don probably told them there were angels up there so they wouldn't go running around up on the platform," I said, and Cyndi and I both laughed.

Sara Beth and Cameron seemed satisfied that they had delivered their message and they tore off again without another word.

RENEÉ WILKINS: For the longest time, I watched Brett run up the steps of the pulpit. Then a crowd gathered in the aisle and blocked my view. I couldn't see Brett. I asked my teenaged daughter to go get him, but after searching throughout the church she came to tell me he wasn't anywhere to be found.

"He's gone into the gym, I bet," I said. So I left to go there.

MYERS BRUSO: After the service, I went on an errand to the church office. When I returned to the sanctuary, a crowd of 50 or so still lingered. I spotted a young man named Travis in a pew toward the back and went over to talk. But as I greeted him, Travis asked, "Did you hear that splash a minute ago?"

I shook my head, then remembered: "There's probably still water in the baptistery."

"Some kids probably snuck up the stairs behind the front wall and threw in a hymnal," Travis said.

"Well, I had better go run them out of there."

I went up onto the platform and then to the choir risers, peering through the open baptistery window. I expected to see a mischievous head pop around up on the landing, and I stood on the top row, straining for a better view. The stairs were empty.

Hearing a soft *bump, bump, bump*, I stood on the chair and looked down into the water. There was a blond child floating on his back in the tank!

He was floating so effortlessly I assumed he was playing. But then I noticed that the boy's eyes were wide open and his arms were spread out, palms up. His legs were slightly parted, and the bumping sound I had heard was one of his hard-soled saddle oxfords hitting against the fiberglass wall.

My chest tightened as I looked at the child's gray, vacant eyes.

"Dear Lord!" It was baby Brett. His hair was wet and washed back; obviously he had been underwater.

A feeling of dread overcame me. Brett's blue lips fell open and he let out several *uh, uh, uh* moans. A terrible thought raced through my mind—that I was hearing his last gasps.

I bent over the partition and reached for Brett. *He's going to sink*, I thought as I grabbed for him. But I was able to get my arms around his back and scoop him out. I flung the little wet body across my shoulder and jumped over the chairs, knocking some down. I vaguely remember hearing gasps and shouts as others realized what had occurred.

I laid Brett on his side next to the podium and gently squeezed my hands between his chest and back. Only about two tablespoons of water came out of his mouth.

RENEÉ: I was on my way to the gymnasium when Sara came running down the hall exclaiming, "Hurry. Myers just fished Brett out of the baptistery!" There were tears in her eyes.

I got to the sanctuary just as Myers squeezed the boy's chest. Brett wasn't moving and he wasn't crying. My husband, Andy, who is a trained paramedic, knelt next to them.

Every horrific thought was framed in my question: "Is he . . . ?"

"He's going to be all right, Reneé," Andy said. "Don't worry."

Andy picked Brett up and the youngster started to cry. It wasn't a scared cry, though. It was more like the cry of a newborn child.

Brett remained limp as we took him into the nursery to get him out of his wet clothes and wait for the ambulance. He barely responded to my voice, as if he were having trouble awakening from a deep sleep.

The EMTs wrapped him in a warm blanket and raced him to the hospital, where X rays showed no significant water in Brett's lungs. After the doctor gave us the news, she smiled. "The baby's going to be just fine," she said. "But," she added, puzzled, "your story doesn't add up. Small children aren't usually relaxed enough to float. They fight the water until their lungs fill, then they sink to the bottom, facedown. And yet Brett had no water in his lungs—I can't explain it."

Little by little, Brett came out of his stupor. I finally picked him up, and asked gently, "Brett, honey, what happened?"

"I thought there was fish in the water," he said. "Even a whale."

I hugged him and said, "Oh, Brett, I'm so sorry."

"It's okay, Mommy. A man put me in a basket. And then I wasn't scared."

Andy and I exchanged glances.

SARA: We went with Reneé and Andy to the hospital, and left when the doctor said Brett would be all right. When we got home, the phone rang—it was Cyndi. "Sara, do you remember what Sara Beth and Cameron said just before Myers found Brett?"

A chill ran through me. In all the excitement, I had completely forgotten. Sara Beth was sitting on a stool at the breakfast counter and I put the phone down so Cyndi could hear: "Sara Beth, do you remember seeing any special guests at church tonight?" I asked.

Sarah Beth straightened up and said in a calm voice full of little-girl wonder, "Yes, Mommy. Jesus' angels."

Don leaned down and looked her right in the eye. "I saw them, Daddy. I really did," she said firmly.

"Where?"

"On those choir steps. They had yellow hair and pink jackets and pink hats and their wings was coming out right here." She touched the insides of her shoulder blades.

"Did they say anything?"

"No, they just looked at Cameron and me. But they were so nice."

When I again picked up the receiver, Cyndi said, "That's exactly what Cameron told me."

When we put the children's story about the angels together with Brett's description of the man who floated him in a basket—and added Myers's puzzlement about the baby floating—we had the only explanation for Who saved Brett and protected Cameron and Sara Beth that March night.

A Message I Could Not Ignore

by Patti Bohlman, Kingfisher, Oklahoma

My home was a two-bedroom trailer, and the winter of 1978 was just beginning in my area of rural western Oklahoma when I heard the weather report on television: An ice storm was coming. In preparation, I gathered blankets, and sure enough, the power went out. I said a prayer that God would get me through the night safely and made myself comfortable on the couch, huddling under the blankets. At midnight I awoke as the TV and lights came back on. Feeling all was well, I turned everything off and stumbled to bed.

Fifteen minutes later, I awakened from a sound sleep. A voice was calling me urgently, a voice I always heeded unquestioningly. "Patti, *get up*," Mother said.

A glow was coming from the kitchen, I jumped out of bed and ran to see flames shooting from the hot-water tank. I rushed outside. By the time the firemen arrived, the trailer was totally engulfed in flames. Numb with exhaustion, I watched as the fire consumed my home.

Other family members arrived from nearby, and we surveyed the ruins. "Thank goodness you got out," my sister said. "What if you hadn't woken up in time?" It was then I told them the story of how I had been roused by Mother's voice. The others stared at me in disbelief.

Why was it so amazing to think that she had saved my life? Because Mother had passed away in March the year before.

God had sent me a message I could not ignore.

"Miracles Happen Every Day"

by Fred Bauer

The father that dwelleth in me, he doeth the works.
—John 14:10

Some people believe that miracles only happened in Bible times, but they are mistaken. Miracles happen every day. I talked to a couple of miracles just the other day. They are David and Barbara Anderson, Christian musicians from Phoenix, who survived a 1993 plane crash in the Bering Sea.

On their way home from a trip to Russia where they had gone on a short mission assignment, their plane went down off the Alaskan coast. Amazingly, the Andersons and five others survived the ditching without serious injury. Amazingly, they escaped from the plane, which sank in seconds, hanging on to floating gas cans that had been loaded on their plane by chance. Amazingly, the pilot of another plane, running late, saw what he thought was a whale splash in the sea. When he heard the crash, he remembered the splash, turned his planes around and "miraculously" located the surviving seven minuscule specks in the vast sea. Amazingly, two helicopters were available and, amazingly, rescue workers were able to pluck the Andersons and their troupe out of the icy sea before hypothermia could claim their lives.

"We can't find enough superlatives to describe the work of our heroic rescuers!" Dave Anderson exclaimed. "Or thank God enough for sparing our group."

The experience gave new meaning to that old Cowper poem: "God moves in a mysterious way/His wonders to perform/He plants His footsteps in the sea/And rides upon the storm."

> *You, Lord, are the miracle of all,*
> *Mindful of our need before we call.*

Cliff Catastrophe

by Barbara F. Backer

Do angels protect kids? Ask the Lunt family of Moncks Corner, South Carolina.

On a 4th of July outing, Tasha and Jeff Lunt and their three children hiked up the Table Rock Mountain trail to one of the highest points in South Carolina. As they started down on a different path, the trail became too steep and they all headed back.

But as 8-year-old Jayme turned, his foot slipped. He lost his balance and plunged head-first off the mountain's side. Stephen, 7, spun around to catch his brother, but Stephen too began falling just as his 10-year-old sister Niki grabbed for him—then found herself sliding.

Fortunately, Niki was caught in a bush a few feet below the trail. But the two boys lay flat on their backs 40 feet below. Neither was moving.

"I thought they were dead," says Tasha Lunt, a nurse. "I don't know how I got down the side of the cliff, but I reached Stephen first."

"I'm OK, Mom," he said. "An angel caught me. Go check on Jayme."

But where was her other son? At last she spotted him. The boys had landed more than 20 feet apart with bushes between them. She dashed over to where Jayme lay, his face covered in blood. Jayme opened his eyes. "Am I in a dream?" he asked. Then, "I'm OK, Mom. An angel caught me. Go check on Stephen."

Tasha Lunt began crying and praying. She was amazed and grateful that her sons were safe, but mystified by their talk about angels. She recalls, "I kept wondering, 'How can this be? How can they be saying the same thing?' They couldn't see or hear each other."

Later Stephen said, "When I started falling, I felt something strong push me to the side. Jayme fell straight down, but when I went sideways, I caught onto a tree, then did somersaults down the mountain."

Apparently bushes slowed his fall. He had cuts and bruises, but his injuries weren't serious.

Jayme says, "When I got near the bottom it felt as if I fell right into someone's arms. It was soft, just like falling into a fluffy pillow."

People who saw Jayme fall said he appeared to be diving headfirst down the mountain's side. Then his body turned as he neared the bottom, and he landed on his bottom before falling onto his back.

A few kids at school teased Jayme and Stephen when they heard about their angelic encounter. "Some bigger boys said I should jump off the roof at school to prove that angels will catch me. But I know that's not right," Jayme says.

Besides, Jayme doesn't need any more proof that angels are watching out for his family.

Chapter Four

Faith for the Family

Look after the children
O Lord;
I pray for them
As I know my mother
prayed for me.

Set a watch over
the days of their lives
When they walk through
the brambles, across deserts,
Climb mountains, swim rivers.

Look after my children
and my children's children;
Look after the children
of the world!

Keep them safe
and finally reconcile
Them to Thee.

– Mary Elizabeth Kennedy
(Twentieth Century)

Homecoming

by Diana Spencer, Daytona Beach, Florida

The summer of 1984 was hot even by South Dakota standards. Parching winds blasted across the plains, raising a storm of prairie dust, and nothing cooled off in the short, restless nights. Each day seemed to melt into the next. Even now, a dozen years later and about 2000 miles away, there is a day from that summer branded into my memory—the day Dallas came home.

A golden haze clung to the morning air as I made my way to our garden, crunching over a swarm of potato beetles that had arrived in the night. I gazed in the direction of a stream that lazed behind my neighbor's house and thought about how cool and fresh a quick dip would feel. Then a movement caught my eye. There on the edge of our property appeared our old Border collie, standing in the shimmering heat, his feathered tail high in the air and his tongue spilling out of his dripping muzzle, as if he had just had a long cool drink from the stream. Sure as I stood there it was Dallas. I would know the quizzical cock of his head anywhere, how he lifted his ears the way humans raise their eyebrows.

"Dallas, where did you come from?" I gasped, going to him. He had taken form almost like a mirage. One minute he wasn't there, the next he was. Were my eyes playing tricks?

He had no business being anywhere near our house. Months earlier we had been forced to give our eight-year-old daughter Charmyn's dog to a farmer miles outside town. I still remembered the look of puzzled concern in Dallas's eyes as they drove away with him. But he had become increasingly hard to handle as he grew up. Not a bad dog, mind you, but an extremely vigorous one. "This dog needs a job," our vet had said with a chuckle. What he meant, he explained, was that the working genes in Dallas were dominant. "This breed was originally developed to herd, and Dallas still has an extra-strong dose of that instinct," he explained.

We tried to make Charmyn understand that her dog would be happier on a big farm, that if she really loved him she would let him go. But she took it hard, and in the end I had thought it better to whisk Dallas off rather than make a big to-do of his departure. Charmyn was heartbroken for a while, then seemed to get over it. I, however, still wondered if I had done the right thing, and in my prayers I had asked God for some reassurance that I had behaved like a good mother.

Now here was Dallas before my very eyes. I had heard of dogs traveling great distances to return to their previous homes, but it would have seemed logical for Dallas to have done that when we first gave him to the farmer months ago. As far as I knew, he was happy. Maybe, on this sizzling summer day, one of God's angels had led him back to say a formal good-bye to Charmyn.

"Charmyn, honey, come here," I called back to the house. "Hurry!" Sooner or later we would have to contact the farmer and let him know Dallas was safe, but in the meantime I couldn't wait to see Charmyn's face when she saw him.

I ran back to the house, met her on the porch and led her down near the stream. Her mouth flew open and formed the word *Dallas*, but no sound came out. Their eyes met and he nuzzled his head into her cupped hands. There was a contented weariness to him. He rolled on his back, and invited Charmyn to squat down and scratch his matted chest. She spoke to him quietly and I left them to themselves for a few minutes. Then I walked back to our yard and I fed him some leftover bacon, eggs and toast crusts from breakfast. He sat politely, as we had taught him. How quickly he made food disappear!

"He needs a bath," I said to Charmyn, crinkling my nose. I sent her inside to get an old towel, a brush that still bore Dallas's teeth marks on the handle, and a bottle of dog shampoo. Then I hauled out the hose I used to water our garden and we proceeded to give Dallas the works. Poised patiently on a patch of grass, Dallas basked in all the loving attention as I combed out the snarls in his thick coat. Running my hand across his fur, I studied his familiar markings: the symmetrical black coloring on his ears, his frothy chest, and his white paws. "He sure was dirty," I told Charmyn as we finished. "That farmer must be keeping him busy."

By then we all needed a nap, so we curled up together in a pool of shade by the lilac bushes. I dreamed of an angel carrying Dallas through a wind-whipped sea of tall grass. A while later the sound of my husband, Jim, coming up the drive awoke us. I waved and called him over.

"Look, it's Dallas!" I cried.

"It's him, all right," Jim declared, giving him an affectionate scratch behind the ear. "I'll be . . . "

We agreed it was time to contact the farmer and Jim went inside to find the number. Charmyn, Dallas and I followed, and the dog waited on the porch as we went in, giving my hand a lick as I closed the screen door.

Jim phoned while I had a little chat with Charmyn about the dog. I was afraid she had grown attached again and I wanted to make certain she understood that Dallas had to be returned. "Honey, maybe we can go visit Dallas on the farm from time to time. Would you like that?"

Charmyn nodded and said, "Sure." I was a little bit amazed at how calmly she was taking it. It was as if she and the dog had come to an understanding.

Jim hung up and looked at me, perplexed. "I just had the strangest conversation," he said. "They won't be coming for the dog."

"What?" I said.

"They won't be coming. The farmer says it's not Dallas."

"Of course it's Dallas!" I insisted.

"He says it can't be," Jim replied softly. "Dallas was badly hurt in an accident a few days ago and had to be put down."

For a moment we were all frozen in silence. Then I went to the porch. "Dallas?" I cried, pushing open the door.

But there was no Dallas to be seen anywhere.

God works in amazing ways in our lives. We can't always explain how. The only indication that Dallas had been there was an old wet towel flapping on the clothesline.

We all have our opinions on how God worked just then and why.

I like to believe that on that lazy summer day, he brought Dallas back to us so we could all say good-bye properly.

We never saw him again, nor did anyone in our neighborhood ever spot a dog looking anything like him. Dallas had gone to his reward—home at last.

Mama's Soup Pot

by Leo Buscaglia, Lake Tahoe, Nevada

T here are too many treasures in life we take for granted, the worth of which we don't fully realize until they're pointed out to us in some unexpected way. So it was with Mama's soup pot.

I can still see it sitting on the stove in all its chipped white-and-blue-enameled glory, its contents bubbling, steam rising as if from an active volcano. When I entered the back porch, the aroma was not only mouthwatering, but reassuring. Whether Mama was standing over the pot stirring with a long wooden spoon or not, I knew I was home.

There was no recipe for her minestrone soup. It was always a work in progress. It had been so since her girlhood in the Piemonte mountains of northern Italy, where she learned its secret from her *nonna* (grandma), who had inherited it from generations of *nonnas*.

For our large immigrant family, Mama's soup guaranteed we would never go hungry. It was a simmering symbol of security. Its recipe was created spontaneously from what was in the kitchen. And we could judge the state of our family economy by its contents. A thick brew with tomatoes, pasta, beans, carrots, celery, onion, corn and meat indicated things were going well with the Buscaglias. A watery soup denoted meager times. And never was food thrown out. That was a sin against God. Everything ended up in the minestrone pot.

Its preparation was sacred to Mama. To her, cooking was a celebration of God's providence. Each potato, each shred of chicken was placed in the pot with grateful thanks. I think of Mama whenever I read Proverbs 31:15, 28: "She gets up while it is still dark; she provides food for her family. . . . Her children arise, and call her blessed" *(New International Version)*.

At one time, however, Mama's soup pot became a source of embarrassment to me, for I feared it would cost me a new friend I had made at school. Sol was a thin dark-haired boy, and an unusual pal for me because his father was a doctor and they lived in the best part of town. Often Sol invited me to his home for dinner. The family had a cook in a white uniform who worked in a kitchen of gleaming chrome and shining utensils. Though the food was good, I found it bland without the heartiness of my home fare served from flame-blackened pots. Moreover, the atmosphere matched the food. Everything was so formal. Sol's mother and father were polite, but conversation around the table was stilted and subdued. And no one hugged! The closest I saw Sol get to his father was a handshake.

In our family, warm hugs were a constant—men, women, boys and girls—and if you didn't kiss your mother, she demanded: "Whatsa matter, you sick?"

But at that time in my life, all this was an embarrassment.

I had known Sol would like to eat dinner at our house, but that was the last thing I wanted. My family was so different. No other kids had such pots on their stoves, nor did they have a mama whose first action upon seeing you enter the house was to sit you down with a spoon and bowl.

"People in America don't do things like that," I tried to convince Mama.

"Well, I'm not people," was her proud retort. "I'm Rosina. Only crazy people don't want my minestrone."

Finally Sol pointedly asked if he could come to our house. I had to say yes. I knew nothing would make Mama happier. But I was in a state of anxiety. Eating with my family would turn Sol off completely, I believed.

"Mama, why can't we have some American food like hamburgers or fried chicken?"

She fixed me with a stony glare and I knew better than to ask again.

The day Sol came over I was a nervous wreck. Mama and the other nine family members welcomed him with embraces and slaps on the back.

Soon we were sitting at the heavy, deeply stained and ornately carved table that was Papa's pride and joy. It was covered with an ostentatious, bright oilcloth.

And sure enough, after Papa asked the blessing, we were instantly faced with bowls of soup.

"Eh, Sol," Mama asked, "you know what this is?"

"Soup?" Sol responded.

"No soup," Mama said emphatically. "It's *minestrone!*" She launched into a long, animated explanation of the power of minestrone: how it cured colds, headaches, heartaches, indigestion, gout and liver ailments.

After feeling Sol's muscles, Mama convinced him that the soup would also make him strong, like the Italian-American hero Charles Atlas. I cringed, convinced that this would be the last time I would ever see my friend Sol. He would certainly never return to a home with such eccentric people, odd accents and strange food.

But to my amazement, Sol politely finished his bowl and then asked for *two more*. "I like it a lot," he said, slurping.

When we were saying our good-byes, Sol confided, "You sure have a great family. I wish my mom could cook that good." Then he added, "Boy, are you lucky!"

Lucky? I wondered as he walked down the street waving and smiling.

Today I know how lucky I was. I know that the glow Sol experienced at our table was much more than the physical and spiritual warmth of Mama's minestrone. It was the unalloyed joy of a family table where the real feast was love.

Mama died a long time ago. Someone turned off the gas under the minestrone pot the day after Mama was buried, and a glorious era passed with the flame. But the godly love and assurance that bubbled amidst its savory ingredients still warms my heart today.

Sol and I continued our friendship through the years. I was best man at his wedding. Not long ago I visited his house for dinner. He hugged all his children and they hugged me. Then his wife brought out steaming bowls of soup. It was chicken soup, thick with vegetables and savory chunks of meat.

"Hey, Leo," Sol asked, "Do you know what this is?"

"Soup?" I responded, smiling.

"Soup!" he huffed. "This is *chicken soup!* Cures colds, headaches, indigestion. Good for your *liver!*" Sol winked.

I felt I was home again.

I Married
an Angel

by Kathleen Faulstich, Arcadia, California

I knew there was something unusual about Vern Faulstich from the moment we met. A peacefulness flowed from the tall, blond man with hazel eyes. After we married in 1967 I discovered how unique he really was.

We lived in Pasadena, California, where he was on the police force. He was widowed with three daughters. I, with a little girl, was recovering from a troubled marriage. We adopted each other's children, and we were very happy.

Vern was deeply religious, and at first I had difficulty accepting some of his beliefs. But the more I came to know him, the more I saw how dedicated to his faith he was. He kept a Bible in every room, and he trusted God so much that he believed God guided him through his guardian angel to people who needed help.

Much of his time was spent counseling errant youngsters and incorrigibles. His manner had such a calming effect that people opened right up to him. Friends and strangers alike unburdened themselves. Sometimes they didn't have to; Vern already knew. One night Vern was worrying about a fellow officer.

"Bill Johnson* is planning to kill himself," Vern explained. Knowing he couldn't approach Bill directly, Vern said, "We've got to concentrate and start praying for him to call me." And that's what we did. Several evenings later the phone rang. When Vern picked it up, I knew who it was. My husband went right over to Bill's house and stayed all evening. Vern talked him out of suicide.

Time and again God used Vern to help others. A young couple with four children came to our house on the verge of divorce. We all sat around our dining room table over cookies and coffee. Husband and wife hurled angry accusations at each other. It seemed hopeless until Vern settled them down.

"Look," he said quietly. "There are three sides to every story: his side, her side and the truth. Let's get at the truth."

He asked each to visualize the other being struck dead by a truck. "How would you feel now," he said, "that this person you loved, with whom you had children and with whom you attempted to build a life, is suddenly gone?"

There was silence for a moment. Then the two fell into each other's arms. To this day they're still married.

Afterward I asked Vern, "How do you think of those things?"

"God just puts these thoughts into my mind," he said.

About a year after we married, we moved to Las Vegas, where Vern worked in law enforcement. One morning in 1972 he came to the breakfast table puzzled. He said during the night his guardian angel had impressed on him that he should look for a boy with a rose.

"Should I look for a boy carrying flowers?" he wondered.

"Well," I said, "I guess you'll have to do what you've always done; wait and you'll be shown."

A few days later at supper Vern told me of an experience he had had that afternoon. He had felt compelled to have lunch at a restaurant in a disreputable part of town. "I wasn't too happy about eating there," he said, "but I went in and sat down at the counter. A surly-looking kid about sixteen years old was sitting next to me. All he had was a doughnut and a glass of water.

"I couldn't help commenting, 'For a growing man, that's not much lunch.'

"Oh, he cussed me out something awful. But then as he reached for his glass of water, I saw a tattoo of a rose on his arm."

"The boy with the rose," I remembered.

Vern nodded. "I began to ask him about himself. He glared at me and swore. 'What's your problem, mister?' he said. 'Are you some kind of nut?'"

Vern smiled in recollection. "'Oh, yeah,' I answered, 'I've been called that lots of times. But you know what? I was sent here to help you.'

"The kid snarled: 'With what?'

"I said, 'You've got a problem. What is it?'

"'Yeah,' the kid spat. 'I'm going to kill myself. Wanna know how?'

"'No,' I said, 'I want to know *why*.'

"The boy calmed down," Vern continued, "and began to tell his story. He was angry at his parents. They wanted him to buckle down on his studies, stay in school, go to church, cut his hair and take out his gold earring.

"Because he wouldn't do it, they had taken his car away. All the boy could say was how much he hated his folks, and how he wanted out."

Vern shook his head. "I tried to explain that his parents were simply doing their best to help and guide him because they loved him so much."

"Do you think you reached him?" I asked.

My husband stared into his coffee cup for a moment, then nodded. "I believe I did," he said. Vern never saw the boy again.

In 1988, at age 63, Vern was diagnosed with terminal pancreatic cancer. I spent all my time with him in the hospital. Eventually, he slipped into a coma. But on December 23, he suddenly awakened, full of life and rational. He took my hand and smiled. "Out of all the days that God has blessed me with on earth, the day I met you was the best." He squeezed my hand. "When it's your time to travel home," he said, "just walk toward the light; I'll be waiting." He died soon afterward.

Hundreds of people came to Vern's funeral. I was standing in the vestibule of the chapel when a handsome young man with his wife and two children approached me. "Please excuse us," he said. "I don't mean to intrude at a private time like this. But I just came to pay my respects to your husband."

As he extended his hand to me, his cuff slipped back and there on his arm was a rose tattoo. I hadn't thought of it in years, but immediately I remembered the boy in the diner. He had never forgotten my husband, as hundreds of others had never forgotten him. Vern knew how permanent one good act can be, and how goodness goes on working. Vern's goodness lives on, and doesn't that make him a kind of angel?

After all, that's why I married him.

Angel in Our Backyard

by Denise Brumbach, Manheim, Pennsylvania

I was working in the beauty shop that I operate out of our home when my husband, Den, came in, a troubled expression on his face. "Look what I found in the girls' tree house," he said. He held out some jeans and a T-shirt. "It looks as if someone's living in our backyard."

"It's those kids," I said, aghast. "Den, you're on the borough council. We've got to do something!"

Lately there had been several acts of vandalism—a shock for our small town—and teenage boys from out of the area had been seen roaming the streets. It was the fall of 1991, and crime had become frighteningly real in the nearby city of Lancaster. Our town was determined to keep the problem from spreading to Manheim.

"I'll report this to the police," Den said.

A few days later I looked out the window and saw a group of teenage boys sauntering out from between our house and the neighbors', heading up the street. I ran out the door and, putting two fingers in my mouth, gave a piercing whistle.

The boys turned around. There were four of them, wearing relatively clean jeans and T-shirts; no gang colors that I could see. "Hi," I said. "What were you guys doing in our backyard?"

"Just cutting through," one said.

"Why aren't you in school?" I asked.

"Don't need that garbage," said another.

But then a tall young man stepped forward. Unlike the others, he looked right at me. "I'd like to be in school," he said. "But not in the neighborhood I'm from." He had a Hispanic accent and was slender and clean-shaven, with cinnamon-brown eyes.

As they headed down the street, I turned back to the beauty shop. At least they didn't seem like gang members or hardened criminals. And there was something compelling about that kid who wished he were in school.

Somehow I wasn't surprised a day or so later when he reappeared as I was raking leaves in our backyard. "Hi," he said. "Can I give you a hand?"

I studied him for a moment, trying to read what was behind those eyes. I handed him the rake. "What's your name?" I asked. "Where are you from?"

"Angel Melendez," he said. "I'm from Lancaster. But things there are getting kind of rough."

"So where are you living now?"

"Sometimes I crash with a friend," he said. "I stashed some clothes in your tree house. Sorry. I didn't mean to cause any trouble."

"You want them back?" I asked. He nodded.

I went inside, leaving Angel working industriously. After gathering his clothes, I watched him from the upper deck. He was so thin. Lunch seemed a fair exchange for raking a huge pile of leaves.

The lawn looked good. Angel sat at the kitchen table and wolfed down the sandwiches as if he could have eaten half a dozen more.

Over the following days, Angel continued to stop by to chat. Sometimes he talked about his dream of becoming a Navy pilot. He started coming around in the evening, while Den and I and our teenage daughters, Haley and Amanda, were watching TV. Whenever I put out snacks he ate ravenously. As he cheerfully said good night, we knew we were sending him out—to where? Nowhere.

Then one night Den said, "Angel, if you have nowhere else to go, you can sleep out in my workshop."

"Thanks," Angel said, smiling. He turned at the door, a bit nervously. "Mr. and Mrs. Brumbach," he said, "I would really like to finish high school. I was wondering if you could help me get in."

As we prepared for bed, Den and I turned to each other with the same questions. What were we going to do about Angel? He seemed like a nice kid. But did we want to get involved?

"Before this goes any further," Den said, "I'll have the police run a background check on him, to make sure he is who he says he is."

In the meantime Angel informed us of what he had found out: To enroll at our high school, he needed a permanent local address as well as a parent or legal guardian who was a district resident.

That night when Den got home he summoned Haley, Amanda and me to the kitchen table. "I talked to the Manheim police," he said. "Officer David Carpenter called Lancaster and spoke with a Sergeant Wilson. It seems the kid's been on his own since he was eight years old. He's seventeen now. But what impressed Sergeant Wilson is that, for a kid who's had to raise himself, Angel's never been in trouble."

"All he wants to do is to go to school," Haley whispered. "How can we not help him?"

It turned out Officer Carpenter had been impressed by Angel as well. Several nights later he called. "I know a police officer isn't supposed to get personally involved in his work," Carpenter said, "but sometimes you have to. I don't have room for Angel to move in, but I'm willing to become his legal guardian."

The rest of our community was harder to convince. We started to receive phone calls—many of them anonymous—that made it clear Angel was not welcome in our town.

The school didn't seem to want him either. Weeks turned into months as red tape continued to block his admission. In the meantime Angel got a job at the local McDonald's. He had breakfast and dinner with us, then spent the evenings doing odd jobs around the house or watching TV.

The weather turned frosty; Den's workshop where Angel slept was unheated. We called another family meeting. As fond as we'd all become of Angel, letting him move into our house was a big step. Maybe too big.

"What else can we do?" asked Haley. "It's getting really cold," Amanda added. It was brave of them. I knew they were being questioned at school by kids who didn't understand the situation. They only saw that Angel was Hispanic and a "city boy."

"If he becomes a member of the family, he'll be treated like one," I said. "He'll have chores and a curfew; he'll have to work hard and obey our rules."

We all agreed that Angel could move in. He was ecstatic at being invited to sleep on the living room sofa. "The doors lock at ten," I warned. "You've got to be in by then."

"Yes, Mom," he said.

That kid had really gotten to me. "Angel," I said, "you've been through some really tough times in your life. How have you managed?"

"God kept me going," he answered. "When I was about seven, I started going to this place called Teen Haven. It was kind of a youth center where they told me about Jesus. As I've gotten older, I know he's still with me. He's kept me safe, and led me to people who care, people like . . . you."

Finally, six months after we had started the process, Angel had a legal guardian and a permanent address. I'd never seen anyone as excited as Angel was on the morning Officer Carpenter and Den took him to enroll in school. He wore his best clothes and held his notebooks as if they were winning lottery tickets.

It was a wonderful victory. But it had taken a real toll. Den and I saw our social life starting to slip away, except for a few close friends. Business had fallen off at my beauty shop. People who normally offered a friendly hello while passing by now ignored us. Sometimes Den and I snapped at each other in misplaced frustration. I began losing sleep. Many nights I paced, crying and praying. Was it all worth it? Should I just ask Angel to go?

One night, depressed and confused, I sank to the kitchen floor in the darkness, and my tears poured forth. "What's the answer, Lord?" I asked. "It would make it easier on the rest of the family to ask Angel to leave. But he's your child—and he's trying so hard. What should I do?"

As the cry for help left my lips, the far side of the kitchen began to glow with a hazy yet bright light. Blinded by the increasing brilliance, I sensed there was a loving warm presence in that kitchen with me. Somehow I *knew* it was an angel. It delivered a message silently but clearly: *Deni, let him stay. It will be all right.*

More amazing than the unearthly glow was how, in the twinkling of an eye, I was enveloped by a blanket of peace. No matter what hardships still lay ahead, I knew God would be faithful to us if we were faithful to him.

When I looked up again, the kitchen was dark and I was sitting alone by the radiator.

That was three years ago. The people at the school got to know Angel. Teachers found an eager pupil; coaches found a first-class athlete; the other kids found a loyal friend. And my anxiety and frustration were replaced by love and understanding for those who had reacted negatively toward a kid who was different. When I was ready to forgive and reach out once again to those who had dropped us, many were more than ready to renew our friendship. People who had been wary of Angel started to help him, providing money for glasses, clothes, shoes. He was even offered a part-time job at a local lumberyard.

Angel worked so hard to catch up in school that he's gotten mostly A's and B's. He played on the school teams until he turned 18; now he helps manage them. When he discovered his poor vision would keep him from becoming a Navy pilot, he set his sights on college; he talks of someday studying marine biology.

The Bible says some have "entertained angels without knowing it" (Hebrews 13:2, *New International Version*). We're lucky—we do know it. I thank God for the day our Angel left his clothes in our tree house, and for the angel in the kitchen who told me to let him stay.

One More Dance

by Christopher Schonhardt, Rosemount, Minnesota

I was a senior in high school when my dad passed away in 1975. Mom had sorted through his clothes and asked me to bring the boxes downstairs for pickup by the local disabled veterans group. *I should save something*, I thought. But Dad was much bigger than I was.

I stared down at one box and saw his brown wing tips, the left heel worn down more than the right, a reminder of Dad's boyhood polio. Dad was a mechanic who wore practical shoes; this one old pair of dress shoes only came out of the closet for church and special occasions. The tops of the shoes were scuffed and as I ran my fingers across the leather, I found myself thinking back to how those scuffs came to be.

We had attended a wedding with my parents' friends Lorraine and Matthew. Multiple sclerosis confined Lorraine to a wheelchair; the disease had also sapped her spirit. As her husband wheeled her into the reception, the eager greetings of the other guests dropped to whispers. "It's a shame," I heard someone say. "She was a dancer— and quite a good one."

The band had been playing for a while when my father bent down to Lorraine's ear. "May I have this dance?" he asked. In one smooth motion Dad lifted her from the wheelchair and Matthew placed her shoes on top of Dad's wing tips. Everyone watched the couple glide across the dance floor. Lorraine, supported by my father's strong arms, stood smiling, eyes closed, head tilted back.

After the last song faded, Dad and Lorraine whirled toward her wheelchair and he gently lowered her into it. Beaming, Lorraine gave my father a vigorous hug.

Now, as I carried my father's wing tips downstairs with the rest of his things, I thought of what he had left me, what I would save. It would be the memories of a man who always tried to make a difference in others' lives.

One Big Dog vs. One Big Love

by Robert Fulghum

A man and woman I know fell into Big Love somewhat later in life than usual. She was forty. He was fifty. Neither had been married before. But they knew about marriage. They had seen the realities of that sacred state up close among their friends. They determined to overcome as many potential difficulties as possible by working things out in advance.

Prenuptial agreements over money and property were prepared by lawyers. Preemptive counseling over perceived tensions was provided by a psychologist, who helped them commit all practical promises to paper, with full reciprocal tolerance for irrational idiosyncrasies.

"Get married once, do it right, and live at least agreeably, if not happily, ever after." So they hoped.

One item in their agreement concerned pets and kids. Item Number 7: "We agree to have either children or pets, but not both."

The man was not enthusiastic about dependent relationships. Kids, dogs, cats, hamsters, goldfish, snakes, or any other living thing that had to be fed or watered had never had a place in his life. Not even houseplants. And especially not dogs. She, on the other hand, liked taking care of living things. Especially children and dogs.

OK. But she had to choose. She chose children. He obliged. Two daughters in three years. Marriage and family life went along quite well for all. Their friends were impressed. So far, so good.

The children reached school age. The mother leapt eagerly into the bottomless pool of educational volunteerism. The school needed funds for art and music. The mother organized a major-league auction to raise much money. Every family agreed to provide an item of substantial value for the event.

The mother knew a lot about dogs. She had raised dogs all her life—the pedigreed champion kind. She planned to use her expertise to shop the various local puppy pounds to find an unnoticed bargain pooch and shape it up for the auction as her contribution.

With a small investment, she would make a tenfold profit for the school. And for a couple of days, at least, there would be a dog in the house.

After a month of looking, she found the wonder dog—the dog of great promise. Female, four months old, blue eyes, tall, strong, confident, and very, very, very friendly.

To her practiced eye, our mother could see that classy genes had been accidentally mixed here. Two purebred dogs of the highest caliber had combined to produce this exceptional animal. Most likely a black Labrador and a weimaraner, she thought. Perfect. Just perfect.

To those of us of untutored eye, this mutt looked more like the results of a bad blind date between a Mexican burro and a miniature musk-ox.

The fairy dogmother went to work. Dog is inspected and given shots by a vet. Fitted with an elegant leather collar and leash. Equipped with a handsome bowl, a ball, and a rawhide bone. Expenses: $50 to the pound, $50 to the vet, $50 to the beauty parlor, $60 for tack and equipment, and $50 for food. A total of $260 on a dog that is going to stay 48 hours before auction time.

The father took one look and paled. He smelled smoke. He wouldn't give ten bucks to keep it an hour. "Dog," as the father named it, has a long, thick rubber club of a tail, legs and feet that remind him of hairy toilet plungers, and is already big enough at four months to bowl over the girls and their mother with its unrestrained enthusiasm.

The father knows this is going to be one big dog. Something a zoo might display. Omnivorous, it has eaten all its food in one day and has left permanent teeth marks on a chair leg, a leather ottoman, and the father's favorite golf shoes.

The father is patient about all of this. After all, it is only a temporary arrangement, and for a good cause. He remembers item No. 7 in the prenuptial agreement. He is safe.

On Thursday night, the school affair gets off to a winning start. Big crowd of parents, and many guests who look flush with money. Arty decorations, fine potluck food, a cornucopia of auction items. The mother basks in her triumph.

"Dog" comes on the auction block much earlier than planned. Because the father went out to the car to check on "Dog" and found it methodically eating the leather off the car's steering wheel, after having crunched holes in the padded dashboard.

After a little wrestling match getting "Dog" into the mother's arms and up onto the stage, the mother sits in a folding chair, cradling "Dog" with the solemn tenderness reserved for a corpse at a wake, while the auctioneer describes the pedigree of the animal and all the fine effort and neat equipment thrown in with the deal.

"What am I bid for this wonderful animal?

"A hundred dollars over here; two hundred dollars on the right; two hundred and fifty dollars in the middle."

There is a sniffle from the mother.

Tears are running down her face.

"Dog" is licking the tears off her cheeks.

In a whisper not really meant for public notice, the mother calls to her husband: "Jack, Jack, I can't sell this dog—I want this dog—this is my dog—she loves me—I love her—oh, Jack."

Every eye in the room is on this soapy drama.

The father feels ill, realizing that the great bowling ball of fate is headed down his alley.

"Please, Jack, please, please," she whispers.

At that moment, everybody in the room knows who is going to buy the pooch. "Dog" is going home with Jack.

Having no fear now of being stuck themselves, several relieved men set the bidding on fire. "Dog" is going to set an auction record. The repeated hundred-dollar rise in price is matched by the soft "Please, Jack" from the stage and Jack's almost inaudible raise in the bidding, five dollars at a time.

There is a long pause at "Fifteen hundred dollars—going once, going twice…"

A sob from the stage.

And for $1,505, Jack has bought himself a dog. Add in the up-front costs, and he's $1,765 into "Dog."

The noble father is applauded as his wife rushes from the stage to throw her arms around his neck, while "Dog" wraps the leash around both their legs and down they go into the first row of chairs. A memorable night for the PTA.

I see Jack out being walked by the dog late at night. He's the only one strong enough to control it, and he hates to have the neighbors see him being dragged along by this, the most expensive dog for a hundred miles.

"Dog" has become "Marilyn." She is big enough to plow with now. "Marilyn" may be the world's dumbest dog, having been to obedience school twice with no apparent effect.

Jack is still stunned. He can't believe this has happened to him.

He had it down on paper. No. 7. Kids or pets, not both.

But the complicating clauses in the fine print of the marriage contract are always unreadable. And always open to revision by forces stronger than a man's ego. The loveboat always leaks. And marriage is never a done deal.

I say he got off light. It could have been ponies or llamas or potbellied pigs. It would have been something. It always is.

"We Can Always Come Home"

by Jennifer Thomas

Homes are built on the foundation of wisdom and understanding.
— Proverbs 24:3 (GNB)

In a few months, I will graduate from college and nervously enter the "real world." This anxiety only increased when I went home last weekend to find that my youngest sister had moved into my bedroom.

As I stood staring at Stephanie's personal belongings mixed in with my own, I was struck by a feeling of loneliness. *Does being in school mean that I am no longer a part of my home? What will happen to me when I graduate?*

I puttered around the house with this question still in my mind when my mother came home from work. Upon seeing the look on my face, she asked, "Are you all right, Jen? You look so preoccupied."

"Oh, I was just thinking about graduation," I answered vaguely, not wanting to reveal my true concern.

When my sisters came home from school a little while later, Stephanie greeted me briefly and went straight to my room. She soon walked out of it, carrying her belongings in her arms. "Your room is back the way you left it, Jen!" she smiled, and went upstairs to her old bedroom.

"Jennifer, please come set the table!" my mother called from the kitchen, just like always.

And as I set the table for all of us, I knew that I had been wrong to lose faith in family, because no matter where I go, I will never really be leaving home.

Assure us, Father, that we can always come home.

Children's Corner

When Life Gives You Scraps, Make a Quilt

by Kanani Beck, Felton, California

Rags! On the brink of adulthood, I stared at the pile of miserable rags my childhood dealt me. I gazed wistfully at other people's lovely fabric. Gorgeous, useful garments were their family legacy. My only hope was piecework. I could use the tattered scraps to construct a quilt or let them sit unused in a pile.

Looking at my pitiful supply of colorless cloth, I noticed a beautiful piece of padded material available for the backing. Surely this was Jesus and His power to transform my life. Dare I let Him try? Materials for a quilt were there, but did I want to examine the pain of the past? Reluctantly, I threaded a needle.

Shaking with fear, I grabbed the *rag of abandonment*. At last count, two failed adoptions and four abandonments earned me the title, "California's Most Orphaned Orphan." Holding the scrap to the backing, I watched in amazement as God's transforming love remodeled the good parts of those fragments into a sturdy velvet nine-patch. Frayed edges disappeared, leaving hemmed seams in their place! My struggle to belong continued, but now God's acceptance and contentment began healing my soul.

Curious now, I reached into the lifeless pile and seized the *fringe of fear*. Severe abuse and neglect left me terrified of trusting people. Placing the fringe on the backing, I yelped with delight as God washed the rag's scarred surface with a shining yellow light. As the snippet changed form, it became a quilt square of courage and friendship.

Next was the *broken dreams rag*. I seriously doubted God could change this decrepit tatter. How often I'd lost everything—my beloved twin sister, a precious baby sister, other siblings, parents, belongings. Dreams turned to ashes repeatedly. Tentatively, I tossed the scrap on the backing. A glistening wave in rainbow colors appeared. Broken dreams became patterns of determination and acceptance of God's will. Suddenly, it wasn't hard to look at the pile of scraps, knowing that God was giving them purpose and meaning in my life.

One by one, I placed pieces on the backing. Anger became the square of forgiveness. Hurt, mistrust, sadness, and failure became soothing patches of comfort, trust, joy, and accomplishment. Tears trickled down my cheeks as I comprehended the change God brought to my pathetic rag pile.

With the loving, delicate hands of the Lord, the rag girl is becoming a work of beauty. I have learned that life is a matter of attitude. We can stare in disgust and self-pity at difficult circumstances, or we can allow God to take our tattered, battered lives, mend the torn parts and sew the healthy pieces together into priceless treasures that bring joy and comfort to others.

"For I know the plans I have for you," declares the Lord, "plans to prosper you, not to harm you; plans to give you hope and a future" (Jeremiah 29:11). Trust Him. When life hands you scraps, make a quilt.

Kanani Beck completed her studies in the Christian Light School this spring, and now attends Bethany Bible College. Kanani has been involved with the Mount Hermon Ponderosa Lodge, a Christian camp that trains maturing Christians to become leaders. Kanani's goal is to become a Christian Camp Director.

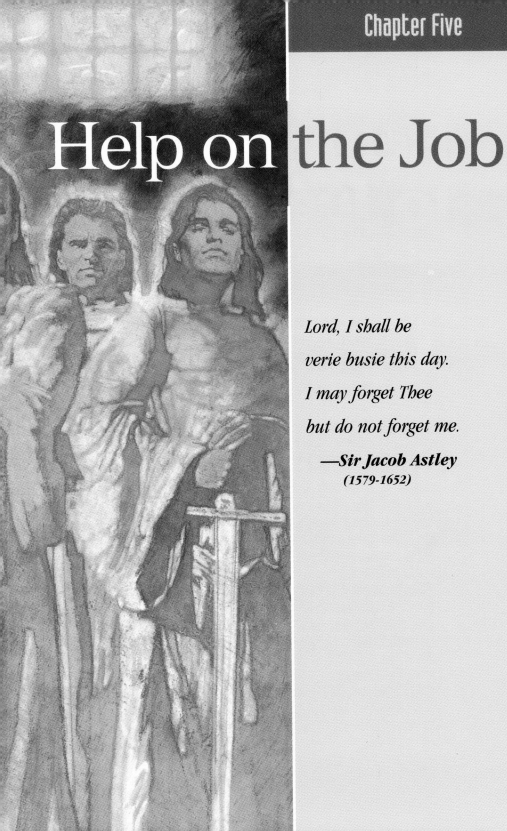

Chapter Five

Help on the Job

*Lord, I shall be
verie busie this day.
I may forget Thee
but do not forget me.*
—Sir Jacob Astley
(1579-1652)

Return to Juárez

by William P. Wilson, M.D., Durham, North Carolina

T he guard slammed the barred door shut in the Mexican jail I was visiting that January day in 1980. He walked off, his footsteps echoing down the concrete corridor.

I was locked inside a huge, reeking room. I looked around. There were about a hundred prisoners in the cell. Some of the men were lying on the bare floor, wrapped in filthy blankets; some leaned against the wall; others wandered about. A cold winter light filtered down from a few tiny, grilled windows high up near the ceiling.

I had come to this jail in Juárez to assist a local lay preacher. The two of us stood just inside that room with its penetrating odor of urine and sweat—me, an American psychiatrist from Duke University, and my companion, a Mexican ex-convict turned evangelist. As the preacher stepped toward the center of the room to address the men, I asked him what he would like me to do. "Pray," he said.

The ex-convict began to preach. I could understand only a few words of his colloquial Spanish and my mind drifted to the surprising fact that I was there at all.

I had been under a lot of stress back home in North Carolina, carrying two careers at the same time: one as a psychiatrist in private practice, another as a professor of psychiatry at Duke. I had taken time off that winter to stay at a retreat ranch friends had told me about near El Paso, Texas. Visitors were invited to take part in the ranch's many outreach ministries. One was to this jail where, I was told, many of the prisoners were mentally ill.

Perhaps in choosing to come along I was subconsciously trying to work through unpleasant memories from my days as a young doctor. I had taken a junior staff job at a state hospital in North Carolina where there was a ward for the criminally insane. In that ward there had been the same angry faces I was seeing here in this Mexican jail, the same aimless roaming, even the same pungent smell of disinfectant. Some of the patients in that North Carolina ward

114

were murderers. One man had killed a fellow inmate with his bare hands and was constantly trying to maim anyone he could, lunging out to bite, kick or stomp. We doctors never knew when one of the patients might turn on us, and we were glad there were guards nearby.

But there were no guards nearby now. The mentally disturbed prisoners were easy to spot. Rousing themselves as we entered, they uttered gibberish, railed at the two of us, and made obscene gestures. There was no way of knowing which of these men might suddenly become violent.

Many of the prisoners were moving toward us now, some grouping themselves around the preacher, some around me. I became aware of one man in particular, hovering at my left. I turned. From two feet away the man was glaring at me, eyes narrowed with rage. The fellow was dressed in a stained, torn shirt; his chin jutted forward. I was used to helping my patients cope with their fears, but now I was the one who was afraid.

The man with the angry eyes thrust his face still closer. I edged along the wall, trying to put some distance between us. He followed. For 20 minutes we moved together in a macabre dance, never more than a foot and a half apart, never closer. At last, quite abruptly—it wasn't until years later that this struck me as odd—the poor creature gave up his pursuit.

With relief, I turned my attention once again to the preacher as he gave his altar call to the now quiet room. Some 30 men responded. Shortly afterward the guard came to let us out. I flew back to North Carolina assuming the whole experience was behind me.

Fifteen years passed. Then last year, in February, I decided to take another break from daily pressures and fly back down to the retreat ranch in El Paso. Once again—perhaps out of some sense of unfinished business—I chose to take part in the ministry of the ranch by visiting the jail in Juárez. As we crossed the Rio Grande into Mexico I felt the old misgivings.

Soon we were walking with the guard down the echoing corridor to the mammoth cell. Once again the barred door slammed shut behind us, the guard's footsteps faded away, and we were locked inside the stinking, ill-lit room. The man with the rage-inflamed eyes was no longer there, but his place had been taken by a dozen others equally restless and angry.

The lay preacher—a different one—began to speak. I took my place behind him and closed my eyes in prayer. And it was then I saw them.

Through my closed eyes I saw in front of us six magnificent male figures dressed in dazzling robes, whiter than any white I had ever imagined. Each held a double-edged long sword, pointed down toward his feet. I noticed little details, like the fact that the sword hafts were not engraved. The figures were peaceable and yet there was an aura of overwhelming power about them. They simply stood there looking at the preacher.

For 10 minutes, unwilling to open my eyes and bring the vision to an end, I gazed at the mighty figures. I felt a sense of exultation but not of surprise, as if it were in the natural order of things that they should be there. At last I opened my eyes.

The shining figures were still there.

I could see them as brilliantly with my eyes open as with my eyes closed. Had they, I wondered suddenly, been in this cell during my first visit too, watching, maintaining a safe space between me and that angry-eyed man as he followed me? Were they protecting both me and him from destructive emotions? Could they have been the reason he abruptly gave up and moved away?

One thing was certain: I felt safe now, 15 years later, knowing the angels were nearby. Bit by bit, as the preacher reached the end of his sermon, peace settled over the cell. In response to the altar call a score or more of prisoners came forward. With the dazzling creatures looking on, the preacher and I prayed with each prisoner and the service ended. A guard arrived and opened the door, and we left that beautiful, holy room.

On the airplane back to North Carolina, I thought about the many professional and personal uncertainties that lie ahead as I grow older. I will face them with a different attitude now, knowing that angels are looking on, robed in white, swords in their hands to protect us against the enemies of doubt and fear. I had seen with my own eyes a heavenly resource I had only *heard* about before that day in a Mexican jail.

I don't expect to see angels again. It's enough to know they are quite near, watching over us in our weakness, strong spirits sent by God.

Partners in a Dream

by Martha Hawkins, Montgomery, Alabama

My eyes were barely higher than the long, broad stretch of butcher-block counter my mother worked over in the kitchen of our rural Alabama home—her hands moving like magic, chopping okra, snapping peas, seeding peppers, stripping corn. Each action, each movement, was deft, with a confidence that can only come from a love for the work. My mother loved cooking the way some people love poetry. As she worked she often hummed hymns and spirituals, a deep resonant counterpoint to the darting movement of her dark, gifted hands. I watched everything she did, and I learned. I dreamed: Someday...

"Someday," I told people, "I'm going to open a restaurant where folks can come and sit and talk and eat good, honest food and enjoy themselves, just as if they were coming over to my house." This was my dream, and most of the people who knew me, including my sons, smiled indulgently whenever I spoke of it. "Mama," they asked, "how you gonna do that?" The answer hung in the air like a wordless accusation: *How am I going to do anything when I can't even take care of myself?*

There was a time when my dream seemed as far away as the moon. My life had taken some pretty hard turns, but none harder than the summer day in 1979 when I sat on the edge of my bed and stared at a handful of sleeping pills. We lived in Montgomery's teeming Trenholm Court housing projects. But that steamy gray morning I could hear nothing but the silent, taunting pain of my own life. I was 31, and tired—so tired I just wanted to sleep forever.

I was married when I was 16. I cried like a baby on my wedding night because it was the first time I had ever been away from home. I was the youngest girl of 12 brothers and sisters. My father was a farm laborer, so we were poor and depended on my mother's poetry in the kitchen to keep body

117

and soul together. My mother always managed to keep us healthy and fed. "The Lord provides, Martha," was the only explanation I got.

I had four boys and a divorce decree by the time I was 23. My husband, who was in the Air Force, and I had drifted apart. After all, we had been so young when we started. "Martha, we're just not the same two people anymore," Reuben told me. I started working at the kinds of jobs that are left for a woman who drops out of school in the tenth grade. I cleaned houses for a while; I was a seamstress. Then I got a job working in a glass factory that paid pretty well and had enough shifts open so I could juggle raising my boys and earning a paycheck.

But it was a terrible struggle. As the years passed I felt myself giving out. The financial strain of single parenthood and all the worry about protecting my children from the evils of the street took a mean toll on me. I saw what could happen to children where we lived, and it scared me something awful. My health began to deteriorate. I developed kidney problems; my appendix ruptured. It was one thing after another, and I started to feel tired all the time. I remember a morning when I just lay in bed staring at my sons, unable to move. "It's all right, Mom," my oldest, Shawn, said. "We'll help you."

It's not a child's place to care for his mother. *You're a failure, Martha*, I began to chide myself. Even church, which had always been a refuge, could no longer comfort me, and I stopped going, telling myself that my faith had never amounted to much anyway. *Like everything else about me*, I thought. I was even a disappointment to God.

There was a horrible ache inside me, someplace no doctor or medicine could touch. I cried for days at a time, refusing to leave the house. In 1976 I was hospitalized for a nervous breakdown and received electroshock therapy for depression. Still I sank deeper into despair and self-blame. I went on disability and public assistance. *Martha, look at yourself. You haven't done a thing with your life but fail.*

Then came that day in 1979 when I gulped down a handful of pills and lay back on my bed, hoping never to wake up. It seemed so easy, so right. *No more pain*, I thought as a cold smothering grayness overtook me.

The next thing I knew Shawn was standing over the bed with his schoolbooks, crying "Mom, Mom, Mom!" They rushed me to the emergency room, where doctors pumped my stomach. When I woke up in Greil Memorial Psychiatric Hospital, I felt like more of a failure than ever.

One afternoon a few days later I was sitting alone in my room when I pulled open a drawer in the nightstand. Inside was a pale-blue Gideon Bible. I knew about the Bible, but I had never really sat down and read it. I mean really read it. I picked it up out of the drawer and dropped it on the bed, where it bounced open to Isaiah 61. A verse jumped out at me: "The spirit of the Lord God is upon me."

The spirit of the Lord God is upon me. What did it mean? I felt scared. I flipped the Bible closed. It fell open again to the same verse. I picked up the book and it felt so good in my hands, so solid and alive. I didn't want to let go of it, ever. I started to read. Day in and day out I consumed that Bible, every cleansing, life-changing word in it, and it consumed me, like new love. I could not get enough. When my doctor, Dr. Case, visited I told him, "There's nothing you can do. I have to help myself because I am the problem."

Then, pointing to the Bible, I said, "This is my solution." As I read the Gospels, I began writing letters to Jesus. I called them love letters, and I emptied my heart of all its sorrow, fear, loneliness and shame. How could I ever have tried to take my own life? Christ had already done the dying for me so I could live.

When I was finally released from the hospital, I returned to the housing project and to welfare. But I was on my way up this time. I found some part-time work. And before me I saw that dream of watching my mother in the kitchen, and a cozy old house—my house—where folks could come over and sit and talk and eat good, honest food. God had renewed my dream, and I talked about it to everyone I could.

That is when my boys smiled and just shook their heads. "Mama... " But they didn't think it was so bad when I drove up to college and gave them and their friends some home cooking. I'd get half the campus looking for a meal. When I cooked, I felt whole. I felt a part of creation.

With three of my boys on college scholarships I decided it was high time I did something about my own education, so I went back to school, got my GED and took some night courses at Troy State University. I kept thinking about that restaurant, and talking about it, but it takes lots of money to start a business, and I was barely getting by on cleaning houses. I applied for loans at some of the local banks, with no luck. One manager said to me, "Martha, what you need is a business partner, someone to handle the financial side of it." I told him that I already had a partner—God—and he would look after what I couldn't do for myself.

Through my cleaning I met a nice lawyer, Calvin Pryor, and I told him all about my dream. One day he led me over to 458 Sayre Street, a beige frame house from the turn of the century, a bit down at the heels but solid, definitely solid, and familiar. It was the house from my dreams. The minute I set eyes on it, I knew. "It's a bit run-down, Martha. It'll take work. But you can have it rent-free for a while, until you get on your feet."

I saved my money and bought paint and wallpaper, a little at a time, and went

119

to work. If I ran out of paint, I baked a couple of pies, sold them, and bought another gallon. My sons and other relatives began hiding from me on weekends for fear I would press them into service—and I did too. I combed yard sales for tables, chairs, dishes and silverware. I sewed napkins and curtains.

There were times when I felt low, when it seemed I would never get my dream. I remember one day when I sat down on the floor and just cried until I cried myself dry. Then I remembered Isaiah: *The spirit of the Lord God is upon me.* I got my Bible and put it down on the floor. Right there in the middle of the half-papered dining room I slipped off my shoes and carefully stepped up on my Bible. "Lord," I cried out loud, "I am standing here on the foundation of your Word. You love me. I am not alone!" The Lord had promised he would be with me, and I could never let myself forget that promise. With him I could do all things—but only with him!

On a fine day in October 1988 Martha's Place finally opened for business, and we've been going strong ever since, giving people that kind of good, nourishing Southern home cooking that I learned from my mother and she from hers. I still have problems these days, but they are good problems, the problems of running a successful business. You see, I am no longer the problem. I am blessed, blessed, blessed! Every morning at four o'clock I'm in my kitchen chopping greens, baking corn bread and boiling turnips. It is the most peaceful hour of my day, when I am alone with my cooking and alone with my Lord. Because when I work, I feel the Lord. That work is his gift to me, and when I feel the food in my hands, I feel his blessings all through me.

I want my customers to feel that too. There's nothing fancy about Martha's Place, but it's mine—mine and my partner's.

The Man in Room 4014

by Ruth Barrow Bar, Stoughton, Wisconsin

Sometimes experiencing something really terrible isn't as difficult as surviving it. I had a chance to learn about that as a nurse at Corpus Christi Naval Hospital. It was there I met John, a Navy flight instructor stationed at the jet base nearby in Kingsville, Texas. Tall, blond, blue-eyed and with a smile that had melted more hearts, I felt certain, than mine alone, he was also wise and funny and full of life. But as we continued to date and our relationship grew, I became aware that it was his generous, understanding spirit I loved most of all.

Our romance seemed like a dream come true for me, and then, very much like a dream, it ended abruptly. Late one gray December afternoon in 1978 word came that a jet had lost power doing low-level landing approaches to the Corpus Christi naval airfield. To avoid a collision, the pilot had banked the plane away from a mobile drill rig moored in the bay, and crashed barely a mile from the hospital where I worked.

Word passed quickly through our small hospital staff that a plane had gone down. But there were a dozen squadrons in our region, and John was an outstanding pilot with years of experience. Of all those pilots, I reasoned, it surely had to have been someone other than John who crashed.

I dialed his office just to be reassured by his voice. A second later I was greeted by John's commanding officer. His words, painfully gentle, ripped the earth from under my feet. "Ruth, I have something to tell you... . " John was dead.

I took time off for the funeral. I felt lost and aimless. How could I go back to working and buying groceries and cleaning my apartment as if everything were just the same?

When I returned to the hospital a new patient had been admitted to our floor, in room 4014, as a civilian humanitarian case. He was a small, round man, with

121

a scrubby beard and hard little eyes. He had a badly infected leg wound that required strict bed rest and intravenous antibiotics. But it quickly became clear that he had another problem, one that was a lot more difficult to treat.

Everything about the man was foul: his filthy body, his groping hands, his horrid language, and more than anything else, the pleasure he seemed to get from making nurses uncomfortable. As hard as we tried to look beyond his behavior, each of us invariably left that room as quickly as possible, practically ejected into the hall by a stream of his obscenities.

The man in 4014 simply didn't care about anyone, least of all himself. He refused baths, refused to dress completely or to shave, and refused to allow us to keep his room in even a marginal state of order. About the only thing he agreed to was being left alone, which our frustrated staff began to do willingly.

Two weeks into his stay I stood at the nurse's station, mixing his last dose of antibiotics for the evening shift and stewing over my latest encounter with him. I had tried to get him to wear a robe over the hospital pajamas that covered him so inadequately. In language as cold and raw as the January wind that screamed past his window, he had made it quite clear what I could do with the robe and my other good intentions.

Now I had to face him again, to administer antibiotics. My agitation must have shown on my face, because one of the other nurses shook her head and said: "The guy in 4014 again, huh?" She grimaced. "I can't stand to be in the same room with him. It must be even worse for *you*."

Her emphasis puzzled me. "What do you mean?" I asked.

She looked startled, then uncomfortable. "I… I thought you knew."

She had my whole attention now.

"That guy," she explained, "was working on the mobile rig that your pilot swerved to avoid. If it hadn't been there John probably could have ejected safely."

I wanted to scream. Tears blurred my eyes and I fought to steady my trembling hands as they mechanically set the medication tray on the counter. How could I face the man in 4014? How could he be alive when John was dead?

I took a deep breath. I had promised myself and God that I wouldn't ask why such unfair things happened. I knew God was our Father, and that he loved me and John. The image of John's handsome, patient face flashed before me, and suddenly I realized: *I haven't lost everything of John. I still have all the sense of meaning and purpose that he so often shared with me. What would he have thought about the man in 4014?*

John believed in God's guiding hand and that every human being had worth. He thought that things happen for a reason, and he believed in handing over to God what we can't manage ourselves.

I made my way down to 4014. I stood just a moment outside the closed door, and prayed silently. *God, I don't know why you've put this patient and me together. I guess I don't need to. Just help me reach him and give him what he needs.*

I opened the door and went in.

"Now what?" he growled.

"Only your shot," I assured him. He nodded curtly and turned to stare out the window. The bay sparkled silver in the distance where brisk winds tossed the waters in the moonlight. His image in the glass reflected a haunted aspect I hadn't noticed before.

"Looks cold out there tonight," I said.

"It'll never look the same to me again." He stared down at his crumpled bedclothes.

"How do you mean?" I asked. He shrugged awkwardly. "Oh, it's just that crash. You know, the jet that went down in the bay a while back?" He pressed on without waiting for an answer, not noticing how I had frozen in place. "I was out there... on that rig when the plane went down."

He was almost talking to himself now, staring out the window. "I've never seen anything like that before. One minute the plane was up there and the next... . " His words trailed off and he looked back at me with another shrug, his expression pained.

I met his eyes, willing myself not to cry. What kind of response could I give him? What kind of answer did I have myself? Before I could gain enough control to say anything, his face changed, shock sharpening his features.

"You're the one, aren't you?" he asked.

I waited for him to explain, though I knew what he was asking.

"You're the nurse who was dating that pilot, aren't you? I had heard one of you here was. I'm... I'm sorry." His rough, sun-browned forehead wrinkled over eyes that seemed to waver between his usual defensive glare and genuine concern.

"That's okay," I told him when I found my voice at last. "It's hard getting past something like that, whether you actually knew the person or just saw it happen. Believe me, I understand."

"I can't stop thinking about the accident. Gone, just like that. Why? Why should that pilot's time be up and not mine? How are you supposed to live with that? I mean... am I supposed to owe somebody something now? They say the good die young." He chuckled—a humorless bark with a nervous edge. "I guess that doesn't say much for me, huh?"

I groped for a response. His questions were ones I had asked myself, and I suppose I might have felt as defensive as he sounded—if it hadn't been for one thing. Beyond all my doubts and questions, I believed in God—not just in his existence, but in his active, caring part in our lives. Words came to me, strong ones. It was as if I had borrowed John's strength and faith.

"I don't have an explanation for why things happen, either good or bad," I said. "But I do believe God has his reasons, and that he didn't give any of us life to waste. We just have to keep going and do our best to make something worthwhile of it. You never know when you might make a difference."

He was still for a moment, then nodded slowly. I finished taking care of him in silence, getting only an absent nod when I said good night.

The next day I made my way down to room 4014 without the old feeling of dread. What haunted my patient wasn't so different from my own ghosts, and I now saw him in a different light. When I pushed the door open I had to suppress a gasp.

The man in 4014 was smiling at me, hesitantly and shyly. He was clean-shaven, his hair was neatly combed, and for once he was dressed in clean pajamas and a robe. For some people these would not have been remarkable changes, but for this man they were bold steps.

I felt happier than I had in a long time. I couldn't help but wonder which of us had learned more. Maybe 4014 had simply needed to know it was all right to have survived when someone else hadn't. Maybe I had needed a reminder that I had to move on and make a new life without John.

But one thing was clear. The man in 4014 and I both had things left to do. They might not be great, world-changing things. But then again, remembering his smile, I thought of ripples on a pond: a tiny impact reaching out in ever-wider circles. *They might be after all.*

I Love My Job

by Eric Youngberg, Mapleton, Utah

I loved my new job, but I couldn't stand my boss. He was popular with my colleagues, but the truth was he worked only while his supervisor was on the floor. His projects piled up on my desk. To make matters worse, he took credit for my ideas while blaming me for his mistakes.

One morning on the way to work, I popped a Bible cassette into the car stereo. "But I say unto you which hear, Love your enemies, do good to them which hate you, bless them that curse you, and pray for them which despitefully use you," the narrator said, reading Luke 6:27, 28. I pressed rewind.

I gripped the wheel tighter, waiting to hear the words again. *What am I going to do about my boss, God? He's driving me crazy, but I can't just quit. My wife and kids are counting on me.*

As I played the tape a second time, Scripture sank in—and I got an idea. Instead of complaining about the boss, I would pray for him.

When I arrived at the office I concentrated on doing my best, without worrying about who received credit for the work. As the days passed, my boss didn't change, but gradually things got better. My shoulders didn't tighten when he swaggered in to toss me his files. I could relax and tackle any project because I didn't concentrate on the man's faults.

We still had our moments, but pretty soon I didn't think of him as my persecutor. And though prayer doesn't always make problems disappear, let me tell you the good news: Not only did the prayers change my perspective, a month later my difficult boss was transferred.

What Was Out There?

by Doug Oldfield, Hamilton, Ohio

I finished the night audit and glanced at the clock: 2:30 A.M. The midnight shift of a motel desk clerk can be lonesome work. You do anything to entertain yourself and stay alert. Patrons rarely check in at such an hour, but sleeping on the job isn't tolerated. So I flipped on the TV set, leaned back in my chair and started to read my new thriller in the wavering blue light. The blurb on the cover promised "deadly suspense."

Not even halfway through the first chapter, the clicking of metal on stone echoed in the quiet. I heard a tap, tap, tap on the counter behind me. *Who in the world...* ? I wondered as I swung my chair around—

I faced a sawed-off shotgun. My eyes moved up to the man who held it. He was large and dirty. Brown, greasy hair fell to his shoulders. His lips curled in a sneer amid a patchy beard. His skin was dark and weathered. An olive-green Army jacket buttoned to the neck hid the rest of his clothing. The man stared back as if he couldn't stand the sight of me.

He waved the barrel of the shotgun toward the door that separated us. "Open it," he said.

Slowly I stood up, afraid my legs wouldn't support me. I couldn't will them to move. My head swam with thoughts of escape. Without taking a step, I reached for the door. Before opening it, I whispered a prayer, "God, please send an angel to protect me."

My hand gripped the doorknob, and I had barely turned it before the man pushed his way through. He grunted, and breathed hard. He could easily have broken down the flimsy door. *He's toying with me.* He shoved me against the wall and kicked the door shut behind him. We were alone in the small back room.

"Open the deposit box," he snarled.

"I don't have the key," I said truthfully. I was trembling.

My head seemed to explode as he slammed the barrel of the shotgun across my jaw. I groped along the wall, shaking my head instinctively, trying to see. Where is he?

The man thrust his face to within an inch of mine. I could smell his stale breath. Flecks of spit dotted the corners of his mouth. Sweat formed on his brow. "I *said*," and he drew out each word, "open the deposit box."

Did he think I was lying? "I don't have a key," I repeated. *Let him believe me and leave me alone.*

Again he hit me with the gun. This time the stock crashed into my mouth, splitting my lip and loosening my front teeth. Did I actually think this man was going to just walk away and leave?

He swung the shotgun around and placed the barrel between my eyes. *I'm going to die. I am a dead man. This is how my life ends.* My mind rolled the idea around. *Dead.* I began to accept it. My muscles relaxed. I went limp.

"Open the box or I'm going to kill you." The words were matter-of-fact. How many times had I heard the same overused expression in everyday life? "I'll kill you if you… " But now it was for real. I waited for the blast.

Who is going to tell my wife and children? I didn't want the police knocking on their door in the middle of the night, scaring them and upsetting them. I didn't want my wife blaming herself for not having talked me out of taking this job. I didn't want to die! Anger began to grow in me, and I spoke up forcefully. "Check my pockets. Go ahead. I don't have the key!"

The man pulled the gun away and punched me in the eye. My head bounced off the wall and I fought for consciousness, sprawled on the floor. I knew that if I passed out I would not wake up. My head ached and my hand shook. I had only one hope and I called on him again. "God," I said aloud, "protect me from my enemy now." I groped in my mind for a Bible verse but couldn't find one.

Just then, the front doors rattled. The gunman took his steely eyes off me. I couldn't see the lobby from my vantage point behind the registration desk, but I listened for the doors to open. Was it a late-night patron? *This can only make the situation worse.*

I looked back at the armed man, and I couldn't believe what I was seeing. The hulking intruder stood staring into the lobby. His eyes grew wide with terror. His weather-beaten skin paled. His back hunched in fear.

"No… " he said, and let the word trail off in a long sigh. The shotgun dropped limply to his side and he backed against the wall. What was out there? I strained my neck, but could see nothing. I figured the police had arrived in force, guns drawn.

The man continued to stare into the lobby as he slowly backed away. He turned to me, pleadingly. He tried to say something. The meanness had left his face. He shook his head helplessly, too terrified to speak. Then he fumbled for his gun, ran down the hallway and out the back door.

I stood cautiously, not wanting to alarm the police officers. "My name is Doug Oldfield," I shouted. "I'm the night manager. The gunman ran out the back." I inched into the lobby, anxious to be surrounded by my rescuers.

The lobby was empty.

I checked outside—no police cars, no movement of any kind. *What the... ?*

I went back inside and called the police. They arrived within minutes, but there was no trace of the armed robber. Later, an officer showed me a picture and asked if it was the gunman. "That's him all right," I said.

"You're a lucky guy," the officer replied. "He's the suspect in several other motel robberies. In every other case, though, he's killed the desk clerk and we had no witnesses. We'll get him this time."

The man was going to kill me. But Psalm 91 says, "He shall cover thee with his feathers, and under his wings shalt thou trust... Thou shalt not be afraid for the terror by night... "

To this day I don't know what my attacker saw in the lobby that made him run away. But I have always believed it was an angel with a flaming sword, or an army of angels ready to protect me.

Doing Well by Doing Good

by Paula Lyons

Hanna Andersson, a booming, mail-order clothing company, is a business with a heart. The "heart" began beating soon after its first catalog went out, in February 1984.

Hanna's founder, Swedish-born Gun Denhart, conceived of "Hanna-downs" as a way to promote her high-end line of brightly colored, cotton garments for children. When their children outgrow them, customers can return their used "Hannas" for 20 percent of the original purchase price, to be applied to their next order. In turn, Hanna donates the used clothing to needy children.

Says Denhart: "This exposed us to a whole world I didn't even know existed. . . kids walking around America today with parents who can't afford to buy clothes for them. That opened up our hearts."

In just 11 years, Hanna Andersson grew to a $49-million business, employing nearly 300.

The Hannadowns program has played a big part in that success: The company has issued in excess of $2 million in credits to customers and has distributed about 500,000 articles of clothing to charities around the world. Since 1993, United Parcel Service has shipped Hannadowns for free.

But Hannadowns was just the first beat of Hanna Andersson's heart. Since 1988, Denhart has paid 45 percent of the child-care costs of her workforce—up to $3500 a year per family.

The company also donates five percent of its profits each year to charities its workers select, matching their contributions up to $500 each. It also allows each employee to volunteer for the cause of her choice for eight hours a year on company time.

Notes Denhart: "You can look at problems and say, 'Oh, too overwhelming; I can't do anything.' Or you can say, 'I'll do a little bit to make this a better world.' "

A Perfect Pot of Tea

by Roberta Messner, Kenova, West Virginia

An impatient crowd of nearly 200 diehard bargain hunters shoved their way into the huge living room of the old Withers' homestead. The sweltering 90-degree temperature didn't deter a single one, all in pursuit of the estate-sale find of the summer.

The lady conducting the sale, a long-time acquaintance, nodded as we watched the early-morning scavengers. "How's this for bedlam?" she chuckled.

I smiled in agreement. "I shouldn't even be here. I have to be at the airport in less than an hour," I admitted to her. "But when I was a teenager, I sold cosmetics in this neighborhood. And Hillary Withers was my favorite customer."

"Then run and check out the attic," she suggested. "There are plenty of old cosmetics up there."

Quickly, I squeezed through the ever-growing throng and climbed the stairs to the third floor. The attic was deserted except for a petite, elderly woman presiding over several tables loaded with yellowed bags of all sizes.

"What brings you all the way up here?" she asked as she popped the stopper out of a perfume bottle. "There's nothing up here except old Avon®, Tupperware®, and Fuller Brush® products."

I drew in a long, cautious breath. The unmistakable fragrance of "Here's My Heart" perfume transported me back nearly 20 years.

"Why, this is my own handwriting" I exclaimed as my eyes fell upon an invoice stapled to one of the bags. The untouched sack held more than a hundred dollars' worth of creams and colognes—my very first sale to Mrs. Withers.

On that long-ago June day, I'd canvassed the wide, tree-lined avenue for nearly four hours, but not one lady of the house had invited me indoors. Instead, several had slammed their doors in my face. As I rang the bell at the last house, I braced myself for the now-familiar rejection.

"Hello, Ma'am, I'm your new Avon® representative," I stammered, when the carved-oak door swung open. "I have some great products I'd like to show you." When my eyes finally found the courage to face the lady in the doorway, I realized it was Mrs. Withers, the bubbly, matronly soprano in our church choir. I'd admired her lovely dresses and hats, dreaming that someday I'd wear stylish clothes, too.

Just two months before, when I'd traveled to a distant city to have brain surgery, Mrs. Withers had showered me with the most beautiful cards. Once she'd even tucked in a Scripture verse: "I can do all things through Christ which strengtheneth me" (Phil. 4:13). I'd carried it in my red vinyl wallet. Whenever my teachers told me I'd never make it to college, I'd take it out and study it, repeating its promise softly to myself.

I'd believed that verse, even when my teachers kept saying, "With all the school you've missed, Roberta, you can never catch up." Perhaps they felt it was kinder not to let me dream too much, since I was afflicted with neurofibromatosis, a serious neurological disorder.

"Why Roberta, dear, come in, come in," Mrs. Withers's voice sang out. "I need a million and one things. I'm so glad you came to see me."

Gingerly, I eased myself onto the spotless white sofa and unzipped my tweed satchel filled with all the cosmetic samples five dollars could buy. When I handed Mrs. Withers a sales brochure, suddenly I felt like the most important girl in the world.

"Mrs. Withers, we have two types of creams, one for ruddy skin tones and another for sallow skin," I explained with newfound confidence. "And they're great for wrinkles, too."

"Oh good, good," she chanted.

"Which one would you like to try?" I asked as I started to adjust the wig hiding my stubbly, surgery-scarred scalp.

"Oh, I'll surely need one of each," she answered. "And what do you have in the way of fragrances?"

"Here, try this one, Mrs. Withers. They recommend that you place it on the pulse point for the best effect," I instructed, pointing to her diamond-and-gold clad wrist.

"Why, Roberta, you're so knowledgeable about all of this. You must have studied for days. What an intelligent young woman you are."

"You really think so, Mrs. Withers?"

"Oh, I know so. And just what do you plan to do with your earnings?"

"I'm saving for college to be a registered nurse," I replied, surprised at my own words. "But today, I'm thinking more of buying my mother a cardigan sweater for her birthday. She always goes with me for my medical treatments, and when we travel on the train, a sweater would be nice for her."

"Wonderful, Roberta, and so considerate. Now what do you have in the gifts line?" she asked, requesting two of each item I recommended.

Her extravagant order totaled $117.42. Had she meant to order so much? I wondered. But she smiled back and said, "I'll look forward to receiving my delivery, Roberta. Did you say next Tuesday?"

I was preparing to leave when Mrs. Withers said, "You look absolutely famished. Would you like some tea before you go? At our house, we think of tea as 'liquid sunshine.' "

I nodded, then followed Mrs. Withers to her pristine kitchen, filled with all manner of curiosities. I watched, spellbound, as she orchestrated a tea party like I'd seen in the movies—just for me. She carefully filled the tea kettle with cold water, brought it to a "true" boil, then let the tea leaves steep for "exactly" five long minutes. "So the flavor will blossom," she explained.

Then she arranged a silver tray with a delicate china tea set, a chintz tea cozy, tempting strawberry scones, and other small splendors. At home, we sometimes drank iced tea in jelly glasses, but never had I felt like a princess invited to afternoon tea.

"Excuse me, Mrs. Withers, but isn't there a faster way to fix tea?" I asked. "At home, we use tea bags."

Mrs. Withers wrapped her arm around my shoulders. "There are some things in life that shouldn't be hurried," she confided. "I've learned that brewing a proper pot of tea is a lot like living a life that pleases God. It takes extra effort, but it's always worth it.

"Take you, for instance, with all of your health problems. Why, you're steeped with determination and ambition, just like a perfect pot of tea. Many in your shoes would give up, but not you. And with God's help, you can accomplish anything you set your mind to, Roberta."

Abruptly, my journey back in time ended when the lady in the hot, sticky attic asked, "You knew Hillary Withers, too?"

I wiped a stream of perspiration from my forehead. "Yes… I once sold her some of these cosmetics. But I can't understand why she never used them or gave them away."

"She did give a lot of them away," the lady replied matter-of-factly. "But somehow, some of them got missed and ended up here."

"But why did she buy them and not use them?" I asked.

"Oh, she purchased a special brand of cosmetics for her own use." The lady spoke in a confidential whisper. "Hillary had a soft spot in her heart for door-to-door salespeople. She never turned any of them away. She used to tell me, 'I could just give them money, but money alone doesn't buy self-respect. So I give them a little of my money, lend a listening ear, and share my love and prayers. You never know how far a little encouragement can take someone.' "

I paused, remembering how my cosmetic sales had soared after I'd first visited Mrs. Withers. I bought my mother the new sweater from my commission on the sale, and I still had enough money for my college fund. I even went on to win several district and national cosmetics-sales awards. Eventually, I put myself through college with my own earnings and realized my dream of becoming a registered nurse. Later, I earned a Master's degree and a Ph.D.

"Mrs. Withers prayed for all of these people?" I asked, pointing to the dozens of time-worn delivery bags on the table.

"Oh, yes," she assured me. "She did it without the slightest yearning that anyone would ever know."

I paid the cashier for my purchases—the sack of cosmetics I'd sold to Mrs. Withers, and a tiny, heart-shaped gold locket. I threaded the locket onto the gold chain I wore around my neck. Then I headed for the airport; later that afternoon, I was addressing a medical convention in New York.

When I arrived in the elegant hotel ballroom, I found my way to the speaker's podium and scanned the sea of faces—health-care specialists from all over the country. Suddenly, I felt as insecure as on that long-ago day peddling cosmetics in that unfamiliar, affluent neighborhood.

Can I do it? my mind questioned.

My trembling fingers reached upward to the locket. It opened, revealing a picture of Mrs. Withers inside. I again heard her soft but emphatic words: "With God's help, you can accomplish anything you set your mind to, Roberta."

"Good afternoon," I began slowly. "Thank you for inviting me to speak about putting the care back in health-care. It's often said that nursing is love made visible. But this morning I learned an unexpected lesson about the power of quiet love expressed in secret. The kind of love expressed not for show, but for the good it can do in the lives of others. Some of our most important acts of love, sometimes, go unnoticed. Until they've had time to steep—for their flavor to blossom."

Then I told my colleagues the story of Hillary Withers. To my surprise, there was thunderous applause. Silently, I prayed, *Thank you, God, and Mrs. Withers.* And, to think, it all began with a perfect pot of tea.

"I Will Know"

by Elizabeth Sherrill

*"Don't do your good deeds publicly, to be admired, for then
you will lose the reward from your Father in heaven."*
—Matthew 6:1 (TLB)

I stopped in front of the light switch in our bedroom this morning, grateful for a gift I couldn't see. It was more than twenty years ago that a white-haired electrician left a gift behind him probably without knowing it.

He'd come to the house to replace some antiquated wiring. We followed him, fascinated, from room to room as he cut through walls, installing wires and switches.

One thing especially intrigued us. Before he closed up the holes in the walls, he carefully lined up the screw heads on the switch boxes. Patiently, painstakingly, he made sure that the groove on each screw was horizontal, exactly parallel with all the others. It was a pleasing pattern, a small work of art really, but who would ever see it?

At last, I couldn't contain my curiosity. "Why are you taking such trouble when it's all going to be covered up? Who's going to know?"

The old man stuck his screwdriver back in his tool belt before turning to look at me. "I will know," he said.

And *I will know* has been a family phrase ever since, reminding us that joy in work doesn't depend on applause. Each little unsung, unseen act today, done with integrity, can affirm like those hidden screw heads that the life "hid with Christ" is the one that counts.

*Father Who sees in secret, I will know and You will know
everything I do today.*

Mama and the Encyclopedias

by Joyce Reagin, Ft. Mills, South Carolina

One day after school there was a knock at our door. Mama opened it. A lady selling encyclopedias stood there. "Come on in!" Mama said.

She knew how much I wanted a set, but I knew we didn't have the money. Still, Mama depended on the Lord for everything—even encyclopedias. In fact, she had cleared and dusted a shelf in the living room to make room for the new books. "They're at the top of my prayer list," she told me. That was Mama for you!

"Do sit down," Mama said to the saleslady. Soon the two were chatting like old friends. Then Mama showed me the handsome sample volumes. I fell in love with the white, leather-bound books.

"I can manage the monthly payments," Mama said, "but it's the money I have to give you now that I'd have trouble scraping together." The encyclopedia lady frowned.

"I understand," she told Mama. "I guess we can't always have the things we want." She began picking up her samples. "For instance, there was this one-of-a-kind pair of shoes I had been admiring but I kept putting off buying them. When I finally got around to it, they were gone—bought on sale for next to nothing! I could've died. Some lucky shopper got a real bargain."

Suddenly Mama smiled. She excused herself from the room and returned with a pair of brand-new shoes.

"Those are the ones!" the lady gasped.

"Try them on," Mama insisted.

They were a perfect fit. "Would you consider the shoes as the down payment for the encyclopedias?" Mama asked.

Two weeks later I was arranging our shiny new encyclopedias on the dust-free shelf. I knew those books would teach me a lot. But they could never teach me as much as Mama did about faith.

O God, You have bound us together in this bundle of life;
give us the grace to understand how our lives depend on the courage,
the industry, the honesty and integrity of our fellow men;
that we may be mindful of their needs, grateful for their faithfulness,
and faithful in our responsibilities to them; through Jesus Christ our Lord.

—Reinhold Niebuhr (1892-1971)

Chapter Six

Pass It On

"Don't Think It. Don't Say It."

by Jackie Clements-Marenda, Staten Island, New York

"Oh, Grandma," I wailed, "I can't!" I was seven years old, learning to sew under the patient tutelage of my grandma Josie. No matter how hard I tried, I ended up with knots and needle pricked thumbs.

"*Can't* is a word this family doesn't know," Grandma told me. "*Can't* is used only by cowards, lazy people and those who don't know God. You do not fall into any of these categories. Remember, Jacquelyn, with God nothing is impossible."

Her mother had taught her to sew, and Grandma Josie was determined to pass the skill on to me. In spite of my ineptitude, she always smiled and showed me once more how to make the intricate stitches. I loved watching Grandma's needle glide through the white material of the dress she was sewing for my First Communion. Although she was 80 and weakened by a heart condition, she refused to allow her only granddaughter to walk down the church aisle in a store-bought dress and veil.

After a month of daily practice, when my handiwork didn't get past the knots and bleeding thumbs, I hoped Grandma Josie would give up on me. But she didn't, and one day she placed a small muslin-wrapped package in my hands. Inside were the last remnants of the family heirloom lace.

The lace was the only possession my great-grandmother Mary Mahoney brought with her from Ireland when she came to America as a young girl in the mid 1800s. Pieces of it had enhanced every bridal and communion veil worn in our clan from then on. It was the special task of the person to whom it was presented to sew on the lace.

There was so little of it left, and the pieces were so fine they would probably unravel in my hands. Worse still, I was afraid I would mutilate them with my clumsy stitches. "Don't think it. Don't say it," Grandma Josie warned, already sensing what I was about to tell her.

I decided to try another approach. "I don't need the lace, Grandma," I said, avoiding even touching it. "The veil is already beautiful enough."

Grandma Josie's eyes twinkled, but she kept her voice stern. "Wearing the lace is a sign to your family that you have the stamina to become the best woman you can be."

I stared at the lace as if it might come to life.

"My mother was fourteen when the great famine swept through Ireland," she said. "Hundreds of thousands were dying and her family knew it was only a matter of time before they too starved to death. There was only enough money to send one person to America."

Grandma Josie's eyes always brimmed with tears when she told this story. I put my hand on her arm.

"I'm sure young Mary Mahoney was terrified to board that ship alone, but she didn't tell her parents 'I can't.' She did what she had to do," Grandma explained. "When I lost two of my children to influenza the same year I lost three siblings to tuberculosis, did I neglect the healthy family I had left while I learned to live with my grief? No."

She took me in her arms, hugging me tightly. "If you don't try to put the lace on your veil because you fear the hard work, how will you stand strong against the difficult tasks that wait in your future?"

How I struggled with that lace from then on, often in tears when what I thought I had sewn straight proved to be crooked. But I didn't give up. Grandma Josie never criticized, and I was determined to please her. After all, my future depended on it.

Ten days before my Communion, Grandma Josie suffered a stroke and had to be hospitalized. She returned home the day before the ceremony, but my parents gave strict orders not to disturb her. I had missed her very much so I managed to sneak into her bedroom and snuggle up next to her in bed.

"I'm sorry you're sick, Grandma," I whispered. "Please, don't be mad. I couldn't finish putting the lace on my veil. I tried, but I got myself into such a thread knot, I didn't know what to do."

She kissed me. "Don't you worry," she said, and touched my cheek with her right hand, which had been paralyzed into a fist by the stroke. "You tried your best. Now just leave your veil on the chair. We'll finish it for you."

I left the room with tears in my eyes. *Who is "we"?* I wondered.

The morning dawned brightly, but there was no joy in my heart.

I was a failure. I tried to sneak past Grandma's room, but she heard my steps in the hall and called me in.

"You'd better get a move on if you plan to be on time," she said. I was surprised to find her dressed and sitting in a chair. "We got the veil done. Now it's up to you."

My veil lay in her lap. I picked it up and ran my fingers over the delicate stitches that held the precious lace in place. It seemed impossible, but the veil was complete. How had Grandma maneuvered the needle with her twisted right hand?

As usual, she answered my thought: "When you do your best and try your hardest, God's angels fill in the rest."

Thirty-five years later I am a competent seamstress. But most important, I live by the tradition of Grandma Josie and those who have worn the Irish lace: When I am confronted with a task so difficult it seems insurmountable, I "Don't think it. Don't say it," but do my best and ask God to send his fill-ins.

Our Brother's Keeper

by Flo Wheatley, Hop Bottom, Pennsylvania

One morning when I was 18, I saw a man who had collapsed on a subway platform. Like everyone else in that swarming rush-hour press of people, I passed him by. The man probably needed medical attention, but I was hurrying to my job as a page at a New York City bank, where I was earning money for school. My dad, a city fire fighter, had always warned me of the streets: "Beware, and look straight ahead." Still, it bothered me. I could have at least tried to find a policeman.

Nearly 20 years later, another subway scene had a lasting effect on me.

My husband, Jim, and I were raising our three teenagers in rural Pennsylvania, when our son, Leonard, was diagnosed with a pediatric type of non-Hodgkin's lymphoma. His treatment at the Sloan-Kettering hospital in Manhattan threw us into a hectic routine: Leonard and I stayed in the city during the day and traveled by subway to my niece's home in Flushing, Queens, at night.

We had taken a cab from the hospital to the subway that rainy Monday afternoon. Leonard was feeling woozy from chemotherapy. I had to stop on the sidewalk outside the subway entrance and prop him up on one of our suitcases while he retched into a plastic bag. People pushed past us with that look-straight-ahead manner that I remembered from my own commuter days. As the rain fell harder, I silently prayed.

"Lady, you need help."

The voice startled me. A rough-looking stranger loomed over us.

"No, we're okay," I responded hastily.

But instead of vanishing into the flow of people, he stood quietly and observed. I clutched the handle of one suitcase tightly; it contained all the money I had for the week.

"Lady," the man insisted, "you need help."

When I mumbled something about being on our way to Flushing, he grabbed a suitcase from me, hoisted it onto his shoulder and headed down the subway steps. I had no choice but to clutch Leonard's hand and the other suitcase and scramble after him. Our week's cash was riding on the stranger's shoulder.

After ducking under the turnstile, the man stepped onto a crowded subway car. I feared we would lose him, but a few stops later he got off, right where we had to change to a local. We followed him.

This car was less crowded, so I had an opportunity to study the man. He wore faded blue jeans, shabby sneakers and an old army jacket. A ring full of keys jangled from his belt.

It was still raining when we reached Flushing. I was amazed that he had come all this way with us. But when I turned to thank him, he had already stepped into the street and was hailing a passing cab. The driver sped by; I could understand why—no one was going to stop for this fellow.

A second cab inched near in the slow-moving traffic, and he grabbed the back door handle. The cabbie yelled, but the man held on until the cab stopped. "Come on, lady," he hollered. He shoved the suitcase onto the seat, ushered us in, then closed his fingers around the five-dollar bill I pressed into his hand.

The whole incident lasted about 20 minutes. I never saw the man again, but his parting words haunted many restless nights. Just before he slammed the door, he had said, "Don't abandon me."

Leonard's recovery was slow but steady. By the time we returned to Pennsylvania to stay, Jim got a job back in New York. Our lives continued to seesaw between the two places. Jim came home on weekends and I made frequent trips into the city.

I was aware of the growing number of homeless people. It troubled me to see them huddled over sidewalk grates to keep from freezing. I wanted to help, but all I did was pray for them. What more could one person do?

For two years I had noticed the same man lying near a bridge that I passed when I drove out of the city. One morning something caught my attention. He was now covered by a pink blanket, apparently handmade. It was a tiny detail against the vast backdrop of life in New York City, but it jumped out at me.

I could do that, I thought. Sewing was one of my favorite pastimes.

That night I searched through my sewing materials for scraps. "What do you have that you don't want?" I asked my children. They dug through their wardrobes and I began to sew.

The result was a seven-by-seven-foot quilt made of old blue jeans. We assembled it on the kitchen table. When folded and stitched, it became a sleeping bag large enough to hold a man and a few possessions.

We sewed eight that winter of 1985. Then Jim and I drove into the city to deliver them on the streets. We had no idea where to begin, so we waited until sundown and started driving around. But freezing rain had left the streets deserted. We finally decided to give up and return to Jim's apartment in Queens.

"Stop," I called out as we neared the bridge.

A solitary figure was huddled in the shadows of an abutment. Jim got out of the car and held up the homemade quilt. "Could you use a sleeping bag?"

That was the beginning of a family craft we dubbed My Brother's Keeper.

Then one day a neighbor gave me a piece of fabric from her sewing. "Can you use this?" she asked. I was unaware anyone had noticed what we had been doing.

"Why don't you come show the women at church how to make those quilts?" she asked.

It took me by surprise. I had never considered asking others to join us in our quilt making. We decided to invite people from all the area churches.

Not long after, I nervously greeted a gathering of women from United Methodist, Catholic, Quaker and Assembly of God churches. I spread the patchwork square of fabric on the table and began laying it with insulation. Then I placed a second square on top and started tying off the quilt.

I stitched the sides and rolled it into a sleeping bag with necktie handles. One woman got up, ran to the phone and quickly dialed. "I want you to come right down here," she insisted to a friend. "You've got to see this!"

From that point on, the project was never ours alone.

Today Jim and I deliver as many sleeping bags as we can. Not everyone wants our help, but most are grateful.

One day we saw a girl standing on the curb, wearing a shawl over her head and holding a paper cup. My husband brought the car to a stop. He approached her and asked, "Can you use a sleeping bag?"

She clutched it and started to cry as Jim quietly walked away.

We were distributing bags outside a shelter as people were turned out into the night, when a young man approached me. He said he was 19 and had stayed his allotted time at the shelter. He was facing a six-week wait on the streets until there was an opening at a halfway house.

I gave him a sleeping bag. Without a word he pulled me to his shoulder and hugged me.

I am still cautious on the streets, but I no longer pass by people in need. I stop, just as someone once stopped for me on a rainy Manhattan sidewalk. These people are as human as their hugs, and they must not be abandoned.

Set Aside a Portion

by Oseola McCarty, Hattiesburg, Mississippi

I was born on a farm in Wayne County, Miss., 88 years ago. I lived there with my mama, grandmother, and aunt. We raised corn, peas, potatoes, watermelons and cane. And we used to wash our clothes outside in a big black cast-iron pot.

When the four of us moved to Hattiesburg in 1916, we brought that pot with us. Like a treasure pot, it helped us make a living. In it my grandmother and mother did washing for white folks. They carried the water from a hydrant and filled up three big pots they had on a bench in the backyard of our little frame house. Mama boiled the clothes—she wouldn't scrub them—then rinsed and hung them on the line with wooden clothespins.

I can remember being just a small child trying to throw some of the washing in the pot. I thought I was helping, but really I was just tossing clothes around and messing everything up. My great-grandmother, who was there at the time, called over to Mama: "Lucy, let that child wash the smaller pieces, the socks and things!" And so Mama let me stand on a wooden box and put a few pieces into the water. That was how I began.

I loved to wash and iron. When I started going to Eureka Elementary School, I washed my own clothes on Saturday mornings, standing on my box so I could toss them into the pot. Then I took my box out to the clothesline so I could reach up and hang the wash in the morning sun. In the evening, I heated up that heavy old iron on the cookstove and did my ironing while standing on the box. And so I had all my clothes ready for the next week.

I loved school and every one of my teachers, especially Miss Hill. I must have been about 10 or 11 when one day she said, "Oseola, come up to the desk." So I went up and she talked to me low so nobody else could hear: "Oseola, who irons your clothes?"

"I do."

"*You* do? Oh, my. Well, I've got a linen dress I'd like you to iron. What do you charge?"

I said, "Ten cents." But when I returned the dress, freshly washed and ironed, she paid me a quarter. As time went on one person told another about my washing and ironing, and the work just seemed to come. The more I did, the more money I made.

Some children in the household where my grandmother worked had discarded a doll and buggy, so Grandma brought them home for me. I started putting my dimes and nickels and quarters under the pink lining of the doll buggy.

When I was 12 my aunt took sick, so I dropped out of the sixth grade to look after her. I was sad to miss out on learning, but felt good about helping my aunt. The next year my classmates had moved on, and I felt so far behind I never went back to school. Instead, I kept washing and ironing and tucking money under the pink lining of that buggy.

I was the one who went round to the grocer and the milkman to pay our bills each month. One day I passed the bank and it seemed to be the thing to do to keep my money there. I took in all my coins and dumped them on the counter— I can't tell you how much I had, maybe five dollars. The teller put my money away in a checking account, and every month, when I paid the bills, I dropped off more coins at the bank. All, that is, except for what I put in the collection plate at the Friendship Baptist Church. Nobody instructed me to do that. It just seemed fitting to give God back something of what he had given me.

The years passed. When I was in my 20s the Depression came, and I kept on taking in washing. I still used the old cast-iron pot, but now I didn't need to stand on a box. On my days off, if anybody needed help for a party or something, I made some extra money. I loved to work. I always asked the Lord to give me a portion of health and a portion of strength and some work to do. And over the years he did just that.

I hear some people today have financial advisors to tell them how to save their money and what to spend it on. Or people want more of this or more of that to make them happy, they just can't get enough. Well, the Lord portioned out the good things in life to me just fine. Who needs any more?

I made a rule that I would always keep up my church giving, and once a year I made a payment on my insurance and on my burial plot. And every month I paid my water and electricity and gas bills, and set aside a certain amount for groceries and everyday needs. Over the years God showed me how to spend a certain portion on this, how to spend a certain portion on that, and how to save the rest. It must have been him because nobody else showed me.

One day, when I went to the bank to deposit my money, the teller said, "Oseola, if you put your money in a savings account, you'll get some interest on that money."

"Yes, ma'am. When can I do it?" I asked. ·

"You can do it now." And I did.

Then on another visit one of the people at the bank said to me, "Oseola, you ought to put your money in CDs and build up more money."

And I said, "Yes, ma'am. When can I do that?"

And she said, "Right now." So I did, and I just kept on adding. Sometimes twenty dollars a month, sometimes fifteen dollars. I only went to the bank to put my change and dollar bills in, not to get them out. As long as I was able to keep working, I didn't see any need to take out that money and buy things I didn't have to have. Once a man down on Third Street was making a cedar chifforobe, and I paid him forty dollars for it. But that was the first and last check I wrote.

I also got my license as a hairdresser, and for about 14 years I washed and fixed people's hair. But when Mama got sick with cancer, I went back to washing and ironing at home so I could take care of her.

Things were changing after the war. I had been charging two dollars and fifty cents for a bundle of laundry, but as time passed people gave me ten dollars a bundle. Some folks were switching to hand-cranked washing machines, but I kept using my cast-iron pot and the line out back. I never needed much. If somebody gave me a pair of shoes that didn't fit, I just cut out the toes. And my Bible got so tattered from use, I had to tape it up to keep the pages in. Never needed a car; I always walked wherever I went. Pushed a shopping cart back and forth to the grocery store about a mile down the road. I've got an old black-and-white TV; it gets one channel. But I never watch it. I'd rather read my Bible.

In '64, Mama died; in '67, my aunt passed on. So I've been by myself ever since. I was alone, except for the Lord.

I kept on working, even after the age most people retire. It was December of '94 when my hand started swelling. I was doing washing for Lawyer McKenzie and his wife, and Mrs. McKenzie asked, "What's the matter with your hand?"

"Creeping arthritis," I said. "I've had a touch of it before, but it's got me now." It was mighty distressing that I had to quit work at the age of 86. But I said, "Lord, I want you to stay by me and guide me and protect me in all things." And he sure did.

At the bank one day they asked me where I wanted my money to go when I passed on. Mr. Paul Laughlin—he's one of the officers there—sat down with me and spread out ten dimes, and he told me that each dime represented ten percent of my money. So I took a dime for the church and a dime for each cousin. That left six dimes for a dream I had always had.

"I want to help some child go to college," I said. "I'm going to give the rest of my money to the University of Southern Mississippi, so deserving children can get a good education. I want to help African-American children who are eager for learning like I was, but whose families can't afford to send them to school."

Mr. Paul looked at me funny and said, "Miss Oseola, that means you'll be giving the school a hundred and fifty thousand dollars."

One hundred and fifty thousand dollars! I had never realized how much I had, and the amount 'bout took my breath away! Lawyer McKenzie talked to me to make sure I still really wanted to follow through with my plan. Then we drew up the papers. He made sure I would still have enough money if I ever needed it, and the rest would be given out over the years ahead, year by year.

When the news of what I had done got out, folks from newspapers and magazines came round to find out who I was. I didn't see what all the fuss was about, but invitations started arriving—to come visit the President in Washington, D.C., and the United Nations in New York City. I had never been outside of Mississippi, except to Niagara Falls one time long ago and the roar scared me so! But I went and got a Presidential Citizens Medal and was honored by the UN. Who would have thought *I* would be making trips like that?

But of all the new people I met, the one who meant most to me showed up right in my own front yard. Last August a lovely young girl ran up and threw her arms around me. "Thank you, Miss McCarty," she said, "for helping me go to college."

It was Stephanie Bullock, about to begin her freshman year and the first to receive a one-thousand-dollar Oseola McCarty Scholarship. Stephanie had brought along her mother, who is a schoolteacher, and her grandmother, who is a seamstress, and her twin brother, who was entering college also—and we all sat visiting on the screened-in front porch. Right off, we felt like family.

Stephanie had wanted with all her heart to go to USM, but since her twin brother was starting *his* freshman year at Jones County Junior College, money was pretty tight. Even though her grades were good and she had been president of the student body at Hattiesburg High, she kept missing out on scholarships. Nonetheless, she had gone ahead and applied to USM on faith, and her family had asked the Lord for help. Everyone in the Bullock family prayed for something to happen. Stephanie's mama, Leedrester Bullock, kept telling her not to worry but to trust in the Lord that something good would come through.

"Lord, you've told us that if we asked, we would receive," Stephanie had said, "so I'm asking for your help." Then she received a phone call telling her she would be the first person to receive an Oseola McCarty Scholarship. "Within minutes," Stephanie's mother told me, "the whole neighborhood knew."

I'm so proud. I told Stephanie right away that I'm planning to be there for her graduation. Now I feel like I've got a granddaughter.

I'm always surprised when people ask me, "Miss McCarty, why didn't you spend that money on yourself?" I just smile.

Thanks to the good Lord, I *am* spending it on myself.

The Nicholas Effect

by Margaret Green, Bodega Bay, California

While touring southern Italy last September, we visited an ancient Greek temple in Paestum. The children scampered up and down the worn steps. Taking my eyes off them for a moment, I spotted four doves perched on top of a column. Two of the birds suddenly flew away, disappearing into the golden sky. *Someday, our children will be gone too*, I thought.

Glad to be reminded of how much I loved my children, I gave seven-year-old Nicholas a big hug. Four-year-old Eleanor ran from the temple and let me hug her too.

It had been a dream trip, especially for Nicholas. Entranced by ancient history, he was thrilled to see the Roman Forum and Colosseum, the ruins of Pompeii and now these beautiful temples. Recalling his mythology, he had announced in a mock-serious voice from the steps, "I'm Zeus!" And then remembering how the Romans had referred to the same god, he ran onto Italian soil and said, "Now I'm Jupiter!"

"We'd better be going," Reg, my husband, said, glancing at his watch. We headed back to our rental car.

We planned to drive all night to the southern tip of Italy and take a ferry to Sicily. The sun hung low when we finally got under way. Reg was behind the wheel while Nicholas and Eleanor settled against pillows in the backseat. Soon they dozed off and, sometime after ten o'clock, so did I.

Angry voices shouting in Italian woke me up. 11:00 P.M. "Something is going on," murmured Reg. A car was keeping pace with ours on the dark autostrada. From the passenger side a man with a black bandanna over his face pointed a gun in our direction.

Worried that we'd be at their mercy if we stopped, Reg floored the accelerator. There was a loud crack, and the backseat window shattered. I heard more angry shouts. "It's too dangerous to stop," Reg said. He pushed the car faster. A moment later another shot blasted his window. But now a gap was opening between the cars, and the attackers dropped farther and farther behind.

Cold night air was rushing in. I unbuckled my seat belt and leaned over the seat to check on the children. Nicholas lay on his pillow, his eyes closed. He had always been a heavy sleeper, so I assumed he was still dozing. Eleanor sat up, complaining, "I'm cold, Mommy." Relieved that both of them seemed unhurt and had slept through the worst of the ordeal, I brushed away granules of glass and covered the kids with extra clothes. Eleanor settled in her seat.

I strained my eyes, looking for help, occasionally glancing into the backseat. Finally we spotted flashing blue lights. Two police cars and an ambulance were stopped at the scene of an accident. We pulled over. An officer tried to wave us on, but Reg gestured to our damaged car.

As we opened the car door and the dome light glowed over the children, I noticed that Nicholas's tongue was protruding slightly. Then I saw blood on his hair. *Dear God, he's hurt. Is he cut from the glass?* Trembling with fear, I looked closer and found a small round bullet wound in his head.

The officer yelled for the ambulance. A medic raced over and lifted Nicholas's limp body into the ambulance. Reg picked up our son's blanket, a small patch of sheepskin, and put it on the stretcher. If Nicholas woke up in a strange place, it would comfort him.

As the ambulance headed toward the nearest hospital, I begged to follow. We tried to explain to the officers what had happened. We still couldn't understand it ourselves. A young Italian man who had stopped his car when he saw the commotion translated for us. We would have to go to the station to make a report. *But what about our son?*

Reaching into his coat pocket, our translator pulled out a string of blue plastic rosary beads. He kissed them and handed them to me. "For you." I gripped those beads so tight they left indentations in my palm.

When we arrived at the hospital, a swarm of medical personnel was standing around the ambulance. Nicholas would need special care, we were told. They wanted to take him to the hospital in Messina, more than an hour away on the island of Sicily. We gave our approval and then made our report at the police station.

I felt as dark and empty as the streets we were driven through. Escorted by police cars with flashing blue lights, we were put on a ferry to Sicily. At the hospital in Messina we could only view Nicholas from outside a window in the intensive care unit. Electrodes were patched to his forehead. He was surrounded by wires, tubes and hospital equipment. I hugged Eleanor close as the neurologist explained slowly and carefully, "The bullet is lodged in an area where it is impossible to operate. Your son is in a coma. All we can do is wait."

As we were taken to a hotel, I longed for home. If this tragedy had happened there, we would have had the support of our family and friends. We would have been better able to understand what the doctors and nurses were telling us.

The hotel lobby was empty except for a desk clerk. We wearily made our way to our room and tossed and turned for an hour or two.

The next day I felt as though we were living in another world. I tried to remain hopeful. When we were not sitting on the hard plastic chairs in the waiting room, we hovered helplessly by the hospital window or waited at the hotel for a phone call that would bring some news. I could be with Nicholas only once, and then for just five minutes. The doctor said I might be able to sit with him the next day—perhaps for 20 minutes.

But the following morning the doctor ushered us into a conference room. The team of physicians looked grave. With the help of a translator the head of the intensive care unit explained that Nicholas's brain had died during the night. The respirator was the only thing keeping his small body going. He was gone.

I held Reg's hand, barely able to comprehend the horrible truth. Was there nothing more we could do? "Shouldn't we give his organs?" one of us said (we don't remember which one). "Yes," we agreed.

"We would like to give his organs," Reg told the doctors. *Maybe this way his death can make a difference*, I thought.

That afternoon, when we returned to the hotel, a crowd of people waited by the front desk. Some stepped aside, too shy to intrude, but wanting to comfort us. The hotel clerk gestured to one young mother who wished to see us. She turned to us with a tear-stained face, and we hugged each other and cried. A perfect stranger but she understood.

We were flooded with kindness until we left Italy. On the street in Messina an old man pressed a stuffed animal into Eleanor's arms. When I asked if I could bring some clothes for Nicholas's body, the head of a department store invited me to pick out anything I wanted for free—I chose a blue blazer, gray slacks and a tie with Goofy on it. The day I wanted to walk Eleanor to get some ice cream, a policeman drove us to the best spot in town and bought it himself. The president of Italy arranged for us to be flown home in an Italian Air Force jet.

Bringing Nicholas's body back home to California for burial, we faced our loss all over again. Little things set me off, like going to the grocery store and grabbing Nicholas's favorite cereal. Or the day a package arrived in the mail with all his toys we had left behind in the rental car. Or when I opened his closet and saw the tricorn hat for his George Washington costume for Halloween—a costume he would never wear.

But the letters and telegrams kept pouring in. Newspapers and TV stations throughout Italy had carried our story. The country grieved for the boy.

Schoolchildren wrote stories and poems. Towns small and large named streets and schools after him.

We had been home for only a few months when we were invited to Italy for a ceremony honoring Nicholas. *How can we go back?* I wondered. *How can we face the pain again?* But I realized we had to go for his sake.

The morning of the ceremony, Eleanor, Reg and I got dressed in our hotel in Messina. We went to the lobby, and a beautiful young woman came over to us and introduced herself as Maria Pia Pedala. Only 19 years old, she had been near death when she received Nicholas's liver. She was alive, thanks to our son.

Next we met 14-year-old Anna Maria Di Ceglie. She had received one of our son's kidneys. At the ceremony, we greeted, one after another, the people whose lives had been changed by Nicholas. There was an 11-year-old boy who had been on dialysis for a year until he was given a new kidney. We met a schoolteacher and a salesman who had each received a cornea from our son. We shook hands with the 30-year-old woman who had received cells from Nicholas's pancreas to help her body produce insulin. The only one missing was 15-year-old Andrea Mongiardo, who was still recovering from a heart transplant operation.

More important were those who had simply been affected by our story. An Italian specialist told us he had done only one transplant every four months, but ever since our son's death, the number of organ donations had risen dramatically. Doctors said Nicholas had changed the entire country: Italy, which has one of the lowest rates of organ donation in Europe, reported the willingness to donate went up 400 percent since Nicholas died. They called this the Nicholas effect.

Of course, I would have done anything to have my son back, but the fact that his young life had made this much difference was overwhelming.

On the last night of our stay, after an exhausting day of visits and speeches, we returned to our hotel at midnight, only to find a man who insisted that Reg come to a disco with him. "Two musicians have written a song about your son," he said. Reg didn't have the heart to turn the man down.

Filled with loud music and youngsters dancing, the disco came to a stop when Reg walked in. In the silence two young musicians started strumming guitars and singing a song. The only word Reg could understand was *Nicholas*. At the end, the people erupted into cheers and hugs for my husband. Everybody wanted to give him their blessings.

"It was like a church," Reg told me later. "There was that much love in the place." All because of a seven-year-old boy.

Prayer at a Truck Stop

by Craig Chaddock, San Diego, California

At a truck stop on a cold rainy day, I sat down next to another driver. I made a few comments about the weather and then he shared his hard-luck story. Suddenly I realized he was no driver, just some drifter hanging around to keep warm and bum a few meals.

I stepped outside and immediately my conscience began to nag me. Although I work with the homeless at our church, I don't like to meet them on the job. But I thought of Christ's comment that we help "the least of these." What was I supposed to do? I was on a tight schedule. Plus, I didn't have the resources. *Lord, you know what he needs*, I prayed quickly. *Help him.*

As I did a final check of my rig before heading out, another driver approached me. He desperately needed to have 2000 pounds of his load shifted in his trailer and was offering fifty dollars for the job.

I couldn't take the time to help him, but an idea occurred to me. "Is the fifty-dollar offer good for anyone who helps you?"

"Sure is," he said. "I can't do it on my own."

Within minutes I found the drifter inside and asked him if he was interested. "Of course," he exclaimed as he popped out of his seat. "Buddy, this is an answer to prayer!"

Later I reflected on how my own prayer had been answered. I had asked God to help one poor man. Little did I know he would help three.

A Widow's Letter to Her Children

by Carmen Gordon

In 1993, Gary Gordon was killed trying to rescue a fellow U.S. soldier in Somalia. Months later, his widow, Carmen, wrote the following letter to their children, Ian 6, and Brittany 3.

My dearest Ian and Brittany, I hope that in the final moments of your father's life, his last thoughts were not of us. As he lay dying, I wanted him to think only of the mission to which he pledged himself. As you grow older, if I can show you the love and responsibility he felt for his family, you will understand my feelings. I did not want him to think of me, or of you, because I did not want his heart to break.

Children were meant to have someone responsible for them. No father ever took that more seriously than your dad. Responsibility was a natural part of him, an easy path to follow. Each day after work, his truck pulled into our driveway. I watched the two of you run to him, feet pounding across the painted boards of our porch, yelling, "Daddy!" Every day, I saw his face when he saw you. You were the center of his life.

Ian, when you turned one year old, your father was beside himself with excitement, baking you a cake in the shape of a train. On your last birthday, Brittany, he sent you a hand-made birthday card from Somalia. But your father had two families. One was us, and the other was his comrades. He was true to both.

He loved his job. Adventure filled some part of him I could never fully know. After his death, one of his comrades told me that on a foreign mission, your dad led his men across a snow-covered bridge that began to collapse. Racing across a yawning crevasse to safety, he grinned wildly and yelled, "Wasn't that great?"

You will hear many times about how your father died. You will read what the President of the United States said when he awarded the Medal of Honor: "Gary Gordon died in the most courageous and selfless way any human being can act." But you may still ask why. You may ask how he could have been devoted to two families so equally, dying for one, but leaving the other.

For your father, there were no hard choices in life. Once he committed to something, the way was clear. He chose to be a husband and father, and never wavered in those roles. He chose the military, and "I shall not fail those with whom I serve" became his simple religion. When his other family needed him, he did not hesitate, as he would not have hesitated for us. It may not have been the best thing for us, but it was the right thing for your dad.

There are times when that image of him coming home comes back to me. I see him scoop you up, Ian, and see you, Brittany, bury your head in his chest. I dread the day when you stop talking and asking about him, when he seems so long ago. So now I must take responsibility for keeping his life entwined with yours. It is a responsibility I never wanted.

But I know what your father would say. "Nothing you can do about it, Carmen. Just keep going." Those times when the crying came, as I stood at the kitchen counter, were never long enough. You came in the front door, Brittany, saying, "Mommy, you sad? You miss Daddy?" You reminded me I had to keep going.

The ceremonies honoring your dad were hard. When they put his photo in the Hall of Heroes at the Pentagon, I thought, *Can this be all that is left, a picture?* Then General Sullivan read from the letter General Sherman wrote to General Grant after the Civil War, words so tender that we all broke down: "Throughout the war, you were always in my mind. I always knew if I were in trouble and you were still alive you would come to my assistance."

One night before either of you were born, your dad and I had a talk about dying. I teased that I would not know where to bury him. Very quietly, he said, "Up home. In my uniform." Your dad never liked to wear a uniform. And "up home," Maine, was so far away from us.

Only after he was laid to rest in a tiny, flag-filled graveyard in Lincoln, Maine, did I understand. His parents, burying their only son, could come tomorrow and the day after that. You and I would not have to pass his grave on the way to the grocery store, to Little League games, to ballet recitals. Our lives would go on. And to the men he loved and died for, the uniform was a silent salute, a final repeat of his vows. Once again, he had taken care of all of us.

On a spring afternoon, a soldier from your dad's unit brought me the things from his military locker. At the bottom of a cardboard box, beneath his boots, I found a letter. Written on a small, ruled tablet, it was his voice, quiet but confident, in the words he wanted us to have if something should happen to him. I'll save it for you, but so much of him is already inside you both. Let it grow with you. Choose your own responsibilities in life but always, always follow your heart. Your dad will be watching over you, just as he always did.

Love, Mom

Dream Big Dreams

by Doris Toppen, North Bend, Washington

B arb Drennen still remembers the phone call that spring morning in 1986. It would change her life.

"Mrs. Drennen," the woman on the other end of the line said, "I'm from the Department of Social and Health Services. I know that you and your husband have had many foster children in your home, and wonder if you'd be willing to help us out?"

"How?" Barb asked.

"We're seeing more and more drug-addicted babies born at University of Washington Hospital, and need someone to devise a program of care for them. Can you do that?"

Barb, 50, was stunned. "I've suspected that some babies my husband and I take are drug affected," she said. Recently, she had seen perplexing symptoms in babies placed in her home. The infants were anxious, couldn't sleep or eat, and cried uncontrollably. One trembled frantically, his tiny arms shaking, his chin quivering, his body wracked with severe tremors. "I can care for the babies in my home," she told the social worker, "but I can't design a program for them."

"Please think about it," the social worker pleaded. "These poor infants are suffering and need help."

Barb talked to her husband, Ken, an engineer, about the phone call, then called her friend Barbara Richards, 52, to tell her. Barbara and her husband, Gary, a reservation clerk for an airline, also care for foster children, mostly neglected or abused children taken from their parents by social workers. The two couples had cared for more than 700 children in their homes during the previous 30 years.

"Oh, those poor babies," Barbara said, tears sliding down her cheeks. "But they need something more than we can design." Years earlier, when she lived in the midwest, Barbara had started a center for medically fragile children, and she didn't want to fight the bureaucratic system again.

But Barb and Barbara couldn't forget the plea. During the next few weeks, they called each other frequently, and called other foster parents in their small community of Kent, Wash., a Seattle suburb of 38,000 people. They found little help.

Barb wished she could just enjoy her comfortable two-story home, and simply love the babies put in her care. But social workers continued to call. "Do you have room? We need more homes like yours where foster parents know how to treat infants with drug problems. Babies are dying for lack of care."

Barb was plagued with doubt. "Why me, God?" she prayed. "I've never done anything like this."

Barbara wrestled with similar questions. Barbara and Gary's four natural children were grown, and the couple now had seven foster children in their home, whose ages ranged from seven months to 27 years. Barb and Ken's two natural children were grown, but they had two adopted children, and were legal guardians to a boy with cerebral palsy.

When two drug-addicted babies died in a foster home within months, Barb telephoned Barbara. "We really need to do something," she said.

"I'm ready to help," Barbara said.

Later that evening, they sat at the table in Barb's kitchen and wrote down all their questions and the problems they faced.

"We would need to train nurses, find a building, raise money, buy all the extra equipment these babies need for round-the-clock care," Barb said. "And we would need a doctor available at all times."

Together, they outlined a facility that would provide care for addicted babies until they were healthy enough to be placed in a family. Because many drug abusers come from stable families who are devastated by the daughter's lifestyle, and who want to keep the family intact, the expectation was that most of the babies would find homes with family members.

Barbara leaned forward, encouraged. "When I think of the hurting babies out there, I know we have to give this all we've got."

"It looks right," Barb said, grinning. "We're just moms, but God prepared us for this. I believe there are people out there who would like to help. God has tapped us, and we'd better believe it—for the babies."

Barbara nodded, and looked over the plan again. "Doctors, nurses, and social workers tried to create a program, but gave up and kept calling us. I didn't think we could do it. But here it is, designed by God."

Barb's blue eyes shone through her glasses. "And this won't be an institution where babies are warehoused. We'll move them back out into family and foster homes as soon as possible."

During the next two years, their husbands provided $4000 and cared for the children at home while Barb and Barbara traveled across the country on and off, attending classes and seminars, and visiting medical facilities. They worked with local doctors and hospitals, met with social-service officials. As they took those first steps, more ideas developed and were made part of their plan.

Finally, in May 1989, they took their proposal to the Department of Social and Health Services, which had asked for their help three years earlier. In a meeting with officials, the two women asked for $200,000 to fund the program. At the end of the hour, convinced the babies would be "warehoused," the officials rejected the proposal.

The two women were stunned. Barb looked at Barbara seated next to her in the meeting room, usually tough and composed, and saw her chin quiver, her shoulders sag. *We've lost. Now what do we do?* They had struck out. During the ride home, they were in shock and couldn't talk.

Barbara cried all night. "What are we doing wrong?" she called out to God. "Are we blundering toward something not meant to be? Is this the best answer for these babies?" It seemed like the end.

But God had other plans.

The next morning, the two conferred over coffee, then put their questions before God, and listened. "You've brought us this far, Lord, but it looks like the plan is dead." As they prayed, they began to realize what had happened during the past three years. They had met doctors, nurses, social workers, even key legislators, preparing to set the program in motion. They realized that even though things didn't seem to have worked out at all, God was behind the scenes working for good.

The pieces began to fall into place. "We're more than qualified to do this," Barb said with a confident smile. They realized that their experience complemented each other's skills: Barbara's 30 years in caring for severely handicapped children, Barb's having worked with newborn and premature infants.

"There's nothing wrong with this program," Barbara said. "It will work." As they talked, a quiet boldness grew within them. "We've got to believe God's view that we can do this," Barb said.

Barbara sat back on a stool and smiled. "I don't feel afraid, Barb. We *can* do this." There was no turning back. They decided to take their plan directly to the state legislature, and began preparing an even more comprehensive proposal.

The women put everything in writing, and solicited letters of support from lawyers, doctors, social workers, nurses, foster parents and hospital directors. They discovered shocking statistics: At the University of Washington Hospital, which has a special program for people with drug problems, eight out of ten babies were born drug affected—compared to the national average of one out of ten babies. In one six-month period, seven hospitals in the Puget Sound area reported that 1500 of the 8000 babies born had mothers addicted to cocaine, crack, heroin or alcohol.

Barb and Barbara knew that state legislators had been studying the problem, so they prepared information packets for each legislator, and drove the 50 miles to the capitol in Olympia to begin lobbying.

"This is what's happening in Seattle," they said. "We have to do something about it." From there, state representatives June Leonard and Margarita Prentice took the reins. "This is exactly what we're looking for," said Leonard.

In August 1989, state officials approved $500,000 for a nine-month pilot program, and funneled the money through the social services department, where officials presented the next hurdle. "Be up and running in thirty days or you don't get the money," they told Barb and Barbara.

"Thirty days!" gasped Barbara. "How can we do all that needs to be done by then?"

But they swung into gear, and found a small medical facility that had been empty for several years. At the same time, a friend told a local newspaper reporter about the program, and a series of stories began appearing in the Valley *Daily News*. Barb and Barbara told reporters what was needed and the deadline they faced, and phone calls began coming in with offers to help.

Volunteers were asked to come to the first planning meeting, held in the empty building. The two women prayed, and that night nearly 90 volunteers jammed the meeting room and spilled onto the porch. They were asked two questions: "What can you do?" and "Who do you know?"

To get the project started, Valley Medical Center donated $32,000. That opened a flood of help from the community. Now the work began. Doors and windows had to be replaced, a sprinkler system installed, the furnace repaired, walls painted, medical equipment purchased and installed, a staff hired-in fewer than 30 days.

The list of volunteers had grown to 200, but Barb and Barbara still didn't know if it was possible to pull everything together in time. When things looked bleakest, the phone rang. "This is Dick West from Boeing. Do you need help?"

"Yes," Barb replied, grateful for one more volunteer to wield a paint brush. But when West arrived the next day, he wore a suit, carried a briefcase, and had an assistant with him. The two men walked through the unit and studied the plans. "We can bring a paint crew in," West said, "but you need a project manager. Boeing understands time lines and management, and you don't have much time. We'll provide a project manager, and if you're not ready by deadline, we'll bring people in from Boeing to help."

The two women couldn't comprehend the extent and effect of such a gift. And when Doug Burroughs, in his 20's, cheerful and handsome, walked in the next day, younger-looking than their sons, they wondered if he was up to the job.

But Burroughs calmly managed eight contractors, all the volunteers, and ran for supplies and permits himself as well. "Listen, everybody," he kept encouraging the volunteers, "we can do this."

One day, an older woman stopped and asked, "Do you have any special need?"

"Would you like to walk through?" asked Barbara. "We're making headway, but we don't have $10,000 for a sprinkler system."

"I have a wealthy friend," the woman said. "He's very particular, and will want to know more about your organization."

The next day, she stopped again. "I have a check for $10,000 to give you, provided you never tell my friend's name."

Pediatric Interim Care Center opened in October 1990. Care for one month for a drug-addicted baby is $4000, compared with $30,000 at the University of Washington Hospital. The Center's costs are lower because so much is donated, nurses work for lower wages and no benefits, and the medical director donates his time. Paid staff is minimal, and more than 100 people are on the waiting list to volunteer their help. The average treatment time for a baby is 36 days. The facility is equipped for 13 babies, and has cared for more than 350 infants since it opened. It is a labor of love for Barb and Barbara to bring the babies to the Center for loving care.

The community rallied around the Center, helping meet each new challenge. When money was needed for a machine that measures oxygen in the blood, a nearby church gave $5000 from tithes and offerings—just the amount needed.

Medical staff and social workers call from across the country for information on funding, staffing, and caring for drug-addicted babies. "It's overwhelming. They have no concept of what it's going to take," Barbara told a volunteer after a siege of calls. The task is so daunting that the Center remains the only one of its kind in the country.

But the Center must care for more than the suffering infants; volunteers must also care for the mothers. When Tanya's baby, Kenny, was born on the kitchen floor, he was transferred to the hospital, and three days later to the Center. Each day, Tanya, 42, with her three other children, rode the bus across town, transferring through winter storms, to sit with Kenny. She rocked her baby while watching her other children play around her chair.

The reality of having her baby taken away at birth had jarred her out of the clutches of cocaine. "The drug tricks you," she said to Barb, "until everything—home, family, possessions—is gone." Her voice broke. "And I hurt my baby."

The Center trained Tanya how to respond to her baby's withdrawal symptoms, which could continue for six months. Babies born drug-addicted are at risk for drug abuse for the rest of their lives, and can suffer inappropriate emotional responses—laughing when they should cry, crying when they should laugh—for a lifetime. But the Center's staff also helped Tanya see what a beautiful baby she had.

On the day before Kenny was to go home, Tanya brought in a gray, stiff undershirt worn through at the arms, the only baby clothes she had. Nurses and volunteers knew it was Tanya's birthday, and put a baby shower and birthday celebration together overnight.

When Tanya arrived the next day, Barb walked down the hall with her. "We have a surprise for you," Barb said. The smiling group gathered around the table covered with balloons and gifts. Tanya stared at the decorated cake, and huddled her children in her arms as tears rolled down her cheeks.

"Are you all right?" asked Barb.

"Yes," Tanya said, swallowing hard, wiping her nose. "It's just that I've never had a party before."

Barb and Barbara hugged Tanya. A new light shone in her eyes. She wasn't going home to a white picket fence, but she was ready for another run at life. Now, three years later, Tanya continues drug-free, raising her family and doing well.

The workday for Barb, the Center's director, and Barbara, its administrator, stretches from 6:30 A.M. until 6:30 at night. Their love for the babies keeps them going. Lives are being changed because two women had a dream, wouldn't give up, and believed that innocent babies deserve a chance at life.

"A Blessing Shared"

by Fay Angus

Always try to do good to each other .... Always be joyful.
—I Thessalonians 5:15-16 (TLB)

I had the grumps. The whole world looked "tattletale gray" in spite of the sun. Today was my day to get at all the old mundane chores that had been piling up. Run a dozen errands. Do the laundry. Dust the living room...the bedroom ... everything.

What's more, it was trash day. Lugging a sack of garbage to the cans at the sidewalk, I felt put out.

An unexpected glint of color on the hood of the car caught my eye. *Is that paint?* No, it was spring flowers—homegrown daylilies, daisies, bright blue periwinkles and tiny pink tea roses—carefully arranged in a small basket tied jauntily to the hood ornament. *Of course! Today is May Day!*

I didn't know where or whom it came from, but no matter. I found myself swinging and whistling on the way back up the drive. The gray mists blew out of my heart. Mundane became fun-filled. I ran my errands with the perky basket wobbling on the car's hood, and got many smiles and waves from pedestrians and other drivers.

I know now that it was my good friend Millie who crept around at dawn to touch my day with wonder, and I am grateful. This year I am passing along Millie's blessing. Early this morning I will fill my own small baskets with flowers from my garden, then hurry around the neighborhood to place one on the doorstep of each house, Nancy and Jack, Lennie and Jim, dear Goldie way up the hill ... won't they be surprised!

A sweet surprise from the heart of a friend
Blesses our day with radiant joy!

Thank You, Lord, that a blessing shared is a double delight!
Help us to send one on its way—to gladden a heart and brighten a day.

The Miracle Pie

by Bobby Livingston

I could hear my mama and the doctor talking in the next room.

"He *must* eat," the doctor said. "He's weak and dehydrated."

"I've given him everything I can think of, but he just can't keep anything down."

Mama came to sit beside me. "Bobby," she said, "Want me to go to the store and buy some Jell-O?"

"No, Mama."

"Can't you think of anything you'd like?"

"Make me some shoo-fly pie, Mama," I said. "I know I could eat that."

I had never eaten shoo-fly pie in my life. But Mama had been reading stories to me about Amish children, and I just knew I could eat one of those shoo-fly pies they were always talking about.

Mama didn't know anything about making shoo-fly pie. And nobody she called knew either.

"Bobby," she said. "I'm going to the grocery store and try to find something else."

"What store are you going to, Mama?" I asked, "I'll ask God to send you a recipe there. He'll send you one."

"The Winn-Dixie." I could see she was worried about my praying such a big prayer.

But as soon as she left, I asked God for that very thing.

Mama returned an hour later with the biggest smile on the face. And then she told me why.

As soon as Mama walked into the grocery, she saw them: Amish ladies. She rushed up to them and said, "Could you write me a recipe for shoo-fly pie?"

"Of course. All Amish women know how to make shoo-fly pie. We will help you find the things you need to make a nice pie."

And so the women did just that.

Mama asked them how they happened to be in a Winn-Dixie in Florida.

"We were just passing through the area," one of the ladies said, "when my friend here said, 'Let's stop at that Winn-Dixie.' So here we are. I really don't know why we came in."

Later that afternoon, Mama spooned big pieces of shoo-fly pie into my mouth. Nothing had ever tasted as good. By morning I was able to drink fruit juice and eat poached eggs and toast.

The doctor could hardly believe it. "That must have been some pie!" he said to Mama.

"You could call it a miracle pie," Mama answered, smiling at me.

And, in fact, that's what we've called it ever since.

Chapter Seven

Don't Ever Give Up

*O Lord God,
when Thou givest to Thy
servants to endeavor any
great matter, grant us
also to know that it is
not the beginning, but the
continuing of the same
until it be thoroughly
finished which yieldeth
the true glory;
through Him that for
the finishing of Thy work
laid down His life.
Amen.*

*—Sir Francis Drake
(c. 1543-1596)*

Will to Live

by Steve McClure, Thompsontown, Pennsylvania

I heard a crash of metal against metal and was jolted by a bone-shaking series of thumps. Clumps of earth and bushes rushed by. With my heart frantically pumping, I clutched the steering wheel as my pickup careered down an embankment. *Oh, my God! I'm off the road—I must have fallen asleep.*

An earthen wall rushed out of the blackness, and my truck slammed to a grinding stop. I screamed at the sharp pain tearing through my groin and lower body. Then in a sudden, eerie silence a cloud of steam wafted through the crazily slanted headlight beams. Numbness seeped from my spine down to my feet until I couldn't feel my legs. I knew I was badly hurt, but I couldn't bear to look down. I was afraid of what I might see.

Why didn't I listen to Brenda? She saw how tired I was.

My fiancée, Brenda Strawser, lived in McAlisterville, Pa., just 20 miles from my home in Spruce Hill. She had asked me to spend the night on her couch rather than drive home, but the biggest blizzard in years was expected to hit by 1:30 A.M. I wanted to get on the road before the snow began.

As I turned around to see where I was, a hot poker of pain raced up my spine. I slumped back in a cold sweat. My pickup was at the bottom of a steep embankment. Shards of glass from the smashed rear and passenger-side windows littered the cab. A shudder racked my body. I was getting cold and knew I was going into shock. My watch read 12:30 A.M. *It's not that late. Cars will come by; somebody will find me,* I thought.

I leaned on the horn, but it emitted only a low, throaty rasp. The light from the headlights dimmed to a dull amber glow. The battery was dying. Then a breeze brought in a few snowflakes, which melted on my face and hands. I gazed in horror as snow flurries flickered through the beams of my fading headlights. The blizzard had begun. If I stayed in the pickup, I would be buried alive.

The whoosh of a passing car was muffled in the gathering storm. Snow was already covering the ground. I grabbed the door handle, but it was jammed. A sharp pain ripped my lower body as I twisted to reach the passenger-side door. I fell back, defeated by the intense pain.

Just an hour earlier Brenda and I had been holding hands and talking about our future. Now I wondered if I would last the night. *Lord, you didn't bring me this far to end it here*, I prayed. I reached over and, ignoring the pain, butted my hands and head against the far door. Finally it wrenched open. Using my arms and shoulders I levered myself out of the cab and slid into the snow and mud. Above me loomed the embankment. Another car roared down the road. "Help! Help me!" I screamed. But my words were snatched by the rising wind.

I struggled to stand against the truck. As soon as I put weight on my legs, pain shot through my body and I crumpled in a heap. But I had to get going. Clad only in a T-shirt, sneakers and a light windbreaker, I was freezing. I began to crawl slowly up the embankment. I was unable to keep my jacket and T-shirt from riding up, and felt the ground rubbing my bare midriff raw. Finally, with a last breathless heave, I pulled myself over the top and onto the road.

"Oh, no," I said with a sob as I saw where I was. I had dozed as I turned off the four-lane highway at the exit ramp. My truck had gone through the stop sign at the end of the exit ramp, then across the Route 75 overpass road, which crossed over the four-lane highway, and finally hurtled down the embankment. The painful climb up the slope had brought me to the edge of the empty, white expanse of the overpass. There was no shoulder. If I crawled farther I could be hit by any vehicle that might come by. If I inched back down the embankment, no driver would see me. I lay there despondent, exhausted and gasping for breath. A car sped around the overpass but the driver couldn't see me—a shapeless snow-covered lump alongside the embankment. I could look down and see more cars on the four-lane highway. If I got down there, I would have a better chance of being found. I had to move quickly. I was getting numb. The snow got thicker, slanting across the road in the moaning wind. I felt drowsy. I shuddered. In my condition sleep could mean death.

I began to crawl down the ramp. My strength was ebbing. It took two hours to crawl 500 yards to the eastbound shoulder of the divided highway. Then I began shaking uncontrollably. I couldn't move. A car came by, then another, then two more close together. But I couldn't raise my body enough to be seen.

"Hey, over here, please. Help me. Help me," I rasped, and waved as each car went by, but it wasn't enough. I had felt so victorious at being able to crawl to the main highway, but I still couldn't get help. Now no more cars were coming.

The other side. Maybe I'll have better luck on the westbound lanes.

I could feel the beginnings of delirium and panic as I worked my way through the growing drifts to cross the median strip. Halfway across, the median fell away into a ditch.

I slipped into a quagmire of mud and freezing water. I swallowed a mouthful of the filthy water as I flailed wildly, clawing the side of the ditch. Just as I reached the top, I fell back down. I didn't have any strength left. *Oh, Lord, don't let me die here.*

Finally, tearing my fingernails along the road's edge, I pulled myself up on the asphalt. But there were no cars—nothing but black night and driving snow. Weak and lapsing in and out of consciousness, I rolled across the highway to the shoulder. It took a long time to cross the highway, but now I had no confidence that I would be better off there. Every move I made had turned out worse than the last. I was beginning to feel warmer—a bad sign. If I gave in to the warmth, I might not wake up. I felt at peace. *If this is the way you want me, Lord, I'm ready.*

Just as a wave of darkness washed over me, I saw a flicker of light. I recognized it as a lamppost in the parking lot of Cedar Grove Church. "Thank you, God," I gasped as I crawled toward the church. I knew God didn't want me to give up. When I was just yards from the church, my fingers grasped a chain-link fence. *Oh, no. No!*

I pulled myself upright and pressed my face into the links. I leaned against the fence and stared at the church, almost invisible in the swirling snow. I couldn't climb the fence and didn't have the strength to go any farther. With a sob I slid down. *Well, Lord, I guess that's it.* I thanked him for all he had done for me during my life. The warm drowsiness returned. I let it come. Soon I would wake up in his arms.

Maybe 15 minutes later I awoke cold and shaking. Then a sudden thought blazed into my mind: I wasn't going to die here! It wasn't my choice to make!

With strength I didn't know I had, I rolled and crawled down the hill back to the shoulder of the highway. There I saw a truck coming on the eastbound lanes across the median strip. *I'll wave him over!* I started to raise my hand. But I couldn't move. I just lay there and stared. Day was breaking and it was getting lighter, but I was dying. The truck drove by slowly. The driver would never see me from across the median strip. Tears burned down my frozen cheeks. *Why couldn't you have been here sooner? I was right where you are a few hours ago.*

But the truck stopped. I could barely see it across the four lanes. No way could the driver see me. Then, through the driving snow, I saw a shadowy form racing across the road. In moments the driver was at my side. "Are you okay?" he asked. I was so astounded I was speechless. Finally, I croaked, "No. I can't move. Can you give me a ride?" He looked at me in astonishment.

Moments later a plow dashed through the blizzard, its blade piling mounds of snow along the shoulder. The plow driver stopped, and the two men covered me with their jackets. By then I was shaking so much I was bouncing, and my hands were so frozen I couldn't feel them. The plow driver said he never would have seen me on the shoulder. If the trucker hadn't flagged him down, I would have been plowed into a snowy grave.

The truck driver told me it was snowing so hard he could barely see the road in front of him. "Then, just for a moment, the snow let up and I saw you lying at the side of the road. There must be somebody watching over you," he said.

"Yes, there is," I said. My last thought as I drifted off to sleep was wondering what God had planned for me now that he had allowed me to live.

Steve McClure spent 16 hours in surgery as doctors repaired a crushed vertebra and nerve damage. Told he might never walk again, he was bedridden for six weeks, then went from a wheelchair to a walker to crutches to walking unaided. Brenda and Steve were married on June 11, 1994, just as they originally planned.

With Every Step She Took

by Pat Van Dyke, Canyon Lake, California

> *Life had been a constant uphill battle for our daughter Mary. But now, as I watched her carefully step down a set of bleachers at her high school homecoming football game, I felt nothing but pride. The captain of the football team, Brian Robertson, extended his hand, and Mary reached for it. She had come a long, long way ...*

Mary's struggles began on a July morning 18 years ago. She entered the world at Loma Linda University Medical Center at 10:30 A.M. and was immediately rushed to intensive care. Twenty minutes later we were visited by our obstetrician and a neonatologist. "Your daughter is severely handicapped," the doctors said.

"What's wrong?" we asked.

"I'm afraid we can't give you all the details yet," we were told. "We'll have to do a complete examination."

The examination, tests and X rays revealed that Mary had a number of physical and neurological disorders. She was missing a hip on one side and had a dislocated hip on the other. She had club feet, a faulty valve in her heart, curvature of the spine, hearing loss, a short left femur, a muscle disorder and jaundice.

Why would the Lord allow a child to be born with so many problems? I wanted to know. I asked my husband, Peter. He was a minister and had worked tirelessly for his church. "We have served God faithfully. Why would he do this to us?"

"Why not?" he asked gently but firmly. "What makes you think we are so special that this would not happen to us?"

The next Sunday, while Mary was still in the hospital, Peter chose a passage in the Gospel of John for his sermon. In it the disciples asked why a man was born blind. And before he healed the man, Jesus replied, "That the works of God should be made manifest in him" (John 9:3). That was the answer to my question. We would pray that the glory of God be made manifest in our daughter. The entire congregation prayed for Mary.

170

But as the weeks went by, when we thought we were making progress, we were pushed back. Mary developed apnea, a condition that made her stop breathing. A doctor stood by her side 24 hours a day and performed mouth-to-mouth resuscitation up to 20 times an hour. A CAT scan revealed underdeveloped areas of her brain. No one could say if she would even be able to hold her head up.

When she was seven weeks old, Mary was released from the hospital. We drove home with a backseat filled with hospital equipment. What we did not know was that the doctors had agreed that Mary would not live beyond six months. Mary's struggle to prove them wrong had begun.

By the age of two, Mary had been in the operating room 12 times. We often grew weary of trips to the hospital, but continued the fight. Mary's sister, Alice, only three years older, helped her accomplish the impossible. When the therapist said that Mary would never be able to crawl, Alice taught her how to climb an entire flight of stairs. When we were warned that Mary would not be able to stand, Alice taught her to pull herself up on the side of the sofa. When we were told that two-and-a-half-year-old Mary would never walk, Alice helped her take her first unaided steps.

"I can do it myself," Mary said.

"No," Alice corrected. "Jesus is showing you how."

One day I lifted Mary in my arms to climb a steep hill. As soon as I set her down she hurried back to the starting point and climbed up herself. "See," she said, "Jesus is showing me how to do it myself."

At the age of three Mary was eligible to be placed in a state-funded educational program for the handicapped. But we insisted on mainstreaming her, so we enrolled her in a private school, where I was also able to find a teaching job. I was grateful to be close to her every day.

The doctors had predicted that she would be a slow learner, but at the age of five she entered the regular kindergarten class. Graduation took place with Mary in a full body cast, pulled down the aisle in a red wagon by her best friend. In first and second grades she excelled in all her academic subjects. But the physical struggle continued.

Unable to do all things, Mary still wanted to take part in every activity her friends did. The simple news of a school roller-skating party brought tears; the dream of someday becoming a cheerleader only resulted in frustration. I watched the pain cross her face each time classmates stared at her or forgot to hold a door open for her. At playtime Mary was always the last chosen for any game, but she played with fiery determination.

Her teenage years came quickly. I remember one night when we arrived at a neighbor's pool for Mary's swimming therapy. Mary heard the sounds of a party from an adjoining house, the home of one of her friends. "Why wasn't I invited?" she asked. I had no answer.

When I was offered a teaching position at another school, we decided that Mary would also change schools. It meant having to battle the stares, questions and comments of a new set of students, but she was ready for this fight.

That September Mary became a tenth grader at Riverside Christian High School. The students there were unusually inquisitive, but they were also understanding. "What happened to you?" they asked her. "Have you always been this way? Will you ever get better?"

They soon came to admire her independence and humor. When she went swimming they noticed the scars on her legs from all her operations. "What happened to your legs?" one girl asked Mary.

"An alligator bit me," she replied, and the other students laughed.

Special allowances were made to give her enough time to get to her classes. Teachers made it a policy to speak of her handicaps only when she was present. The other students planned activities in which Mary could take part. Her height of four feet eight inches was accepted. The five-inch buildup on her left shoe was viewed as just Mary's shoe. Whenever she fell, which happened frequently, a student was at hand to help her stand and continue on her way.

Even though there's no separation between her thumbs and index fingers, Mary won the award for best typist. In her senior year she was editor of the yearbook, secretary of the student body, a member of the honor society and ranked third in her class.

Some of her handicaps will never be corrected, but we continue to be awed by her faith and determination. Through Mary we have learned more about God's grace than we ever thought possible.

Her father, sister and I were not the only ones touched by this extraordinary child. Her indomitable spirit has inspired our community. Our church has grown dramatically and as the members have watched Mary overcome many of her handicaps and adapt to others, their faith has grown. God's good works have been made manifest.

Mary strained to reach Brian's outstretched hand. He helped lift her billowing dress as her hair blew in the wind. The two walked to the center of the football field and the crowd cheered. The words came over the loudspeakers, "Presenting our 1994 homecoming queen—Mary Van Dyke!" The crowd roared and tears rolled down my cheeks. The crown was placed on Mary's head. Brian lifted her into his arms and carried her off the field.

You Can Climb Higher

by George Sweeting, Chicago, Illinois

God calls us to climb higher, to pursue excellence. It takes hard work and constant commitment, but we can do it, because God gives us the tools we need: faith and prayer. I learned how to use these tools when I was a boy.

Not long after my dad arrived in this country in 1920 as a Scottish stone mason, America experienced the trauma of the Great Depression.

For about five years, little construction went on in the United States. My father couldn't find work for three-and-a-half of those years, so we all took any jobs we could find. I remember as a boy, selling magazines, and delivering milk every Friday night and all day Saturday for a dollar a day. Our family made paper flowers and sold them door-to-door, just to get a quarter, fifty cents, or a dollar. My parents put our house up for sale because we could not make the payments.

As a family, we found the strength to keep going because we had faith that the Lord was in complete control, even in times of poverty and want. Mother would remind us, "God is too good to be unkind and too wise to make a mistake." During our daily family prayer time, we found unity and renewed faith as we identified with the humiliation and poverty of the children of Israel in their desert wanderings—and their ultimate possession of the Promised Land.

Eventually, building resumed, and my dad got a job laying brick, and went on to lead a significant company. But without his—and our family's—faith and trust in God, we never could have withstood the hard times of the Depression.

Have Faith. Little in this world is worthy of our complete trust. The stockholder who depends upon stocks to help him climb higher often learns that stocks go down as often—or sometimes more frequently—than up.

Long ago, I made the decision to believe in God and Jesus rather than in the visible things of this world. One basic decision everyone must make for himself is, "Shall I believe in Jesus Christ?" If you do this, you will have begun to walk the path to excellence. Excellence can never be achieved without the Lord, because climbing higher is not just wishful thinking; it is God's intention and plan for us.

The next decision of life is, "Am I willing to trust God no matter how impossible the situation seems, no matter how long my difficulties continue?" Too often, we have faith for the short run, but not for the long haul. We make it through the first few months of crisis, but we become desperate by the fourth or fifth month.

It's difficult to keep going when you're worried about whether your spouse or child will live or die. No matter how hard you try to displace your doubts— What if he should die or become handicapped for life? What would I do?—they rise to the surface.

God calls us to conquer such panic, which is really doubt grown larger until it turns into fear. "Fear not, for I am with you." God's promises work now, just as they did in Bible times when the Apostle Paul said, "If God is for us, who can be against us?" (Rom. 8:31). Memorizing these words has helped me experience the strength that comes from understanding and believing the promises of God.

Don't Quit. Another barrier to a faith that leads to excellence is the tendency to quit. Recently, I rented a car to travel to a small town north of Indianapolis, Ind. My friend had given me directions over the phone. I took Route 70, as my friend had instructed, rather than Interstate 465, which the rental agent told me to take. My friend had explained that 70 went straight across the city and ran into 465, which circled the city and would add extra miles to my trip. However, as 25 minutes went by and there was still no sight of Interstate 465, I began to doubt.

Had I heard my friend correctly?

Highways began to turn to Louisville, then to Columbus, Ohio. My friend had admitted that she didn't get to the city much. I worried that maybe her way wasn't right.

I finally gave up and turned off the highway to ask directions. As usual, I wished I had trusted my friend's directions just a little longer. Only a few miles ahead, 465 did join 70. I had avoided circling the city by taking Route 70. I had had some faith—but not quite enough.

What mistakes did I make?

First, I wondered if I had understood my friend properly. This nagging feeling of doubt is similar to the questions of false theology that we have all heard. "Did God really say that? Does He really mean that? And while we're thinking about it, we all know that miracles in the Bible can be explained by natural phenomena. Furthermore, such miracles don't happen today; they were just for biblical times.

Slowly, doubt creeps in and destroys faith because we do not trust God and His Word in Scripture.

Second, I questioned my friend's ability. We need to believe that God is able. Abraham had so much faith in God's power that he believed God was able to raise Isaac from the dead. (See Heb. 11:19.)

When we doubt God, we cut ourselves off from His help. Without faith, we cannot achieve excellence. The Christian life begins by faith in Jesus Christ (see Eph. 2:8-9), and it must continue by faith. In fact, without faith, "it is impossible to please Him [God]" (Heb. 11:6). I can build a house without faith. I can marry without faith. I can earn a million dollars without faith. But it is impossible to please God without faith. The greatest challenge of the Christian life is to keep the faith—until the end.

Keep on Praying. When the Pacific Garden Mission in Chicago faced threats of rezoning by the city, local news reporters wasted no time arriving at the 107-year-old mission to interview Superintendent Harry Saulnier. "How do you feel about the planning board's claim that the mission is drawing undesirables into the South Loop and is responsible for neighborhood crimes?"

One reporter from a local news station thrust a microphone into Mr. Saulnier's face and asked, "So what are you going to do now?"

The white-haired man, his features and slight frame gnarled by rheumatoid arthritis and 80 years of living, didn't lash out or cite legal defense tactics. He didn't refer to the mission's outstanding contributions: thousands of men rehabilitated from drug and alcohol addiction. Instead he replied, 'Well, there's nothing I can do but pray."

The future seemed bleak as he heard the planning board's threats, and they must have been magnified by the news reporters who badgered him with questions. But while his opposers descended on their prey, he descended to his knees to pray.

What happened? Within a few weeks, the city dropped its case without any explanation.

Alfred Lord Tennyson once said, "More things are wrought by prayer than his world dreams of." I agree. And so did well-known leaders like D. L. Moody who claimed, "Every great movement of God can be traced to a kneeling figure."

Why is prayer important to the pursuit of excellence? The answer is simple. Prayer enables us to achieve excellence because it changes the events of this world. It also changes us; it is God's cure for caving in. We should always pray and never give up, Jesus said. (See Luke 18:1.)

Jesus prayed in the face of decisions. When He set out to select the 12 disciples—the men who would continue His ministry under persecution and pressure—He knew the choice was far too important to make without prayer.

We need to pray specifically and wisely. We should determine what we really want from God. When I consult my doctor, I carefully prepare a list of questions so all my needs will be met. Why should a consultation with God be any different?

Robert Cook told of a missionary who was evacuated during World War II from a South Pacific island. He was put on a freighter that zigzagged through enemy waters in its journey to safety. One day, the periscope of an enemy submarine appeared directly in front of their ship.

"That's when I learned to pray specifically," said the missionary. "While the enemy was looking our ship over (probably trying to decide whether to sink us), we prayed over every inch of that sub.

" 'Lord, stop his motors! Jam his torpedos!' "

Miraculously the submarine submerged, never to be confronted again.

Specific prayers can perform miracles, as long as we pray with wisdom. One of the programs on Moody Bible Institute's radio station is "A Cup of Cold Water." It is a prayer program in which listeners are asked to pray for a specific person the entire week. They often send cards and letters to that person. Early in June of 1981, listeners began praying for Barbara Cummiskey of Wheaton, Ill. Barbara, 31, had had multiple sclerosis (MS), the "young person's disease," since she was 15 years old.

MS attacks the central nervous system and hardens tissues in the brain and/or spinal cord. It can result in paralysis, and an early death. When Barbara was in her late 20s, one lung collapsed, her other lung labored at half its potential, and her bowels became dysfunctional; thus her case was confirmed as the rare, severe type of MS that attacks the body's organs.

Barbara's breathing had become so difficult that doctors had to perform a tracheotomy. Then a respirator was attached to the hole in her neck. Her green eyes were useless; her legs were spindly and dangling, her arms and hands turned in, and her body was twisted.

Tumors grew on her hands and feet. Barbara was admitted as an outpatient at a nearby hospice. She and her family were preparing for her to die.

On the morning of June 7, 1981, Barbara's Aunt Ruth took her 450 cards and letters that had been mailed to their church by listeners. Almost all who wrote said they were praying for Barbara. After church service, two women also visited her and brought additional cards and letters with them. As Barbara talked with them, she sensed the Lord telling her, "My child, get up and walk!"

"I'm not sure what you're going to think about this, but the Lord just told me to get up and walk," she told her friends. "Please run and get my family," she added. "I want them to be here."

But Barbara could not wait. She unhooked her oxygen supply and jumped out of bed, just as any healthy person would. Barbara's once-atrophied legs were normal again, as were her hands and arms. She had been healed instantaneously.

Barbara's doctor, Dr. Harold Adolph, confirmed her experience. "The patient now has none of the findings of multiple sclerosis, is walking normally, and has no pulmonary problems."

Since then, Barbara completed intensive study to become a registered surgical technologist, and 30 of the 40 hours of her work-study program were spent assisting surgeons in the same hospital that administered her longtime care.

The heroes of the Cummiskey story seem to be God and Barbara, and they are. But what about the hundreds of people who prayed for Barbara and encouraged her with their letters and cards? They are dynamic participants in this drama. They answered God's call for excellence.

We are "the eyes of the Lord." He is looking to us to bring the concerns of His people before Him. And you do not have to be a government leader or a well-known writer to achieve excellence. It's the quality of what you do that counts, not your occupation. Prayer is necessary to excellence. It is the lifeline between earth and heaven. Any army is stranded without its shortwave radios, walkie-talkies, and computers. And God's army is no different. Prayer provides the instant communication and the ultimate power to enable us to accomplish His work here on earth.

Mission for Mikey, Age 3

by Mabel Grayson,* Riverside, California

My oldest daughter, April, was a sweet girl. Innocent and vivacious, she enjoyed playing mommy to her younger brothers and sister. Working with the Special Olympics was her passion. I had never seen a teenager with more patience and with such an affinity for kids. From the time April was little, she dreamed of raising a family of her own.

But when she grew up and got married, things began to change. She became less and less like the April I knew. She stopped seeing her old friends. Her behavior became irresponsible, her answers evasive. It didn't take long for me to realize she was on drugs. It turned out that her husband had been an addict before she was. Saddest of all, when she finally had the children she had always wanted—three of them—she wasn't in any shape to be a mother. There were times when I could see that she really loved those kids. But they needed to be loved all the time, and drugs ruled April's life.

Often, she dropped off the children at my place, promising to return in a couple of hours, which became days, even weeks. April would simply vanish, running, I learned later, from her abusive husband. Finally, she just handed over my three grandchildren. I was relieved that I could protect them and keep them together as a family. We saw little of April, and finally nothing at all.

One winter Saturday in 1992, I was running errands with three-year-old Mikey, when he made a strange announcement: "We have a new brother," he said from the backseat.

"What are you talking about?"

Mikey stood up behind me. "He was born today, Grandma. We have to go find him."

178

Blond, blue-eyed Mikey was as mischievous and unpredictable as any three-year-old, but he had never come up with an odd statement like this one. Another grandchild? *Born Saturday, January twenty-fifth, 1992,* I noted.

Then I caught myself. *Surely Mikey is making this up.* Lord only knew what went through Mikey's mind, with parents who had dropped out of his life. When we had last seen April—six months ago—she didn't look pregnant. Since then, I had tried to track her down; I had called her friends and visited her hangouts. Nobody had said anything to me about April being pregnant. And surely Mikey had not heard from her.

"Mikey," I said as we pulled into our driveway, "you have one brother and one sister, and you three kids live with me. You're all together, safe. Grandma's going to take care of you." Helping him out of the car, I saw he was thinking hard.

That winter Saturday was a sunny and warm southern California day. A neighbor child ran over to play with Mikey in our front yard. *Maybe he'll get his mind off this foolishness*, I thought. I spread out my sewing on the living room table and opened the French doors so I could keep an eye on the children.

I didn't pay much attention to their conversation until I heard Mikey say it was his new brother's birthday. Exasperated, I called my grandson inside. "Mikey, how on earth did you come up with such a story?"

Silently he studied me. "Well?" I demanded.

Mikey huffed, "The angel told me so."

"Told you what?" I asked. "When?"

"An angel and Jesus came to me when I was asleep last night, Grandma, and the angel said I have a new brother. We have to go find him!" Mikey was so adamant, I found myself almost believing him. *But since when do angels bring important messages to three-year-olds?*

"What did Jesus look like?" I asked, testing.

"He was all shiny. I couldn't see his face because it was too bright."

"And the angel, Mikey? What did the angel look like?"

My grandson smiled and ran his hands down the length of his outfit. "All white," he said. "And big and shining!" Then he ran back outside to play, leaving me to sort it all out. Now, more than ever, I wished I could find April—if only to set my mind at ease that I had all her children safe in my care. *Lord*, I asked, *if there was an angel, why didn't you let me see it?* I mulled this over until one of the children needed my attention, and to tell the truth, with the constant activity, I didn't have much trouble putting the whole mysterious episode out of my mind.

Four days later, we received an unexpected bill from the hospital. *What's this about?* I wondered, ripping open the envelope. None of us had been sick. When I unfolded the invoice, I couldn't believe my eyes. "Patient: April Franklin," it read in bold letters. And then, "Ultrasound." As far as I knew, there was only one reason for a young woman to get an ultrasound reading. And then I remembered Mikey's dream.

Perhaps this was all one big mix-up. What were the odds of April being pregnant again—and Mikey knowing about it without having had any word from her? I decided to call the hospital and find out.

"Is April Franklin your patient?" I asked the operator. She checked the list and said no. Another dead end. I started to hang up when I remembered Mikey's urgent request to find his new brother. "This is an emergency," I blurted out. "I must speak to Admissions."

On hold, I listened to droning Muzak. Was I on a wild-goose chase? All because of a little boy's dream?

"Admissions," said the woman on the other end. "April Franklin was discharged."

"I am her mother," I said quickly. "Do you know how to reach her?"

There was an uncomfortable pause on the other end. "She was brought in from county jail," the woman explained. "I assume she has been taken back there."

I hung up brokenhearted. Part of me didn't want to know what had happened. But I could not shake the feeling that Mikey knew something important.

I took a deep breath and looked up the number for the county jail. How many times had I dialed the telephone, dreading what I was going to learn about April?

"County jail," a gruff voice answered. I explained who I was, and finally the matron came to the phone with some answers. I found out that April had been arrested for failure to pay fines on innumerable parking and traffic violations. "Is my daughter all right?" I interrupted. "Is she… pregnant?"

"April's baby was born prematurely."

I caught my breath. *Born?* "Where is he?" I asked, realizing I had assumed the baby was a boy, just as Mikey had predicted.

"I'm sorry," the matron said. "I'm not allowed to give out that information."

"I have custody of April's other children," I said, keeping my voice steady, "and I don't want this one to fall into the system."

There was silence on the other end. Finally she said, "If I were you, and no one was allowed to tell me the whereabouts of a premature baby, I would start at the county hospital."

I couldn't keep the smile off my face. "Thank you for the advice," I said.

Driving my car, I needed every ounce of self-restraint I could muster to stay within the speed limit. Still, I wasn't sure what to expect. Had April really brought another child into this world? *If she has, God, what do you want me to do? Can I handle one more under my roof? I'm not sure I can love another baby.* I flew into the hospital and into the neonatal ward. "I've come to see the Franklin baby," I said, not fully believing the words coming out of my own mouth. "I'm the grandmother."

"I'm so glad you've come," the nurse said. "The baby's kidney infection is clearing up and he's due to be released to… " As we walked, she checked the chart and read the name of one of April's friends. I had arrived in the nick of time!

The nurse led me through a maze of incubators and stopped in front of one. "Here we are," she said pleasantly. Inside lay a tiny but perfectly formed little boy. Mikey had been right after all—he had a new brother. A precious miracle, just as each of April's other children had been. "When was he born?" I asked the nurse, although by now I knew.

"Last Saturday," she said. "January twenty-fifth. He came early."

I immediately fell in love with his tight, pink face, his eyes not quite open. His arms and legs moved herky-jerky, and he seemed to stick his chest out, saying, "Look at me, Grandma." *There's plenty of love left in my heart for you, little one.*

It was hard to tear myself away from him, but I had no time to waste. "I'll be back," I whispered.

From the lobby, I called our lawyer and asked him to seek immediate custody. "I'll do what I can," he promised. In less than 24 hours, he was able to get an injunction against giving the baby to April's friend, who had a police record for drug possession. The child would be put under my protection upon release from the hospital.

Now I had to go see April. I waited for her in the visitors' room at the county jail. When she walked in, I could see that she was furious. She said she had done everything she could to keep the baby a secret because she was determined to raise him herself. "I want my children!" she said through clenched teeth. "And I'll keep having babies until I get to keep one!"

"You should know by now how much God loves you and your children," I answered quietly. "If you keep having them, he'll keep taking them away—using angels if necessary—until you quit using drugs." Then I told her about Mikey's prophetic dream.

April cut our visit short. She seemed truly touched by what I had told her.

When we brought the new baby home, Mikey fell easily into his role of big brother. Of course, he had already fulfilled his mission: He had heeded the angel's message.

We didn't hear from April for a long time. When she finally called, it was from a rehabilitation clinic. She had been off drugs for three months, and was separating from her husband. "I'm going to make it this time, Mom," she said. She sounded different; she sounded like April.

I went to see her recently. She looked great, and she spoke of how she had returned to her faith. She's been running five miles a day, praying as she runs. After so many years, she said the words I never thought I would hear: "I thank God every day for a mother like you. I want to show my children that I love them as much as you love me."

There's a long, hard road ahead for April, but I believe that someday I'll be able to return the children to her. Meantime, the heavenly messenger made sure I had charge over all her babies. That day in 1992 when I first found the little one at the hospital, I asked the nurse the name of my new grandson. She smiled and said, "I'm not sure. We just call him Baby Angel."

"You Can't Quit Now"

by Sharon McCollick, Philadelphia, Pennsylvania

I am a businesswoman who believes in angels. Both the biblical kind and the modern kind who sit behind desks. In business, people who back beginners are often called angels. But my angels did more than back me. They rescued me from catastrophe.

Two years ago, my husband, Steven, faced me across our kitchen table. "Sharon," he asked, "what's going to happen to us?"

I had just hung up on my mother. Crying and sick with worry, she had questioned my recent business decisions. Earlier in the day, my sister Joanie had called to give me a rather forceful scolding on the same topic.

In two and a half years I had gone from a lifestyle that included a stable job and savings in the bank to a state of disastrous debt. I had already lost my car and was about to lose our house. I could not even pay the telephone or electric bills. My marriage—and in fact, my entire life—seemed on the brink of collapse.

In desperation, I asked God, "What should I do?"

An inner voice replied, *"You can't quit now."*

I never dreamed in October 1991, when I began exploring how I might become a fashion designer, that I would find myself in such a nightmare. I had been an executive in the computer business, rising to marketing manager at Intel Corporation. But I commuted three hours daily every week and worked too many weekends. I wanted to have more time to spend with my daughter and husband.

I also had a long-running love affair with fabrics and shapes. Growing up poor in a family of seven children, I had bought most of my clothes in thrift shops and redesigned them. Later I had learned firsthand that no one was making reasonably priced suits successful women could wear to work. Most suits were monotonous in color and design, making their wearers look like would-be men.

183

From the beginning of my working career, I had designed my own suits. Again and again, other businesswomen had asked me where they could buy them.

I started my quest for independence in a sensible way. I consulted experts at the University of Pennsylvania's Wharton School of Business. I spent a year doing market research. I talked to women at conventions; I canvassed department stores; and I soon convinced myself and Wharton that my intuition was right: There was a hole in the market. No one was making the kind of suits I envisioned—feminine in style without being flashy, made well enough to wear frequently—selling for around $200. So many women I interviewed liked my designs, I had $50,000 worth of orders before I opened my doors.

I quit my job and launched Essential Suits. I knew that starting a business would be hard work, and I was prepared. I got off to a good start, but then I found out just how hard things are in the women's-suit business.

The field is dominated by two huge companies; everyone else is practically invisible. Department stores hesitate to deal with the small-fry because the giants know how to keep the racks full. The buyer for the retail colossus JCPenney, for instance, liked my designs but wanted me to install a computerized order system. That was well beyond my resources.

I learned banks were even less interested in my start-up operation. Lynn Ozer, the loan officer at my neighborhood bank, told me in a nice way that I had no collateral, no track record and, as far as she could see, no future.

Desperate to finance production, I turned to a factor—someone who puts up the money you need. In return you pay exorbitant interest rates, which eat up all your profits.

In 1992, I sold 1000 suits. The factor agreed to finance me for another year at an interest rate of one percent a week. I had no choice; I had to prove my business was viable. I sold 2500 suits in 1993, adding a few big customers, such as the Dayton Hudson stores.

I vowed to make 1994 the year I escaped from the factor. I found a venture capitalist in Pennsylvania who agreed to back the company for $300,000 if we sold a minimum of $250,000 in suits in a single sales season. With $150,000 in sales, I again signed a contract with the factor and began production of 3500 suits. Just as the suits were being manufactured, my backer called to inform me he couldn't raise the working capital. Our contract was in default.

Frantic, I mortgaged our house, threw in more of my savings and borrowed my sister Jeanine's life savings. I was still far short of completing production of 3500 suits and fulfilling my factoring contract.

Soon I was missing mortgage payments. My mother lost faith in me. Jeanine, who had been working as my partner, quit. So did my other partner, my pattern maker. Even my husband, whom I had loved since girlhood, started to question my judgment—and I couldn't blame him. That's what brought us to the confrontation at the kitchen table that day. Would things ever turn around?

My mother's anguish troubled me most. In the late 1960s, my father had gone broke trying to become a major player in the cable television business. The blow had wrecked their marriage, leading to a divorce that left my mother as the sole supporter of seven children. She was horrified to see her daughter heading off a similar precipice.

Somehow, by the grace of God, I finished shipping all 3500 suits and closed the factoring contract. The next day, I sat down with the Sunday paper. *God, I need an angel of mercy to rescue me from despair. I need a job!* I opened the paper and the first thing I saw was an ad for computer consultants. The woman who ran the employment agency was an angel in human form. She sat there calmly while I gave her a brutally honest account of my dilemma, frequently interrupted by cascades of tears. Instead of calling me a reckless idiot, she said, "Don't worry. I'll get you a job."

Thanks to her and the wonderful people for whom I consulted, I was able to keep Essential Suits alive. We sold out our 1994 line and paid most of our debts. But where could I find the money for my 1995 line? To miss a year in the clothing business is as bad as missing a century.

We entered a nerve-racking contest run by Pennsylvania Private Investors Group (PPIG) which studies 3000 business plans each year and invites 30 to make presentations to potential backers. Essential Suits was one of the 30, but no one offered to put up a cent.

Again I asked God if I should quit. I got the same tough answer. The next day my telephone rang.

It was Lynn Ozer. Her bank had been taken over by a bigger bank that wanted to lend money to small businesses. Lynn had heard about my PPIG presentation and thought she could help me get a $250,000 working-capital loan from the Small Business Administration.

With $250,000 I could finance a new fall line for 1995 and continue business operations! We filled out the paperwork and waited five agonizing months. Then came the worst news yet. Because I owed the IRS $2000 in back taxes, the loan was rejected.

I could not believe it. I had worked so hard all my life. I had paid my own way through school, and had always thought of God as my friend and supporter. "What are you trying to tell me, Lord?" I asked.

For two days there was no answer. I began to spiral into despair. Then I found myself driving past the bank. *"Don't quit now,"* whispered that voice. Was God telling me to make one more effort?

I leaped out of the car and charged into the lobby. "This is my whole life!" I shouted at Lynn. "I can't take no for an answer."

Before my eyes, Lynn Ozer turned into another angel of mercy. For the first time in 17 years she called the SBA and asked them to reconsider a decision. After a few days of stony silence, they said I could get the loan if I paid off the IRS. I begged friends and family, and raised the money. When the loan came through, the bank threw a party to help me celebrate.

Good things began to happen. My mother and father, who had barely spoken to each other for more than 10 years, volunteered to help ship those suits in the summer of 1994. I think some of their bitterness dissipated in that joint expression of love for me. For the first time I got to know my father as a person.

To help me, Steven left his job with a computer software maker. He persuaded Philadelphia's Thomas Jefferson University Hospital, one of the best in the nation, to give him a job with a five-year plan to computerize all aspects of their nutritional operations. This enabled him to spend far more time at home, and it has turned out to be a major step forward in his career.

The 1994 Essential Suits lines sold well, and in 1995 JCPenney, Federated Department Stores and other major outlets placed hefty orders for our line. We are able to deal with these big stores thanks to another angel—my friend and mentor, Richard Seitchik, who is CEO of one of the nation's largest makers of men's suits. He has allowed us to use his company's computerized order system.

We have a permanent showroom in New York City, and in the spring of 1995 we hired a group of models for our first fashion show. We let the models take the suits home and match them with skirts or trousers of their own, demonstrating how much confidence we had that our clothes have the kind of flexibility a businesswoman wants.

I go to New York twice a week to talk to buyers. The rest of the time I work in Philadelphia, only 10 minutes from home, with time for my family. Although Essential Suits is far from out of the woods financially, I have stopped worrying about the future. With the help of God and his angels I am sure I can cope now.

Shoot for the Moon!

by Norman Vincent Peale, Pawling, New York

Three weeks before his 92nd birthday, one of the most famous alumni of Ohio Wesleyan University delivered the commencement address to the Class of 1992. His advice to the graduates is an inspiring challenge to young and old alike.

As I look over this great assembly, I have decided that you folks are a better audience than I spoke to the other night. On that occasion, I was the speaker at the annual dinner of the Missouri State Association of Funeral Directors and Embalmers.

This exciting gathering was held in Kansas City. When I arrived, I went to the little room off the main ballroom, where the head table was gathering. They were the leading undertakers of the state. They were all clad in tuxedos, and everyone had in his lapel a white carnation. I was in a tuxedo also. It only remained to affix a white carnation on my lapel.

A lady undertaker was assigned to do this job. She was very charming and quite diminutive and had some difficulty, from a standing position, in affixing this flower. She fumbled around and finally, in exasperation, she said, "You know, Dr. Peale, I could do a much better job at this if you were lying down!"

A commencement speaker must be brief. So I'm going to be. My role model is the late Prime Minister of Great Britain, Winston Churchill. He was prevailed upon by the headmaster of his old school, Harrow, to give a commencement speech.

The boys were told that this would be an event they would long remember because Churchill was one of the greatest orators of his time. They were to come prepared to take notes and to listen attentively.

Churchill arose, went to the podium, let a silence fall, then said: "Never, never, never give up." Then he sat down.

When asked, "Why did you do it that way?" Churchill said, "As I sat looking at this class and realized how much each of them would go through, I wanted to prepare them for the discouragement they might feel in the years to come."

Now, I'm not Churchill, but I am going to emulate him by saying just two things to you today. Considering the world you are soon to enter, I want you to remember that on your graduation day, the speaker said, "Always be a thinker. You can think your way through anything, and come out victorious, if you don't yield to emotion, but are a creative thinker."

Thinking is important. Buddha, a great scholar of antiquity, said, "Mind is everything; what you think, you become." Marcus Aurelius, the Roman emperor, said, "Our life is what our thoughts make it."

So, think, think, think your way through life.

Thomas A. Edison, the inventor, was a great thinker. I never met him, but I knew his son, Charles, governor of New Jersey. Charles idolized his father. He once told me, "Norman, Dad often said that the primary purpose of the human body is to carry the brain around."

That means the thing about you that is sovereign is your thinking mind. Remember that, and do everything in your power to enhance the creative ability of your mind.

My second point, one I hope you will never forget, is: Be a believer. Believe in the destiny of your country, the United States of America. And believe in its economic system, even when it is in trouble.

You are looking at a man who lived through the Depression, which lasted five years. During that time, I heard a distinguished economist predict, "America will never have prosperity again." My belief was severely tested by that remark. But my positive attitude was right, because we soon moved into the greatest era of prosperity this country has known.

So, believe in America's economic system. It is the best in the world and it will produce untold prosperity when the citizens think and believe.

And most importantly, believe in God. If you are Christian, believe in Jesus Christ, the greatest intellect known to man. Believe in your family; believe in your community. And, finally, believe in yourself.

This commencement means a great deal to me, for I once received the same diploma you will soon be given. It was 72 years ago, in 1920, that I sat where you sit. It was a June day, for we went to school longer in those days. But I can see my classmates even now. It was the springtime of our young lives; we were enthusiastic, we were positive thinkers, we were believers. We were a great class of men and women. And you are a great class here today.

I have lived in New York City for more than 60 years, and have known every mayor of that city over that time. The greatest of them all was Fiorello La Guardia. His name is now connected with an airport, but La Guardia was quite a man. He was of stalwart character, a great leader, an enthusiastic believer, a creative thinker.

A young woman worked for La Guardia when he was a Congressman, before he was mayor. She went to lunch one day, overwhelmed by her inferiority complex. At four feet eleven, she regarded herself as a shrimp who couldn't do anything.

Returning from lunch, she happened to get into the elevator with La Guardia. Always interested in young people, he said to her, "Young lady, what are your goals?"

"I have no goals, Mr. La Guardia. Look at me. I am a shrimp. What can I ever do?"

That was too much for La Guardia. "Young lady, listen to me," he said. "If you trust God, believe in Him, and believe in yourself, you can do anything."

Then, with a wave, La Guardia exited the elevator. She looked at him and realized that he, too, was short! La Guardia was five feet two, but that interchange worked a miracle. The young woman saw him as a giant of a man, which he was.

You, too, are a giant. Go from this historic campus and do great things. To quote a friend of mine, "Shoot for the moon! Even if you miss it, you will land among the stars."

I hear a bell. That must be a class bell. It tolls for you. I hear it saying, "Be a giant. Go change the world."

God bless you.

"Perseverance and Faith"

by Marion Bond West

For your perseverance and faith in the midst of all your persecutions
and afflictions which you endure.
—II Thessalonians 1:4 (NAS)

Just across the road from our church in Monroe, Georgia, is Mt. Vernon Service Station. It's a neat, white, very small gas station operated for more than fifty years by Ossie Mobley and her son. Donnie is in his late fifties and has spent his life in a wheelchair. He helps his widowed mother run the station and really enjoys the folks who stop by. The station has long been Donnie's window on the world.

Recently, because of some red tape, the people who fill the huge buried gas tanks have refused to fill Ossie's tanks any longer, Ossie can't sell gas now. She fought a long, hard battle and lost.

Early each morning Ossie and Donnie still arrive at the station from their house next door. A few cars stop by for a paper, soft drink or candy, Donnie has never been able to speak clearly, but his bright eyes, winsome smile and quick hand motions enable most folks to understand him. Often Donnie manages the station alone and signals his mother (with a buzzer) when she is needed. Ossie is a small, frail woman, always in a neat cotton dress. Inside their station are two ageless straight chairs and a marvelous little heater. On the coldest day of the year, it's snug in the minute station. Ossie and Donnie make anyone feel special and welcome. She still carefully, even lovingly, washes down the empty gas pumps and faithfully sweeps away the leaves.

They don't complain—ever. Each Sunday, Ossie and Donnie are in church in their regular places singing praises to God and asking me after church, "How are you? Is everything all right?"

Oh, Father, teach me about endurance and perseverance. Amen.

Josh Davis, From Worst to First

By Tom Felton

At the Pan-American games last year, swimmer Josh Davis worried as he waited for the U.S. team's fourth and final event, a relay. The U.S. swimmers weren't favored to win; the Brazilians were. Besides, Josh had already competed in one event that night, winning a gold medal, and he was tired. To make matters worse, he'd been swimming poorly and feeling "horrible" in the weeks before the meet.

But when the gun went off and the race started, Josh and the rest of the U.S. team swam like a dream, beating the Brazilians by one second!

But Josh Davis's swimming career hasn't always been a dream. In fact, long before he became a University of Texas Longhorn and began winning gold medals, his stroke was more of a joke.

"I joined a swim club when I was 12," recalls Josh. "The coaches had to take me aside and teach me the strokes because I only knew one of the four we did.

"Without a doubt, I was the worst swimmer in my group of friends. I was way behind, and I wasn't winning any ribbons or prizes."

All that changed when Josh was in eighth grade. Up until then he had played lots of sports—baseball, track, basketball and gymnastics. But in eighth grade Josh decided to focus on swimming. His goal was to make his high school's JV team the following year. But his swimming coach didn't really think Josh had what it took. So Josh switched coaches—and by the end of the year, he qualified for the school's varsity team!

Since then, Josh has seen plenty of success both in the pool and with the books. (He just finished a bachelor's degree in speech/communications.) But what made his life complete was giving that life to Jesus Christ. "God gave the courage to respond to his truth," Josh says. "I realize that I don't need swimming to make me feel loved and accepted, because I'm already loved and accepted by God, who created me."

If you dream of making a big splash as a swimmer, take a tip from Josh!

Lord, purge our eyes to see within the seed a tree, within the glowing egg a bird, within the shroud a butterfly: Till taught by such, we see Beyond all creatures Thee, and hearken for Thy tender word, And hear it, "Fear not: it is I."

—Christina Rossetti
(1830-1894)

Chapter Eight

Glimpses of His Presence

Journey to Lourdes

by Lorraine Echevarria-Hendricks, Kintnersville, Pennsylvania

I was only 14 years old, but I was sure I was going to die. As a high school freshman I was a cheerleader, played varsity softball and was involved in other teenagers' activities. When I first came down with the flu in October 1975, it didn't seem like a big deal. But after a week or two, I was still having severe headaches, dizziness, violent nausea, and excruciating pains throughout my body.

Hospitalized, I was given a battery of tests that were inconclusive. Mom and Dad consulted several specialists. None could find out what was wrong. One put me in traction to relieve my neck pains; it didn't help. Another thought my illness might be psychosomatic, but tests indicated I was well adjusted. I developed kidney problems, and because of the pain I couldn't sleep. I was told that my schoolmates, as well as people all over the area, were praying for me. That meant a lot, but I couldn't imagine ever feeling well again.

Then one afternoon Mom came to my bedside. "Lorraine," she said, placing a cool hand on my fevered brow, "we're going to take you to Lourdes."

"Is it farther than Pittsburgh?" I asked.

She smiled. "Just a little bit." Mom explained that Lourdes was a small city in southwestern France. There, in 1858, a young peasant girl, now known as Saint Bernadette, had seen a vision of the Virgin Mary 18 times over a five-month period.

Near the grotto where the Virgin Mary appeared, muddy water had trickled from under a huge rock. When Mary instructed Bernadette to "drink and wash in the spring," clear sparkling water gushed forth. Since then countless thousands have made pilgrimages to Lourdes, hoping to be healed by those same miraculous waters.

Healing wasn't on my mind that March day when we took off for France.

I was so sick I wanted to die. At our Paris stopover I was wheeled to the airport dispensary, where a doctor gave me a shot that helped me sleep until we landed at Lourdes. When we arrived, the flight attendant asked if we wanted an ambulance. Mom said we could manage with just a wheelchair and taxi—but the driver took one look at me and wanted to take us to a hospital. "No, no; the grotto," Mom persevered, and finally we arrived at the front gates of the grounds surrounding the sacred shrine.

But I was too ill to go on. The nuns brought me to the infirmary, where I collapsed on a bed. A young American volunteer named Louise said she would sit with me. As she read to me from her Bible, I fell asleep.

Suddenly I was standing alongside my bed looking down at my own body.

Louise still sat reading in a gentle voice, unaware of my "other" presence in the room. The next thing I knew I was outside, moving with a freedom and joy I had never known before. What was happening to me? I felt no anxiety, only a bliss that was as real as life and definitely not a dream.

Somehow I became aware she was beside me—a lady in a long flowing gown, gliding along with me as I continued on my journey. I couldn't see her face because a hood hung over her head, but she exuded a love that transcended anything I had ever experienced.

There was no talk between us, just a kind of intuitive communication.

We floated about five feet above the ground, moving along over a sweeping green meadow sprinkled with exquisite purple violets. My eyes were drawn to a lone tree whose branches spread like loving arms.

The lady spoke at my side; her voice was almost musical yet firm. "You must go back now," she said.

"I don't want to go back," I pleaded. "The body I left is dying."

"You must go back to prove to others that God still exists today."

The next thing I knew I was back in my body. I opened my eyes and looked up into the anxious faces of Mom and Dad.

"We've been trying to wake you," Mom said, "but you weren't responding."

"It's time to go to the baths," Dad said. My limbs were as weak as ever, and I felt as nauseated and sick as I had before. My parents wheeled my chair outside and we walked with Louise through the grounds of the shrine. There before my eyes stretched the same beautiful green field scattered with purple flowers. And in the distance stood the majestic lone tree with its sheltering branches.

"It's the tree on which Saint Bernadette leaned when she had her last apparition," Louise explained. I smiled. I had seen it all before.

We passed the rocky grotto and reached the building housing the baths. Inside were separate areas for men, women and children. There was a moistness in the air like that over a mountain brook in the morning. I was undressed, and a blue cape was wrapped around my body. Then some women helped me to the bath—a long, wide marble tub full of the Lourdes water. My mother knelt by my wheelchair and prayed. The women eased me down two steps into the knee-deep water, where I was led to the statue of the Blessed Mother. Someone poured water on my head.

When I was helped out of the water, I realized to my surprise I was already dry. "Ah, yes," one of the women said. "That's one of the little miracles of Lourdes." I was dressed and bundled in the wheelchair, feeling as bad as ever. The nuns gave the taxi special permission to drive in and pick us up for our return trip to the hotel where we were staying.

At the hotel, I got into bed and instantly sank into a deep sleep.

Hours must have passed. Slowly I awakened. I moved my legs, stretched my arms. I sat up in disbelief. There was no pain! I felt strong. I put my feet on the floor. I could walk! I stepped to the bathroom mirror. My eyes were shining and my cheeks were rosy.

I was no longer trapped inside an unhealthy body. I was whole again. Mom and Dad came running in. We all cried with joy and laughed in exultation. Later that day I walked confidently through the gates of Lourdes once again. Louise, who had sat with me, and several of the sisters who had been with me the day before, were stunned. They told me I seemed so sick that they had feared I would not make it through the night—and now here I was full of life. As I entered the shrine's basilica, I knelt before the altar and gave thanks to God for my healing, and for the beautiful lady I had met at Lourdes.

The Divine Touch

Nancy Sullivan Geng, Bloomington, Minnesota

That winter ten years ago it got so cold that ice formed inside the kitchen windowpanes. Gasoline froze in the tank of my husband's car. Bare, brittle limbs snapped in the breeze and newscasters warned of windchill and frostbite. Despite the bitter weather, I walked each morning, alone, through our new neighborhood, dressed in layers of down and wool. I walked and I walked.

Maybe defying the elements made me feel I had some control over my life. That year I had lost two loved ones to death, and our first baby was born with Down's syndrome. As much as I loved our child, I still felt stunned. God seemed concealed, hidden somewhere in this cold winter of death and disappointment. So I trudged in solitude, day after freezing day. Only in front of a stranger's blue-shuttered brick house did I become gradually aware of a presence, a kind of peace. While my breath froze in the air, a spiritual warmth filled me. Here, for a brief moment each morning, I felt something promising, hopeful, reassuring. I didn't know why.

Spring came. Children pedaled bicycles on the sidewalk, men swung golf clubs on the green fairways and I exchanged my down and wool layers for jerseys and faded blue jeans. One morning I took my newborn, Sarah, with me on my walk. In the bright sunlight in front of the brick house, I saw a mother playing with her young twin daughters.

I watched as she gently guided the girls' hands over rough bark and offered them lilac blooms to smell. Just when I realized the children were blind, the mother greeted me with a wave.

"May they touch your baby?" she asked. While the girls softly stroked Sarah's face, brushed her fine chestnut hair and held her tiny pink hands, their mother spoke about what it had been like when her children were born, and what unexpected blessings she had found in those early years. "In adversity we must be alert," she said, "for God will find a way, somehow, to touch us."

I wondered if I should tell her about my walks. Finally I said, "Last winter when I passed by your home each morning, I felt strangely reassured and comforted. Warmed."

My new friend smiled. "You must be the person I felt compelled to pray for this winter," she said. "I thought someone in this neighborhood was going through a difficult time. Now I know it was you."

Trapped in a Fiery Blaze

by Katie Clarke, Hanover, Pennsylvania and Doug Saylor,
Pottstown, Pennsylvania

KATIE CLARKE: As soon as I woke up on Friday, July 7, last year, I remembered that my three-year-old son, Jordan, and I wouldn't be following our usual schedule. Instead of dropping him off at day care and then going to my job at an attorney's office, I would be taking him to The Milton S. Hershey Medical Center, about an hour and 15 minutes away from where we live. Jordan was born with SVT—supraventicular tachycardia, a condition that causes the heart to race uncontrollably. Medication has stabilized him, but every six months I have to take him to the hospital for cardiac testing and monitoring.

When I got out Jordan's clothes for the day, I smiled recalling how at breakfast the previous morning he had climbed into my lap and asked to wear my angel pin. As a single parent, I struggled to find the energy and time to get everything done. My church gave me much support, but for a reminder of God's constant presence I had taken to wearing an angel pin with an aquamarine stone, given to me by a friend. It reminded me that God was watching over us. For more than a year I had worn it every day. But that day I forgot to put it on.

I dressed Jordan in a gray one-piece outfit I had bought. It had short sleeves and red and white lettering reading EXTRA, EXTRA LARGE ATHLETICS. With his red sneakers and red baseball cap, he looked like a miniature coach.

DOUG SAYLOR: Working as a truck driver for our family's feed-and-seed company in Pottstown, I usually get an early start, hitting the road by 5:00 A.M. So I was surprised that summer morning when I picked up the phone to hear my dad asking why I hadn't started out yet. I checked the clock and saw it was already 7:00 A.M. I could hardly believe my eyes. I seldom oversleep, but apparently this day was going to be different.

In fact, that wasn't the only unusual thing that day. First, I needed to pick up a load in Camp Hill and then drive to Thomasville. In all my years of making deliveries, I had never taken the road between those two locations.

As I drove, I thought about my wife, Robin, and our three children: Scott, Amber and Jamie. I considered all the fun things they would be doing on a warm summer day and, looking at my watch, I hoped that I would be home for dinner.

At Camp Hill I loaded up, got advice on the best way to Thomasville, then headed my 60-foot rig out of the loading area. As I switched gears I reviewed the directions for Route 15.

KATIE: It was 9:00 A.M. when we left our home in Hanover and headed for Route 15. There had been rain, but it had stopped. I had a fleeting thought of the freak accidents people have, but I reminded myself that I was a very careful driver. Surely people could avoid accidents if they stayed alert and drove carefully.

After turning onto Route 15 in Dillsburg, as we approached the first stoplight, I thought, *There's the McDonald's where we usually eat. That's where Jordan plays.* People have told me that I came to a complete stop at the red light, but I can't remember anything except slowing down. Then there is only blankness.

DOUG: As a truck driver I learned to be alert and watch out for the drivers around me. I remember where cars are and look for them out of the corner of my eye.

Heading south on Route 15, I downshifted as I approached the red light in Dillsburg. I noticed two cars stopped at the intersection facing me, but behind them a truck was coming, going too fast to stop. It was a triaxle bulk feed truck with a tank as big as most folks' living rooms. What was wrong? Had his light already switched to green?

I glanced up at the light, then heard a crashing thud. I saw the front car fly about 100 feet across the intersection. It had been hit by the second car, which had been hit by the truck. Flames leaped from under the hood of the second car, racing around it. I wondered if it would explode.

KATIE: I can't recall the accident, but I remember heat—terrible, intense, overwhelming heat—and a sickening stench of burning rubber, paint and plastic. My eyes stung, my nose burned, my throat was parched. I'll never forget that horrifying smell.

DOUG: I pulled my rig off the road, grabbed my fire extinguisher and ran toward the burning car. I emptied the fire extinguisher onto the flames. Others came to help. Through thick smoke I glimpsed what looked like an arm in the driver's window, but all the doors were jammed.

"Get back," I shouted to the person inside the car. "I have to smash the window."

I broke the window with the fire extinguisher. A young woman was in the front seat; there was blood on her face. Leaning through the window, I pulled her out. She was alive! Someone carried her to the embankment.

Relieved, I stood back and looked at the car. Then, through the smoke and flames, I thought I saw movement. There was someone else inside. It looked like a child!

I dashed back to the car but it was too late. The heat had intensified. The flames were leaping out of the car. Another man tried, but he couldn't make it either. I tried again, but the heat was too much to bear. The ground was littered with fire extinguishers others had brought and emptied. Still the fire blazed.

KATIE: I don't remember being lifted out of the car, but I do remember being taken to the embankment. I saw people running around and the ambulance crew arrive. I noticed my car with smoke and flames billowing around it. But something was wrong, terribly wrong. Suddenly I realized Jordan was not beside me.

I heard a scream coming from me, louder than I had ever screamed in my life: "My baby! My baby's inside! Somebody get him out."

DOUG: From somewhere behind me, I heard a scream, "My baby! Get my baby!" In my mind flashed an image of my own children. What if they had been in there?

I had to try. I dashed toward the car again, bracing for the terrible heat. But then the strangest thing happened. It was as though something from above had blown down on the car and driven the heat and flames back.

Climbing through the window, I could see a young boy in an infant seat. I fumbled for the buckle on the straps. It wouldn't give. I grabbed the child and pulled, but he was strapped so tight I couldn't get him out. I pulled and pulled. Nothing.

I slid back out. We needed something for cutting. I took out my pocketknife and headed back in. Strangely enough, the breath of cool air was still holding the heat and fire back. I maneuvered between the steering wheel and seat, my legs sticking out the window.

Frantically I cut at the cords, straps, the seat belt—anything I could get my hands on. I prayed I wouldn't hurt the child. Finally, I pulled again. He was free! Holding him close, I pushed my way out the car window.

KATIE: Jordan and I ended up at Hershey Medical Center that day, but not exactly the way we had planned.

We both had concussions, cuts and bruises, and I needed staples to close a wound in the back of my head. But neither of us were seriously burned. And Jordan's heart remained stable. More amazing to me, Jordan hasn't suffered from any bad memories or nightmares. Looking at pictures of the crushed and burning car, I shudder to think we were inside.

And the angel pin? It was with us all the while—in Jordan's backpack, where he had put it that morning. But God sent another angel to be with us and protect us. His name was Doug Saylor.

DOUG: After the ambulance took Katie and Jordan away, someone brought me a bandage for a cut on my arm, and said that I looked sunburned. My hands were a bit shaky. Other than that, I felt okay. McDonald's offered me breakfast, but I still had a lot of driving to do, so I had a glass of orange juice to get the taste of fire extinguisher out of my mouth, then hopped in my truck.

Looking back, I still think of the strange, cooling breeze that provided relief from the terrible heat. Sometimes I think that God just gave a puff and blew the heat back. People also point to a series of remarkable coincidences—my over-sleeping, the unusual destination. I was right where I needed to be at just the right time. And I had plenty of help.

What Prayer Can Do

by Tammy Walker, Moore, Oklahoma

M y seven-year-old son, Shane, made it through a four-hour operation to remove a brain tumor. "But we won't know whether the tumor was malignant until tomorrow," the doctor said.

That night I didn't leave Shane's bedside. Around midnight an intensive-care nurse suggested I go home to try to get some rest. "Here's the phone number of the hospital," she said, handing me a piece of paper. "You can call us anytime."

I hated to leave, but I had been awake for more than 24 hours, so I went to my house, where I dozed fitfully. Somewhere around 6:00 A.M. I dialed the number the nurse had given me. When a female voice answered I identified myself as Shane's mother. "How is he?" the woman asked.

I was puzzled. "Is this Children's Memorial Hospital?"

"Honey, this is no hospital," the woman said. "We're just a group of women who heard about your son and decided to keep a prayer chain going for him. My friends and I have been on our knees all night praying for that little boy and one of us just asked God to give us a sign that he had heard. Then you called. Praise the Lord."

The tumor was benign and Shane made a miraculous recovery. I've tried to get back in touch with that woman: I've dialed every possible variation of the hospital's number and never again heard her beautiful, velvety voice. But I'll feel connected to her always.

A Call
for Help

by Theresa Morel Hudler, Waldorf, Maryland

A rainstorm had just ended that late January 1968 morning when the UH-1 "Huey" helicopter settled into the mud by the 12th evacuation hospital at Cu Chi, South Vietnam. The chopper was a troop carrier, a "slick," not the medevac type we were used to. It was full of wounded men who only minutes before had been in battle. Their comrades had hastily loaded and flown them to us. Most would remain with us, but the urgent cases would be flown to another unit not far from Cu Chi.

Nurses and medics ran under the rush of blades to lift the wounded through the open sides of the helicopter. Triage was begun. There was the sickly smell of blood and mud, the shouts of medics, the moaning of men in pain, the down-winding whine of the chopper's engine.

I had just finished a 12-hour shift and should have been headed back for the "hooch," the nurses' barracks, but someone called to me.

"Lieutenant Morel, come here, please! Tell us what to do with this one!" I slopped through the mud to a medic standing beside a low stretcher.

Crouching beside the soldier on the stretcher, I observed a massive head wound. He would die if we did not get him to a head-trauma unit. I motioned for the IV equipment and leaned toward the soldier's ear. "Don't worry, sweetheart. We'll get you out of here. We'll get you someplace safe. Just hang on."

Glancing up through the confusion, I saw crew members heading back to their slick.

"Wait!" I yelled. "We have to take this man on and take him up north!"

I jumped to my feet and ran toward the chopper, waving. The pilot glanced at his crew; flying the wounded was not their usual duty. He looked back at me and nodded.

Soon hands lifted the litter and slid it into the open chopper, loading it against a projecting bulkhead near the rear. It took up all but a few inches of

204

the width of the chopper's floor. The door gunners, heads bulky in huge protective helmets, climbed onto narrow benches behind the litter, facing outward, sliding in behind mounted M–60 machine guns.

It was not common for nurses to fly evacuation runs, and I had never been in a helicopter before, but there was no one else free to go. I scrambled up to the metal floor behind the pilot and copilot's seats. Someone tossed me a flak jacket and a standard steel-pot helmet. I noticed the gunners and pilots hooking their helmet headsets into connectors. The crew would now be able to communicate with each other. I had no headset, no ear protectors. My helmet flopped back and forth as I struggled to snap the flak jacket on over my fatigues and then checked that the patient's IV was securely attached to a hook overhead.

The copilot told me to bang on his seat if I needed something once we were airborne. He would then swing his helmet mike out so I could speak into it.

I sat down flat on the vibrating metal floor, my back to the pilots' seats. The doors had been left open; it was as if the chopper had no sides. Sweat trickled down my face and under my uniform. I watched my patient closely as the engine wound up to full pitch. The helicopter lifted up slowly just above the trees, the nose dropping a bit. It moved forward. We were flying.

The engine and rotors throbbed through the metal roof, and the wind rushed past the open doors. The sounds were deafening. The roar increased as we began to move a hundred miles an hour. We bobbed just above the contours of the terrain, up and over the jungle, down over rice paddies and canals.

Suddenly the pilots shouted something about enemy troops below. Simultaneously the gunners opened up with their machine guns. The pilot began to fly evasive maneuvers—banking the chopper steeply, first to one side and then the other. The staccato pounding of gunfire, the roar of the wind and the whine of the engine mixed in an earsplitting clash.

I forced myself to concentrate on my patient. Hours earlier, I had begun my shift with my daily visit to the chapel area. Now I prayed again, crying out silently: *O dear God! Don't let my patient die here in all this! Let us get him to a safe place!*

Suddenly I noticed the IV had come loose from his arm. He would die! I banged on the pilot's seat to get him to level off, but he did not hear me.

I clawed across the pitching deck to the litter. As I leaned over to reach for the IV needle, my helmet slipped forward. It would come off and hit the wounded man! I pulled it off with one hand and flung it behind me.

Now I was bent over, helmetless, tearing tape with my teeth and one hand, trying to hold the IV in with the other, screaming silently over and over, *O dear God, don't let him die here. Don't let him die here!*

Suddenly the gunner on my left stopped firing. He pivoted sharply 90 degrees and bent over until his head covered mine and his mouth was within an inch of my ear. *Why is he here? Does he want to speak to me?* I wondered in the split second he was poised there. Then there was a *ping* and a *pang.* A bullet headed for my left temple ricocheted off his helmet with enough force to knock him out. The gunner slumped unconscious over me and my patient.

His weight was suffocating us. I shoved his body to the left and he rolled onto the litter handles, inches from the open door. I didn't know if he was tethered or secured in some way or not, so I grabbed him with my left hand, still holding the IV needle with my right. I was crying.

O dear God, he'll fall out! Don't let him fall out! Help us, dear God! The prayer screamed through my heart.

It was a little while—a minute? an hour?—before the other gunner realized what had happened. He spoke to the pilots on his mike, and they broke off firing and flew straight to the hospital. We landed. I unclenched my cramped fingers from the gunner's fatigues and the patient's IV.

Medics pulled the gunner down and placed him on a stretcher, then slid the patient's litter to the ground. I headed first to my patient. The IV was still attached and he was stable, still alive. I touched his arm. "Peace," I whispered.

He was rushed off. I never learned if he survived.

I ran to the other litter and bent over the gunner, grabbing his wrist, feeling for a pulse.

With his helmet off, there was no sign of a wound. In fact, he was only dazed. His eyes opened and focused on me as I bent over him.

"What is it?" he asked. "What do you want?" This was the soldier whose helmeted head covered my bare one in a single bullet-splintered second. I just looked at him; what did he mean?

He spoke again, struggling to rise up on his elbow: "You called me!"

A few days later the gunner and I met to talk over what had happened. The Tet offensive was now fully under way. He offered me the bullet-scarred helmet as a souvenir, but I insisted that he keep it. I do not remember his name. But over the years, even as I repressed most of my Vietnam memories, I always remembered that when I needed protection, a gunner heard my call for help so loud and clear over the cacophony of noises in the helicopter that he stopped firing, turned and bent down to see what I wanted.

Tearing tape with my teeth, I had not spoken a word. I had only prayed in silence, to a God who heard and answered me.

The Unseen Visitor

by Lori White, Hickory, North Carolina

"**B**e careful!" I called over my shoulder from the bedroom as my two sons, Jordan, five, and Hunter, three, made a beeline outside to play in the yard.

It was Friday afternoon and we were moving that weekend from Conover, N.C., down the road a ways to Hickory. My husband, Chan, had just pulled into the driveway towing a rugged metal trailer that he had brought home from our family car dealership to haul some boxes and small pieces of furniture.

The house and yard were in complete disarray and the boys were having a blast poking around. But just as my friend Joyce and I started cleaning out the closet, a sickening thud reverberated through the house.

"What in the world—" I started to say to Joyce. An instant later I heard Chan shout in a voice pinched with panic, "Lori! Lori! Come quick!"

I ran downstairs to the front hall. There I saw Chan, ashen-faced, holding a limp, unrecognizable figure of a little boy covered in blood. Blood streamed from his mouth, his ears, and from a terrible gash in his head.

"The—the trailer ramp," Chan stammered. "It slammed down on him when I wasn't looking . . . "

"Dear God . . . " The boy wore green tennis shoes. It was Jordan.

"Lori, we've got to get him to a doctor."

I snatched a blanket off the sofa and we wrapped it around his unconscious form. Joyce stayed behind to watch Hunter as Chan and I leapt into our car. I gunned the engine and the car roared out of the driveway. Chan grabbed the cellular phone and called 911 to have them alert our local hospital that we were coming. As we sped down the road we exchanged frantic glances and tried to soothe Jordan. Chan told him over and over again how much we loved him.

At the emergency room attendants scooped Jordan from Chan's arms. We watched helplessly while medical personnel worked over our boy. Just minutes before, he had been an exuberant child. Chan wrapped his arms around me and I buried my face in his shoulder. A doctor glanced over at us. "We need to transfer him to Frye," he snapped. "They're better equipped." *Equipped for what?* I wondered, my whole being churning with fear.

Chan and I waited in the treatment room with Jordan and a nurse for the ambulance to Frye Regional Medical Center across town. As Chan signed some documents I stood over Jordan and told him that no matter what happened, his daddy and I loved him and that we were praying.

Suddenly Jordan moved. At first I thought it was my imagination but Chan and the nurse saw it too. Then, slowly, almost eerily, Jordan raised up to nearly a sitting position, as if someone were gently supporting him with an arm behind his back. His soot-black lashes fluttered open and in a weak but clear voice he said, "Jesus take care of me . . . " His eyes closed peacefully and he sank back down, motionless once again. The nurse looked at us in bewildered disbelief.

Chan half stood, and a cry gathered in my throat. We had taken our boys to church and taught them to pray, but usually they said their prayers at the table and bedtime. Here was Jordan reaching out in a moment of terrible, desperate need. I too would have to reach out with such sure faith. Just then the curtains swept back and Jordan, Chan and I were rushed to a waiting ambulance.

The evening dissolved in a blur. At Frye, Jordan was wheeled straight in for a CAT scan of his brain. Chan's parents, Steve and Jane White were at our side, as were mine, Keith and Paula Turner. Other family and friends had gotten word and come. A minister, Rev. John Misenheimer, and people from church gathered in the emergency room. We were surrounded by folks who loved us and prayed with us. Yet Chan and I didn't know whether our little boy would live.

Finally, Dr. Gregory Rosenfeld, a neurosurgeon, spoke with us. X rays revealed that Jordan's skull had been fractured by the heavy trailer gate, crushing fragments of bone into the area of the brain that governs speech, hearing and memory. "There is no telling the extent of the damage," Dr. Rosenfeld explained, "until we go in and look." It was only fair, he said, to warn us that the injury was very serious. As Jordan was sped into surgery I broke down and sobbed.

The people who had gathered held hands in prayer. We prayed that the surgeons' skilled hands would be blessed and guided. The love of our friends and family flowed through Chan and me, and an incredible, almost spontaneous feeling of peace and acceptance overpowered our fears. Six hours later Dr. Rosenfeld emerged and, pulling down his surgical mask, motioned us down the hall to a room and opened the door. "Come say hello to Jordan."

Chan and I moved to Jordan's bedside. He was pale and his head was swathed in a turban of bandages. I reached out to him. *Oh, Jordan* . . . It was then I heard the sweetest sound of my life: A tiny burp erupted from my son, followed by a whispered, "Excuse me."

Not only could Jordan speak, but he still had his manners! By the time they sent him up to the Neuro Intensive Care Unit, he was asking the nurse for a toothbrush. "The doctors don't know what to think about this boy," she said. Still, we were warned that Jordan could take a turn for the worse at any time, and that seizures were a serious possibility with such an invasive head trauma.

Most worrisome, though, was the fear that his brain might develop an infection. Ahead of Jordan lay a series of intravenous antibiotic treatments to fight this potentially fatal complication. We were cautioned that the sessions would be painful for Jordan.

I stayed at Jordan's side all night but could not sleep. Once, near morning, Jordan moaned with nausea and everyone came rushing. I held him and he said, "Mommy, pray with me." Over those next few days, any time he was frightened or suffering, he said, "Mommy, Daddy, come pray with me." That was the beginning of a spiritual journey, with Jordan as my guide. The stronger his faith was, the stronger mine became.

Eventually Jordan was moved from the ICU to the pediatric wing, where the staff was eager to finally meet this "miracle boy." Shortly after his arrival a new therapist pulled me aside. "Mrs. White," the young woman said, "we need to plan your son's treatment. There's a lot of work to be done." Confused, I said, "I don't understand."

She checked her chart. "Isn't your boy the one with the depressed skull fracture?"

"Yes, but he just got up and walked to the bathroom. He's been talking non-stop all day and he's building a house with his Legos."

"That's incredible," the therapist replied and went to see for herself.

The technician who had done Jordan's initial CAT scan also stopped by. "I felt so sorry for you that night," she told Chan and me. "I never thought you'd get your boy back this well or this quickly. I wasn't sure you'd get him back at all. I've never seen anything like it."

In fact, the only thing keeping Jordan in the hospital was the intravenous antibiotic treatments—a harrowing twice-daily ordeal that took thirty minutes for the burning, powerful medicine to be completely transfused into Jordan's body. Every time Jordan wailed out in pain he begged, "Pray for me, Mommy. Pray." And I would, as hard as I knew how. Poor Chan. After a while he couldn't stand to be in the room.

The ordeal exhausted me too. One night before the next treatment, while Jordan was sleeping, I felt as if I couldn't possibly endure another minute. Yet I knew he was counting on me. Kneeling by Jordan's bed I buried my face in his blanket. "Lord," I quietly pleaded, "all I can do is trust you the way Jordan trusts you. Please protect Jordan from the pain."

The door opened quietly behind me as I got up and lay down on the bed beside Jordan. I wrapped my arms around him. When the nurse shifted his arm to put the IV in, he started to move. I patted him and whispered, "It's okay. Mommy's here. Mommy's praying." He closed his eyes again.

Nurses stood by ready to help when the burning and crying started. The room was still and dark and hushed. Drip by drip the medicine entered Jordan's vein. Ten minutes. Twenty. Thirty minutes passed and it was over. Not once did my little boy stir.

The doctors were able to release Jordan after only ten days in the hospital. There was no sign of infection, and we brought him home to complete his recovery. He is continuing to heal, with only some loss of hearing in his right ear.

For a time Jordan didn't remember anything about the accident, but then one day while he was playing with a toy truck he suddenly said, "Mommy, I pulled the pin out. That's what made the trailer ramp fall on me." I stopped what I was doing. "It really hurt," he went on, "but then Jesus came."

I tried to sound calm. "What did Jesus look like, honey?"

"He was just . . . all white. Then Daddy came and lifted the ramp off my head." The gate had weighed nearly 300 pounds and Chan had said many times that he was amazed he had been able to raise it so easily.

"Jesus came to see me when we got to the hospital too," Jordan continued. His delicate features were set in an expression of deep, unperturbed seriousness. A feeling tingled up my back. "He lifted me up and hugged me and said, 'Jordan, you're going to be okay now.'"

My mind flew back to that moment in the treatment room waiting for the ambulance to Frye when Jordan mysteriously rose up in bed, as if cradled by an unseen visitor, and spoke. Had he really seen someone at that instant, someone only a hurt little child could see? I knelt and wrapped my arms around Jordan, and as I did I could sense another set of arms enfolding us both, arms that are always close when we are in need.

"Grant Us Eyes to See"

by Mary Brown

Remember the wonderful works that he has done....
—I Chronicles 16:12 (RSV)

After reading about the world's fourth-best bird-watcher, Peter Kaestner of Lansing, Michigan, who has seen almost seven thousand bird species, my husband Alex and I were inspired to start a list of our own sightings over the years.

As we reminisced, delighting again in scarlet rosellas right on our balcony in Australia and pretty pine grosbeaks that visited our feeder here in Michigan one winter, I thought of other sightings I wished I'd recorded over the years: glimpses of God's presence. I told Alex about God's miraculous protection when camping with my college friend Joann in the Porcupine Mountains. Two drunken men started unzipping our tent—we prayed very hard, and they suddenly fled.

Then Alex mentioned our rescue in a blizzard in Wisconsin. "Remember that state trooper who followed us on the shoulder and guided us to an exit?"

I found another notebook, and we began recording our sightings.

God's bringing Alex and me together, and helping us through our long, dark tunnel of infertility, wondrously answering our prayers for children; His leading us to a loving church family; shining a light of guidance on when and where to go for Alex's sabbatical; providing a renter for our house two weeks before we left; hearing Him in the laughter of our children....

We want to keep recording our "sightings" for grandchildren to read someday, but also for those dark times when we feel God has flown, so that we may recall glimpses of His golden wings.

Lord, help us recall special sightings of the past, and grant us eyes to see Your wondrous presence today.

Children's Corner

The Snakebite!

By Debbie Durrance

"Can I go play with Bo?" Mark asked. Outside, his dog Bo barked impatiently.

"Just be careful," his dad said. Living 30 miles out in the brushland of southwest Florida, Mark and his brothers had learned to watch out for themselves.

"I'll be careful," Mark yelled, letting the screen door slam behind him. "Come on, Bo."

Soon he and Bo came upon a colorful bird sitting in a cabbage palm. "Look at that," Mark whispered, jumping across a small ditch. "Let's get closer." Just then something slammed down hard on his foot. A big rattlesnake had hold of his shoe, biting his foot.

"Help me!" Mark screamed. Bo barked and jumped at the snake, tearing into its head. It let go and crawled into the bushes as Mark sank to the ground. He tried to think of what to do, but he was getting dizzy. He was a long way from the house. No one would hear, no matter how loudly he yelled.

Snakebite. What was it Dad said about snakebites? The more you move the quicker the poison will reach your heart. "How can I get home?" Mark mumbled. Bo whined and licked his cheek, but Mark just sank deeper into the tall grass.

That's when it happened. Mark felt strong arms reaching under him, lifting him. "You're going to be sick, Mark," a deep voice said. "Awfully sick. But you'll be just fine."

Mark tried to focus on his helper's face, but the pain was so bad it was hard for him to see. Was it a white robe that this stranger was wearing? It all seemed so strange.

The next thing Mark knew, he was on his front porch. He held onto the door and turned around. No one was there. He pushed the door open. "Mom! I've been snake bit!" Mark hit the floor, unconscious.

Mark's family rushed him to the hospital. He slipped into a coma as his body began to swell from the poison. But, finally, the worst was over. He was going to be all right!

The doctors couldn't explain how Mark got back to the house. His mom didn't know how he'd gotten up the 13 steps to the porch. But Mark knew. And so did the mysterious stranger.

Index

──── A N o t e   f r o m   t h e   E d i t o r s ────

This original Guideposts book was created by the book division of the company that publishes *Guideposts, Plus, Positive Living, Guideposts for Kids,* and *Angels on Earth.* Each magazine contains faith-filled stories to help the reader live a more fulfilled life.

For more than twenty years, the book division has edited the annual devotional book *Daily Guideposts,* which contains new devotionals every year to inspire and uplift.

If you are interested in subscribing to any of the Guideposts family of magazines or *Daily Guideposts,* all you have to do is write to Guideposts, 39 Seminary Hill Road, Carmel, NY 10512.

Guideposts is also available on the Internet by accessing their homepage at http://www.guideposts.org. Send prayer requests to their Monday morning Prayer Fellowship. Read stories from recent issues of their magazines or read today's devotional from *Daily Guideposts.* Excerpts from some of their bestselling books are also available.